THE OLD ONES

ANTHONY HENDERSON

Cover photograph by Lalesh Aldarwish
https://instagram.com/lalesh.aldarwish

To Ira and Noelle, the two hearts that keep this one beating.

And to the extraordinary families we create

T hat first breeze caused folks sensitive to these things to know that summer was tipping its hat to fall. You'd almost miss it, and most did, as the wet flames of August bore down, obliterating every sense except misery. But the old ones, the ones who sat fanning themselves on various porches throughout Louisa, Kentucky knew: they knew that this particular breeze they fanned past their faces was different from the last, and they would close their eyes hoping to intensify its touch. If they were sitting together, a glance or a nod might be enough to acknowledge that a landscape of watercolor was on its way. They would talk about times imagined, when pain wasn't pain and truth was softened through eyes that would never cry their last tears. But as for today this was one for imagination. Today the wind gathered them 'round and whispered, as only the wind knew how, listen...

Anthony Henderson

PART 1

CHAPTER 1

The breeze continued on, through leaves and branches of the huge oaks that shaded a 30-acre plantation, then down through the rows of tobacco that undulated in appreciation, then on to Cumberland Falls fed by mountains of the same name. The snowmelt was warm enough in August to nudge the falls to just above frigid.

It swept along the surface and through small fingers extending themselves up, in the throes of grasping. Seconds later a heap of blond hair broke the surface, then disappeared, but not before the wind snatched away her cries, rendering them inchoate.

***

Tommie Kincaid had had a bad night, like everyone else who pretended to sleep through the cloying wetness of a Louisa summer evening. She had given up trying at about 5am, her clawing bed sheet having won the battle. She must have slept, she figured, *'cause you can't have a nightmare if you don't.*

Her heart was just now slowing, and her sweat smelled different. Maybe it was that smell of fear that she had heard about or maybe it was what happened when tears mixed with sweat. Either way, her clammy bed and airless room were a profound comfort as the nightmare faded.

She wouldn't tell her mama or her daddy. She had bad dreams before and she knew they didn't mean nothin', not most times anyway, no matter how real they looked to be, and this one was scary real. Her Nana told her that nightmares was just a way for your mind to take out the trash and get clean. This always made her feel better, like she was safe from the make-believe monsters, but not tonight.

She lay stone still willing herself to embrace the slightest movement of air as one would a zephyr, but all she felt was heat, oppressive and thick, like the murky swamp water just past the schoolhouse. She could hear her mama downstairs, taking advantage of the minuscule dip in temperature.

After a few minutes, Rabbit, the family pit bull, trotted into her room and sensing she was awake, placed his muzzle beside her pillow. Normally his very presence could make most things right, but this nightmare was too off-putting, badder than anything ever, and now her head hurt. She gave him a perfunctory scratch behind his ears, and he stayed put as she lay back on her pillow.

Her thoughts then went to the stifling firebox that served as a classroom, and this made her feel even worse. She flung the sheet off in frustration, startling Rabbit. It was as if she could feel that tiny room moving from a simmer to a boil, the two windows gaping open for a nonexistent breeze.

She threw her legs over the bed, yawned and stretched as Rabbit looked on suspiciously. They made their way downstairs where she collapsed onto a kitchen chair.

"Bad night?" noted her mother.

"Yeah, I guess."

"I'll hang your bedding outside to catch whatever breeze it can. If you get to school early, you can get a spot that won't be in the sun most of the day."

"Maybe," was Tommie's sluggish response. "But Mrs. Gloadstone will probably move me back to my seat."

Her mother maneuvered around Tommie's chair in the small kitchen, took a couple of pieces of toast off the stove and put them on a plate. She brushed the back of her hand across her moist forehead and placed the plate on the table. "And how do you think I'm gonna answer that, young lady?"

"Can't happen, if I don't try."

"Better finish up now and get a move on in case somebody else gets the same idea." Tommie picked at her eggs and toast, listless and uninterested.

"Where's T, Mama?"

"You know they're planting turnips today."

"If he takes Martha to the falls maybe I could go with 'em."

"Maybe."

***

"Okay, Daniel, you see where you have nine dollars so far?" Kincaid was sitting on a stool with a plank of wood over two chairs that served as his portable desk. He pointed to a line on the page of a thick ledger book.

"Yes, Mista Kincaid," answered Daniel.

"So, when I add the three dollars for this month…."

"That make it twelve," Daniel added quickly.

"That's right. So, I'm going to add that to your bank account this month and it will be there whenever you want it."

"Thank you, Mista Kincaid," and he left the barn. Like most of the other blacks, Daniel didn't believe it was his money until Kincaid let him spend some of it. He was one of several black "workers" on the plantation that had been enslaved. Kincaid freed some when he inherited the property, others had

4

subsequently earned their freedom, and the rest were working towards theirs. He offered salaries to those that decided to stay on.

Daniel's was the last transaction of the morning. Kincaid set the ledger book on one of the chairs, then he moved everything against a wall at the back of the barn and headed into the house.

He entered the stifling kitchen wiping his brow, "Made it again this month. Let's hope prices are up for tobacco or next month won't be as easy." He kissed his wife on the back of the neck as she prepared his eggs. Grace was unresponsive. He put it off to the weather and took a seat at the table.

As she dished the eggs onto his plate she turned to Tommie. "This weather might make you get some crazy idea that you can go to those falls by yourself. I hope you know better."

Undeterred, Tommie turned to her father. "Daddy, can I go if T can't come?"

"Absolutely not. I'm with your mother on this one. You stay clear of those falls if T can't watch you and Martha and that's the end of the discussion."

Then that strange quiet came back. It always seemed to happen when she asked to go to the falls. Something passed between her mama and daddy that changed any happy feeling in the room into something different, like some strange secret only for grown-ups. But they never got mad at her for asking, so she put it in the overflowing file of strange grown-up behavior and let it go.

Martha was a couple of years younger and an orphaned slave. She tried to call T "Daddy" shortly after they first met, but he was firm about being called "T". If anything happened to him, Martha would lose a friend and not a daddy. She also couldn't swim, which meant T had to watch her closely. Tommie hated this because T said she was a really good swimmer and she couldn't go out far when Martha was there.

She tried a different tactic. "Can you let him go early, Daddy? Please?".

"Don't think so. How do you think it would look if I let the foreman go cool off at the falls and everybody else has to stay in the fields? They'll be plenty more hot days for you to go swimming."

"Enough," declared her mother with irritation that made them both look up. "You better show some spunk and get a move on it if you want to find some shade in that classroom."

"Won't make no difference anyway," Tommie said.

Kincaid tousled her hair. "T hasn't been foreman long. Now's not the time to be taking him out of the fields early. Come hug me and get a move on it like your mama told you."

"How much longer?" Grace broke the extended silence after Tommie left.

"What are you talking about?"

"I just want to know how much longer we are going to have to live like niggers so you can save the world?"

"I don't know a lot of them that are preparing breakfast in their large homes right now. We live a lot better than they do."

"Well, it won't be for much longer at the rate you're giving our money away. You walk in here every month and talk about how hard it is to pay these niggers while our furniture looks like we pulled it out of a ditch. You need to start thinking more about me and Tommie. So what we live better than they do? Would you like to see me and her in one of their shacks? You take it too far."

"That's not what I'm saying."

6

"I know it's not, Roland, but I'm getting tired of living like a pauper while you try to be a saint. If you paid them nothing, they would still be better off here than anyplace else. Do you know anybody else who treats their niggers like we do?"

"No, but they're free. They don't have to stay, and we need the help."

"Only because you made them free."

"That part won't change, Grace. Every man I have to purchase will have a chance to earn their freedom."

"Well, something's got to change. God made us white, and it wasn't my doing and I'm not sorry for that. I'm also not sorry for wanting a house I can be proud of. I married you because you're a good man, Roland, and I've been willing to stand by you, but when you come in here and talk about how we don't have money to pay the niggers and I think of all the things we're going without, I just think me and Tommie deserve better."

She turned away as he tried to approach her.

***

Years prior Kincaid had been called away from a budding law practice in Frankfort, Kentucky to see his father through his final days, with every intention of returning. Then his brother, Leon, was murdered.

A female house slave that he had relentlessly terrorized, stole his gun during one of his perpetual blackouts and shot him through the heart. She then turned the revolver on herself.

While her enslaved brothers and sisters mourned her untimely death, they sent out shouts of thanks to Lord Jesus for Leon's overdue demise. He had devolved into a drunken and violent master and most viewed his death as additionally self-inflicted. Including his brother. He was buried without ceremony. That left Kincaid, an abolitionist, master of the plantation.

He had no intention of stepping into his inheritance. He would free the enslaved, sell the plantation and be done with it. A simple, clean solution that would keep his moral compass intact.

And it would have all gone to plan if the plantation sold quickly and the enslaved were strangers to him. But he struggled to get a fair price and many of his enslaved had watched him grow from boy to man and were closer to family than stranger. In the process of working out their futures, his became a new life in Louisa.

He wore a strong sense of moral superiority to his slave-owning peers, assured that his arrangement restored a sense of humanity to his own enslaved, where all others had failed. But this morning his wife put his self-satisfied image in check. She reminded him that she had sacrificed too and that he had allowed his guilt over the accident of his birth to create a sense of duty to the blacks above his duty to his own family.

Her accusation prompted minimal self-reflection, though. Every man knew women were prone to emotions, especially in this heat.

CHAPTER 2

Tommie dragged herself along the dirt road to school, trying to think of anything but the nightmare, which ensured its place front and center. The horrors were too big and demanded their own space in her imagination.

As the details came flooding back and her very real fear returned, she marveled how *somethin' that could seem so real just be all made up. What God go n' do that for?* she thought, *especially if nothin' bad was really gonna happen. Just seemed mean.*

It was 90 degrees at 9am and the sweat dripped into her eyes, stinging them before she could wipe it away. She had almost run into her mama and daddy's room last night and was really glad she didn't. She was 10 and was too old to be doin' that baby stuff, but this nightmare was a really bad kinda scary that ain't never happened before.

She passed houses, trees, fences, dogs and the occasional person. Everything she was seeing now was in the nightmare, except in the nightmare, there was fog. It was a whirling, tactile presence, infused with premonition that held horrors Tommie could feel but not see, and a will that pushed her forward. She remembered that she had stopped moving, determined not to see whatever was beckoning her on, convinced it would be the last thing she ever saw.

She was as sure of this as she had ever been about anything. So, she stayed stock still except for the shivering that crept through her like an angry infection. If she could just stay where she was then whatever lay ahead would never come into view. She planted her small feet and willed them to grow roots, but the fog pushed her forward. She reached behind and grabbed at it.

It misted through her fingers and continued to glide her forward. It was now more solid under her feet, moving her forward like a macabre magic carpet. She watched her familiar neighborhood pass by like images swirling the smoke of fire.

Then she heard a repeating pattern, a thump followed by silence, then another thump. It had been faint but was growing in intensity as if she were closing in on some horrible climax. The sound seemed to be coming from the last house on the left, where Crazy McKinney lived. He was mean and had no time for children and made it known to everybody.

Thump, silence, thump. The sound echoed and lingered and became the entire nightmare. It joined with the fog in a dance that seemed choreographed from evil, and that's when Tommie felt smoky hands on her back. She screamed but remained in the purgatory of the fog that now planted her in front of Crazy McKinney's house, and she saw what was making the noise.

A slight breeze that she hadn't noticed until now was moving a pair of legs away from the trunk of the tree. The thump she heard was the sound of the legs falling back again, and when they hit, they now boomed like a cannon shot. She followed the legs up and saw what was left of T's face. Crows had had their way with his eyes and bullet holes riddled what was left of his torso.

A host of souvenirs had been cut and pulled away, leaving flesh and muscle hanging from what large parts were left. His muscular body had pulled down on the rope, stretching his neck unnaturally several inches below it. Tommie stared soundless;

breath sucked from her lungs. Then his torso dropped, followed by his head.

No, she could never tell her mama or daddy about that dream. Not ever, not never. She decided right then and there that if you tell a nightmare too much then it could become real. This was her new rule, and she would let everybody know.

She collapsed against a tree. Her sticky and wilted dress bore no resemblance to the crisp garment her mother had sent her off in. After a few disorienting minutes she rose from the tree and continued on.

What had been an uncomfortable start to the morning now reached a new level of agony as the nightmare gave way to the wet oven of a day that lay ahead. It was all too much. There was no way she would get to school early, she thought. The only way her dress would dry out was if she walked slowly enough to let it. But when she slowed, the elements seemed to clap their dripping hands in celebration, the sun now had more time to torture every piece of exposed flesh.

Then she stopped, and with nearly the same joy of hearing those magic words, "schools out", she remembered Mrs. Gloadstone would not be there today. She had completely forgotten that a substitute would be there in her place, and almost immediately the lure of the falls rose up again and died away just as quickly.

There would be really big trouble if her parents found out. And it would be a different kind of trouble, she sensed, a worse kind of trouble because of that strange silence that happened whenever she asked to go to the falls. But just as most good Christian children knew their 10 commandments, very few knew the 11th: "All children must disobey thy parents often and without remorse."

She performed the quick calculus: distance to the falls, minus parents finding out, divided by school equaled a chance worth taking. Still, she didn't move. At heart, she was a good child, still more fearful of her parents than succumbing to the desire to disobey. Ditching school would be a first. There would be big trouble for that alone, so she stayed planted against the tree. The mosquitos buzzed and she grew increasingly despondent.

She heard him before she saw him come trotting up. If there was nothing to chase, Rabbit was known to show up at school where he was content to sit under a large oak tree until Tommie was done. She wrapped her arms around him while he lapped at her salty face and much of the morning's tribulations faded from view with his solid, intelligent presence. She backed away and grabbed his cheeks. Looking intently into his eyes she asked, "Ok. I need you to tell me, should I go swimmin' or to school? If you lick my face one more time the answer is swimmin'."

He cocked his head, looked at her looking at him, and licked her face.

CHAPTER 3

T was tall and muscled but not the tallest or most muscled. God knows he was not the first to be stripped of any remnants of family, nor was he the first to have suffered the sting of the whip that cut through his flesh the way a scythe cuts through wheat.

But he was the only one he knew named T. Like a rare jewel or bright new star given a name that was its own, "T" was of his own making and equally rare. It was an act of ownership, and it was the one and only thing no white man had ever thought to take from him. He may have also been a nigger, darkie or coon but so were the thousands of his brethren. There was no other "T."

Curious folks stayed curious, though his unbending frame and solitary countenance ensured that those weren't great in number. "Don't you got somethin' better to do?" was his usual response to queries about his single letter and helped to efficiently spread his reputation as someone to move past for casual conversation. He was neither cruel nor violent, though many deemed him both. Those being the default descriptors of any black man with his bearing.

This also made him an unlikely candidate for childcare. His relationship to Tommie was frowned on by most of Kincaid's peers who could not imagine leaving their precious progeny to wander around, unsupervised, with the likes of T. Neither could the Kincaids until T proved himself to be a fiercely loyal, intelligent and engaging companion to Tommie.

The two discovered a chemistry that was heartfelt and innocent. The Kincaids were watchful and sensitive in the beginning, and ultimately T passed the test. Also, where Tommie went, Rabbit followed. The Kincaids had known a cousin or an uncle and even a brother who had a reputation with children that was unseemly.

If someone became overly self-righteous about T's relationship with Tommie, Mrs. Kincaid would politely thank them for their concern and assure them that she was watchful. Then she would mention that just the other day she heard rumor of someone's favorite uncle Bob or that unusual cousin Stewart who seemed to have a special fondness for their little Sally or Sam. This seemed to abruptly end most questions.

T strode through life on rhythms of his own. He was quiet and self-possessed, with a sheath of outright insolence if need be. The cross, sweet Jesus and other imaginary oases held no sway. Life and common sense seemed to work just fine. He was unimpeded by professions of eternal salvation. If some unfortunate soul engaged him in a conversation about God's plan, they were most often driven to hurling accusations of blasphemy as they walked away, a little less sure of their pompous footing as his closing salvo echoed: "You be a fool if you want to."

He defined his world by what was, not by what could be and certainly not by a soul's salvation. He was adept at protecting his psyche from a world where justice was defined by degrees of injustice. He refused to create an alternate universe full of magical thinking, as he stepped on ground where the blood of his people mixed with the excrement and rot of the pigs and chickens. Which he was considered no better than.

He was content to have no one and didn't pine for family trees chopped to pieces and scattered to the wind. What was done was done. Nothing could be gained by traveling down that road. If he could not fix a thing or change it, he locked it out of his life and moved on. He struck most as a man who thought himself superior, but it would be more accurate to say he didn't lack confidence or crave approval. There were plenty of men easier to talk to, so little conversation ever came his way.

There had been kindnesses. One in particular happened about the time he was first hauled in to stud as a teenager and would serve as a foundation for the man he would become.

One afternoon as the rancid stench of the barn and the painfully satisfying aftermath of the act were occupying his thoughts, his eye caught sight of a grizzled ancient waving him over. It was too late to pretend he didn't see the old man, so T looked directly at him and defiantly turned the other way.

"You may think I'm an ol' fool but you be a young fool to disrespect yo' elders."

"I ain't no fool," T defended himself.

"You say so." This came out as a challenge and T sized the old fool up, then sauntered over with his arrogance fully intact. The old man was scooping up mush with the three fingers that remained on his right hand. He was so adept that T was momentarily transfixed.

"You ain't never seen a man eat before, son?" The spell was broken.

"What you want with me, ol' man?"

"How you 'spect you die, son?" T cocked his head.

"I don't be thinkin' 'bout dyin'. You the one be ol'."

"Not the dyin' you do from gettin' hanged or bein' shot. What you want yo' life to look like when yo' time come? That's what I be talkin' 'bout."

"Never thought on that. I don't know," he answered as he drew shapes in the dirt with his boot.

"Maybe you should think on it. You got the look of a boy who tryin' to learn his own mind. Tell me."

T didn't answer immediately, unexpectedly intrigued and unsure."Tell you what, ol' man?" The arrogance had vanished, replaced by the shock of fear. He had so much to say, so many questions and this old man would listen.

"You on yo' own most times I see you, but you got questions behind those big eyes that other boys don't. Am I right?" T stopped drawing shapes in the dirt. The old man repeated, "I said am I right?"

T looked away, looked back, then asked, "When come the time you start rememberin' yo' mama and yo' daddy?"

The question landed hard. The old man recognized that T was at the place where he needed to put away childish things and for folks of their lot, that had to start at birth. "Don't be nothin' wrong with hurtin' for yo' kin, son. But you got to know that a time of 'rememberin' might never come. After a while, life gets filled up with plenty other things and you forget how to remember." He let this thought sit and simmer then continued

. "You got to let go the hate. That what I want to say to you. It follow us around all day and all night. Now, I ain't sayin' it don't make sense to be full with it, I just see it destroy more than it create."

"Don't you never get mad? Don't you never wanna fight?"

"'Course I get mad! I get real mad. All the time. But you know what I do?" He raised his mangled hands toward the heavens. T thought they looked like gnarled wheels with missing spokes. "Got to let the Lord have all that evil what's in yo' heart, to put it where He will. You let Him into yo' life, He help you say, "My life my

16

own. Not my mad, nor nothing, nor no man will take my life from me." Then a long time from now, or maybe not so long the way you be growing, you be sittin' on a stoop tellin' this story to a young one even smarter, even angrier, even uglier than you be."

T grinned and this started several lazy afternoons of the old man's grizzled mentorship. This relic became the closest thing to a relation he had ever known, and he found himself revealing those delicate psyche spaces of adolescence and getting the wisdom and guidance that would forever set him apart from his peers.

One night the old man, who T had come to know as Ol' Pete, was run over by a wagon that was driven by the drunken overseer. To the few slaves who witnessed the tragedy he shouted, "Who can see you darkies when there ain't no light? Pick the nigger up and put him in the ground." They gathered Ol' Pete up and took him to a shack. He stayed there, out of the way of animals, until he could be laid to rest the next day.

On a cold November morning a meager funeral party laid him to rest in a grave where no marker was allowed. T did not attend. Ol' Pete had been the only one to listen, the only one to break through his hardening scar tissue, and he was inconsolable.

He needed to be alone with his shuttering grief. The tears and curses streamed out of him with the desperation of a final act. It would be the last time the world would be allowed in and he shouted out to a God he didn't believe listened, "How you let a good man like Ol' Pete be run down like an animal?!"

In the silent minutes that followed, he became the man that would no longer excuse a God that demanded total devotion. One who might decide, seemingly on a whim, that heaven needed some unsuspecting child or some kind old man with life left in him. Often leaving behind shattered remnants of souls. A God that demanded that these injured and pathetic survivors ask Him for comfort and understanding, or risk eternal damnation.

The cruelty of this was brought home with Ol' Pete's undignified death. That's when God truly lost him to simple common sense, where the morality of God and man would forever be measured by their actions. Then he remembered one of the most important things Ol' Pete taught him and would guide him to the man he would become: "*My life my own. Not my mad, nor nothin', nor no man will take my life from me*".

His first act of defining his place in the world was to choose what the world would call him. He had heard his bill of sale read aloud many times, and initially the line that always caught his attention was: "...for the purchase of one negro slave named Thomas". Before he grew used to hearing it, he often wondered "*Who was Thomas?*" He knew what a "T" looked like and to him it represented a man flexing his arms, a strong man who was unafraid to show it, and he became T, just T. It symbolized an act of defiant control, an ownership of his existence that he wrestled away from the white man and that no one could ever take from him, and through the beatings, shackles and life that was to come, no one ever did.

***

His inauspicious start with Kincaid happened at the Cheapside Auction Block in Lexington, Kentucky. Hyacinth and magnolia were making their spring appearance and the air carried their sweet fragrances over the chained, scarred and petrified property up for sale that afternoon.

T stared out at the crowd with a left eye that was far-off, purplish and grotesquely swollen. He was joined by three frail, cowering middle-aged mulatto women and one older male. The three women were chained together and struggled to stay upright. They clung to each other, vainly trying to cover their nakedness through their ripped clothing. T stared straight ahead, emotionless.

Kincaid thought he might be able to get that injured, but powerful looking young slave for a bargain. This was not his first visit to the auction block. He quickly discovered that the plantation could not be run properly without occasional replenishments. He had instituted an arrangement that he felt was an appropriate compromise and also allowed him to continue imagining he was mortally superior to his slave owning peers.

He was outbid for the older male with two good eyes before he could raise his hand. The crowd thinned to a spattering after that. Kincaid's bid for T was low but it went unchallenged. The clinging women would be dispensed with last. Kincaid ushered T out quickly, having no desire to witness what was about to occur.

As they headed toward the wagon, a simple buckboard, they passed a large, enslaved woman carrying a bag of vegetables. She was being trailed by a young female who looked close to T's age. They passed each other close enough so that when she stared at his injured eye, his good one took in a pair of shocking green eyes. He wanted to hold those eyes in the gaze of his good one for as long as he could.

"We gonna have problems?" Kincaid pulled him to the present. T did not answer. He wanted to establish his fearlessness up front, and silence always seemed to unnerve white people. Kincaid showed no frustration as he led him to the wagon. He knew this game.

A cacophony rose up from the interior of the auction house. The mulatto women were being pulled apart and the force used to wrest them from each other was savage. Unchained, they started clawing for one another. The few rags that covered them were ripped off in the struggle, and scratches left blood. Through screams of "Sistah! Sistah!", Kincaid kept his focus on T amid this disembowelment.

"How you come by that eye?"

T, again, said nothing.

"Look, young man, you don't know nothing about me. I bought you 'cause I need the help. I will treat you with respect as long as you do the same with me. As far as I see it, we are all the same in God's eyes. I can promise a clean place to sleep and regular meals, like I do for everyone that works for me. You ain't seen none of that yet but that's who I am."

Suspicion on high alert, T responded, "There be no problems."

"Good to hear. But since I don't know you and you look like you got some anger, I'm thinking I need to chain you to the bench in the back of the wagon until we get to know each other. Either that, or I can take a chance and have you ride with me in the front where you can catch a breeze."

"You ain't have no problem with me."

"Does that mean you would prefer the front?"

"Yes." He deliberately left off "sir" to give this white man the opportunity to reveal himself.

"Then hop on up. Gonna keep those wrists chained up until we get home. Still need to get to know you some." T didn't move. This kind of sadistic ruse was common with some slave holders. He would attempt to sit up front only to be pulled to the ground

20

for his foolishness and kicked in the head for good measure. "I know what you thinkin'. But you gonna have to take a chance like I'm doing. Ain't nothing behind what I'm saying. So, what's it gonna be?" Keeping Kincaid in his sights, he struggled up with his shackled wrists and they rode away to the snap of whips and the howling terror of those three gentle women who never expected this would be their end.

The bill of sale stated that T was 17. *If this boy is still growing, I'm gonna have quite a stallion on my hands,* thought Kincaid. About a mile into their journey, he broke the silence. "You ready to talk about that eye?"

"Somebody tried to steal my food."

"Did they get it?"

"No sir."

"Kinda figured that. Can you see out of it?"

"Some."

"That's a good sign. When the fever in it goes down you might have a good eye. So, I see here you're called Thomas?"

"T."

"What's that?"

"Jus' T," *and this is the moment it will happen,* he thought. The one where massa would accuse him of being an uppity nigger and threaten him with violence if he didn't answer to "Thomas".

"Let me explain something to you, T. Everybody who works for me is there because they want to be. I believe you have a right to be a man in this world like anybody else. So, here is my offer: Soon as you work off what I paid for you, I'll give you your freedom and pay you to stay on, if you want to." T whipped his head around and stared in disbelief. "Yeah, I know it's not what you expected, and you have no reason to trust me. Only way to settle that is for you to see for yourself."

In about an hour, the wagon drew to a stop in front of a two-story saltbox structure with unpainted clapboard siding. It was a far cry from the majestic Georgian mansions they had passed but T expected it carried its own brand of depravity, as they all did. He sat motionless, while several slaves started unloading the back of the wagon and warily regarding this new purchase. His eye and bearing ensured that he wasn't paid too much attention.

A no-nonsense looking woman stood on the porch eyeing him with a neutral expression. Her ruddy blond hair was tied back. A little girl with the same blond hair peaked cautiously from behind her apron.

The sun was hot on his back, as though all the rays were directed through a prism, to one spot. He didn't move, awaiting his first order.

"He looks like a monster, Mama," the little girl observed.

"He's no monster Tommie, he's just got a bad eye. Looks to be recent too. Roland, who's our new worker?" she shouted.

He looked at T. "Go ahead and tell her."

"My name T, ma'am," he mumbled, barely audible.

"That ain't no real name," shouted Tommie. "You can't call yourself by no letter."

T stared rigidly ahead, silent and waiting, as always, for folks to work through their discomfort. He would be of no help.

"He can call himself whatever he wants, Tommie. Though that is different. Well, T, how's that eye?"

"Hurtin' some, ma'am."

"Roland, take him out of the sun and I'll get something for that eye and something to eat."

"Thank you, ma'am." This fairytale would end. He was as certain of that as the air he was breathing. He knew what was coming and was strangely looking forward to it. The violence and degradation that was around the corner was familiar, his body knew how to respond, how to shut down. There might be some surprise new form of torture, but it was all of a piece. These people unnerved him, like not knowing when a bomb might drop so you could never prepare.

"Gimme those hands." T was startled out of his musings. Referring to the wrist restraints Kincaid said, "Think it's safe to take these off now. What do you say?" T nodded. Kincaid took off the wrist restraints and exited his side of the wagon.

T didn't move. He stared straight ahead and after a minute started rocking back and forth. The slaves stopped their work and backed away from the wagon as if witnessing a possession. He was in an emotional vortex. These people were trying to earn a trust he had no capacity to give. The last person to acknowledge his humanity, to pierce that piece of granite in the shape of a heart, was Ol' Pete and that seemed like a lifetime ago.

He wanted to simply step down from that wagon and into his new life, but what was happening was incomprehensible. A sense of self-preservation kept him on that wagon, as if insisting he go back to the life he knew, because the one in front of him was not real. Then the wails of the mulattos joined his internal firestorm, as if to remind him of what he was, and a familiar, comforting rage started settling in. This would be a betrayal. These people would be like all the others.

"Come on down when you're ready. I'm going inside." T looked at Kincaid as if waking from a dream.

He spoke with no accusation or anger. He didn't pull him down or hurl frustrated accusations. It was as if he knew what was happening, understood that what he and his wife had created was so foreign to the likes of T, as to be otherworldly. T watched him walk off and after a few minutes, lightheaded and on unsteady legs, he stepped down from the wagon and onto the Kincaid Plantation and instead of proving him right, the Kincaids proved to be exactly who they appeared to be.

CHAPTER 4

"**I** ain't seen a eye look like that for a while."
Joraye was sitting on a stump while she braided the hair of a friend. "It was all different colors, and he couldn't open it. No wonder he look so mad." She was preparing her friend for a rendezvous with a lover and was recalling her sighting of T. When the sun caught her eyes at the right angle it was like looking into the middle of a pair of emeralds.

"You say he just was sold?" Her friend asked.

"Hu-huh."

"He got a whole lot a reason to be mad then."

"I guess."

"Ow! Don't pull so hard."

"Well hold still then! I ain't doin' no different than I always do."

"I be tender headed. You know that. Put some more grease on it."

Joraye reached into a tin of bacon grease and rubbed some of it into her friend's hair. "So, where you gon' meet?"

"I ain't tellin' you. It be just for us. It be a special place that he find."

"You can keep yo' special place. I'm gon' have me a right wedding, just like white folks. Lots of flowers in a big church full up with people from all over. Might even let The President come if he want."

"And some angels from heaven too?"

"Long as there be room." After their laughter died down Joraye asked, "You think you jump the broom with him?"

"He ask me to I will. And I hope he do. I love that man, Joraye. God don't make 'em too much better.

And I don't know what you be waitin' for. You got all kinds of men after you."

"How you know I be waitin'?" Joraye answered demurely.

Her friend leaned forward in surprise, momentarily forgetting the vice grip Joraye had on her hair. "Ow!" She screamed, then, "You lyin'. You know you be lyin'."

Joraye laughed. "Maybe, maybe not."

"Come on, Joraye, tell the truth."

"I be finished now you can go on and meet yo' man."

"I hate you. You better tell me when I get back."

Her friend would never find out because the next day Joraye was sent off to the auction block.

***

T had been with the Kincaid's for a month when he passed Tommie one day on his way from the beet fields. She was trying to make a slingshot by tying two sticks into an X. He watched her get frustrated with each unsuccessful attempt until she reached her limit and threw the unsteady mess to the ground and stomped off with Rabbit at her feet.

A week later he presented Mrs. Kincaid with a beautiful oak slingshot, complete with leather thong. He mentioned he saw Tommie trying to make one and thought she might like to have it.

"Tommie! Tommie, come on out here," she called out. Tommie ran to the front door and stopped dead in her tracks when she saw T standing on the porch. "Come on out and see what T made for you."

She looked at her mother wide-eyed and

cautiously opened the door. Rabbit stepped out, which didn't go unnoticed by T. He handed her the slingshot.

She gasped. "You made this for me?! Really you did?!"

"Only if you want it Miss Tommie."

"Mama, please can I have it? I won't aim at nothin' bad. I promise."

"Well seeing as how he was so kind as to make you something so beautiful I guess it would be rude not to take it. This is a fine piece of work T. We thank you kindly."

"Yes ma'am," he said and walked away.

One afternoon Tommie and Rabbit found him taking a break and she plopped down across from him and started talking in sentences that had no periods. "I ain't never heard nobody named for the alphabet sounds like a piece of a name to me I did know a boy named Tookey once but that still had more letters than your name but I guess it don't take long to write T my name begins with a T too you know I wish I could just be T like you it would be a lot easier to write than Tommie."

"Uh," he tried to comment with no luck.

"but Tommie ain't too long what happened to your eye how did it get all busted up looks like you been in a fight."

He didn't know what to make of this little chatter box, but her fearlessness and innocence quickly won him over. Very few adults had ever been interested in getting to know him.

T proved himself to be a dependable and honest man and earned the Kincaid's trust with their only child, and there was always Rabbit.

Just as he promised, Kincaid had worked out the timing of his freedom, which came and went, and T remained on the plantation. At this point he was getting

27

a salary, had just been made foreman, and had grown to love that little girl.

CHAPTER 5

The Cumberland Falls was surrounded by Rockcastle Sandstone. A flat shelf close to the water served as shoreline, launch pad and sunning surface. The rest of the perimeter was surrounded by a jagged version of the same stone that was dangerous and mostly avoided. The falls were powerful and would become known as "Little Niagara" later in the century.

Tommie stood on the shelf and pulled her dress over her head. After she took off her high-top leather boots and stockings, the only thing she had on was her shift. The roar of distant water crashing at the mouth of the falls made her slow down just a minute to reconsider. She could actually feel some slight spray on her face even though she was several hundred feet away from the drop.

The water directly below her was a shimmering pool of black calm that gave no indication of the violence that flowed just a short distance away. Her planned route would take her in an east-west direction and not the north-south that flowed toward the drop. Still, there was always a current pulling in that direction, though it was negligible from where she stood. She mouthed a quick, silent prayer, then jumped.

She was instantly rewarded with a thousand fine needles piercing each cell of her tiny, thrashing frame. The overall sensation was that of electrocution. No matter how blistering its rays, the sun never seemed able to reach the water that sat in this hole, as if melting the snow and getting it down the mountain were the entirety of her responsibilities.

Even as every living soul seemed vulnerable to the Kentucky heat in August, the water of this one pool stayed stubbornly near freezing. On any given day, some idiot or innocent or innocent idiot could be heard cursing the moment they landed in the near ice-bath. For most this was the last resort against the summer onslaught.

Her arms and legs jack-rabbited in a furious attempt to bring her body temperature up as quickly as possible. After forever, she was able to relax enough to stretch into a traditional crawl, reaching out with one arm and turning her head in the opposite direction just as T had taught her in the yard where the corn grew. She was gliding now, smooth and steady, and the water moved from glacial to refreshing. Rabbit paced the shelf, yapping his encouragement and concern. He sensed the risk and was not entirely comfortable.

She paused and began to tread water, this time without the jerky desperation to ward off hypothermia. The nearby rocks threw off glints of sunlight that struck at the corners of her azure eyes. She blinked and turned her head away from the harsh light that would be the blessed source of warmth when she lay on the rocks at the end of her adventure.

She took in the unique solitude of this airy and majestic setting. Normally any natural sounds would be drowned out by the screams and shouts of the frustrated and joyous hordes, but today it was only her. The trill of robin calls were the only sounds echoing off the rocks, as if playfully answering themselves. Submerged and alone, she was able, at last, to prevail over the morning's earlier trials. The nightmare, the heat and her concern over her disobedience, all faded as she gave herself over to the serenity of the setting.

She set off from the east, keeping the west side in her sights. She had never made it from one end to the other. "They're too far apart. Don't you even think about it," was her mother's tedious admonition whenever Tommie bragged about being able to do it "real easy". The distance wasn't the sole peril or the most worrisome. The 50-foot drop at the south end was. Any object, from the smallest shoe to the largest branch, vanished when it hit the turbulence at bottom. A relentless current pulled the water in that southerly direction, and the pull, though subtle, was strong enough to worry the most seasoned swimmer. The boys of The Bluegrass Swim Club, a group of elite young swimmers, had a healthy respect for that drop.

Tommie wasn't concerned. Even though she could feel the subtle but relentless pull, she felt strong today. She hadn't been in the water since T had taught her the new way to move her head and how to keep her body straight and her arms strong. Concentrating real hard on what he said, she seemed to be moving through the water with a new fluidity since the last time she braved the pool. *Ain't no boy can beat me now,* she thought in triumph as she set a strong pace.

And it wasn't like she'd lied to her mother at breakfast, not really. For the past month, she'd been telling her she could get from one end to the other and that one day soon she would. It just so happened that today was that day. She'd even told her how T said she was getting to be a real good swimmer. Yet, her mother said "No." She always said "No." "No" was her answer to everything, at least everything Tommie seemed to want most. Even though her daddy also told her not to go near the falls without T, he also told her, "The way you learn is by doing stuff you have never done before." So, he was sort of sayin' it was ok 'cause she ain't never done this before, and that's what she would tell him if he found out and got mad.

The way she figured, even Rabbit gave her his approval. Besides, she had gotten so good she figured she could make it all the way across and be out and dry before Rabbit got back from chasing the squirrels and lizards.

T was gonna be mad, at least at first when she told him, she thought. And she would tell him. He was the one person she told everything to. He had a way he listened like most people don't. First, he'd give her that mad look and tell her she should know better than to be out there all by herself. Then she would look at his face, get real close, almost to his nose, and he would smile 'cause she knew he would be proud of her.

Even as she tried to convince herself that her mama and daddy might not be mad like she thought, something about this still made her nervous. This was about the most wrong thing she ever did, she figured, 'cause of that strange way her mama and daddy got about her coming here by herself. T might think he really needed to tell on her this time, even though he never did nothin' like that before. He could keep a secret every time she asked him too. He threatened to tell on her all the time, but he never did. Never. Not once that she could remember, anyway.

As she continued her steady glide through the water, a refreshing stasis occurred between the warmth of the sun on her back and the cold underneath. It was a sensation unique to swimming in the falls and a small reward for the death-defying act of entry. While plotting her scheme she had thought there might be an audience, actually kinda hoped there would be.

She envisioned whoops of surprise and encouragement coming from her friends that lined the rocks as they witnessed the miraculous event, but then Stanley Mitchell might show up. He was always appearing out of nowhere. *"Please God keep him away,"* she prayed silently. He was bad. It wasn't just that he ditched school a lot. He teased her and called her names and his daddy was a drunk who lived in a barn because nobody wanted him in the house. Sometimes, when Stanley Mitchell's mama got mad at him, she told him to go sleep out with the pigs and chickens too. Matter fact, Mrs. Gloadstone once kicked him out of the schoolhouse because he smelled so bad. Well, if he showed up today Rabbit might have something to say to him, she thought.

Even her head was moving the right way. That funny thing T showed her about moving it side to side was real hard to get used to but wasn't no problem today. When he first showed her she told him, "It felt 'bout as natural as a gator holdin' hands with his lunch," something her granddaddy said about stuff that didn't make no sense. He said, "jus' practice moving yo' arms and yo' head in a rhythm and it come to you." *If only he could be watchin' me now*, she thought. She would holler, *do you see me, T? Do you see how I can make my head move?*

Maybe it was a sign she was supposed to be here, 'cause she felt 'bout as good as she ever felt as her small frame moved purposefully toward her goal.

Then her mental kaleidoscopic changed views to the nightmare with a force that pushed aside all other thoughts, and the fog and the sounds and the fear descended on her like a shroud. Didn't matter what her Nana said about bad dreams being like your mind takin' out the trash. T wasn't no trash. T was T. That mutilated thing hanging from the tree could not be him. No way. Could it? She clenched her jaw in concentration and increased her speed but could not completely free herself of the nightmare's cloying presence.

She had been moving at a good clip so was surprised to see that her goal was still a significant distance away. All those stupid thoughts about Stanley Mitchell and T and the other stuff had made her lose her purpose and slow down. She also noticed that the sun no longer seemed to be able to keep the chill at bay and she realized, with an inkling of fear, that she felt colder. Well, she thought, she would have to just swim a little faster, that's all, and stop conjuring up all the crazy stuff. She had a job to do, like her daddy had jobs to do. Like T had jobs to do. She had a race to win against those boys at the Bluegrass Swim Club who wouldn't let her in. She took deeper breaths so she could turn her head to the side with every other stroke and she pulled harder. For a minute or two it worked. She felt a renewed energy and focus that collapsed just as quickly as it came.

She felt it in her arms first, a dragging feeling that had her struggling to pull them out of the water. The water seemed to be getting heavy, like a thickening pudding. Each stroke became a herculean task, it seemed, in a matter of seconds. The drag on her arms crept to her legs which began to feel like they were in the grip of two large, gloved hands that would loosen for a second then press down and make buoyancy impossible.

She struggled on with all of her 10-year-old will and determination but could not stave off a growing sense of terror. She caught a glimpse of the west end. It looked as far away as when she had first jumped in, maybe even farther. Impossible. Then, as if in answer, she felt the inextricable pull of the current dragging everything it caught toward the drop below. It had been working all along to slow her progress and was now aggressively forcing her into its current as she tired and struggled against it.

She imagined Stanley Mitchell standing on the bank pointing at her and laughing. Alone only briefly, he was joined by a throng of naysayers all following his lead, pointing and laughing. No way, she thought, even as her limbs became more like cement with each monumental inch of progress.

She grew aware of Rabbit barking in the distance. He was in distress, pacing from one end of the pool to the other barking out a warning that she was barely able to hear. But she heard enough to know that he was in a panic. She searched the shoreline and caught his eye and even from a distance she could sense his panting anxiety and see that he was alone. There was no one there to call out for help and leap to her rescue. She watched the west end move further and further away and the drop loom closer.

The rest happened quickly. What had been a slow drift, gained speed pulling her and various twigs and branches swiftly toward the drop. But there was nothing she could grab onto. Insubstantial pieces of debris bumped her and hurried past as if in eager anticipation of the drop below. Still, she grabbed onto anything she could catch only to let it go as she flailed about wildly, kicking and slapping the water in uncontrolled terror, aware of the yawning blackness hungry to claim her. The cold knifed through to her core and the water seemed to take on a thickness that pressed hard against any attempt to move through it.

Something brushed against her leg and her scream was cut off as the blackness pulled her below the surface with a sudden final abruptness. She was seized by an adrenaline rush that gave her just enough strength to kick and claw her way back up until her face was barely breaking the surface. Then she heard Rabbit and was flooded with relief until she realized that she could no longer see him on the shoreline and that the barking must have been her imagination crying out for rescue. *"This is all a dream."* The thought came to her suddenly and gave her fleeting seconds of hope that this was just another episode of her mental "waste removal" and she would wake up in her sweltering and safe bedroom.

It was the barking that brought her back to her hopeless reality. Then she heard splashing behind her and was seized with images of every monster she ever imagined until she turned to see Rabbit swimming toward her, his squat, powerful legs fighting the current and miraculously making progress. He was panting with exhaustion but unwavering in his single-minded focus on saving his master.

"Come on, Rabbit, I know you can do it. Come on boy," she got out in a gasping staccato. She saw a large oak branch advancing on him, moving faster than he was moving toward her. "Rabbit, hurry! Please!" The sound of her voice excited him, and he sped up as best he could but was losing the fight. The impossible pace required to get this close, the current and the cold were now working against him, and the branch was gaining speed, almost on top of him.

Her last memory in this life would be of her best friend, her Rabbit, being struck unconscious by the tree branch and heading toward the drop. She was able to get out one more desperate, barely audible, "Help", before the water choked shut her nose and throat. Vague images came to her in a flurry. They were dark, jarring, indescribable things. She had always loved reading horror stories about bottom dwellers taking unsuspecting souls as their supper, and now she felt those spindly, slimy appendages wrap around her ankles, pulling her into their pit and then, nothing.

CHAPTER 6

"You gon' dream them seeds into turnips?"
August was planting time for turnips, not only a kitchen staple but a dependable cash crop. T had paused and was leaning on his hoe, wiping his brow. He had evidently paused too long for a worker in the next row. This particular gnat was resentful of T's elevation to foreman, thinking the position belonged to him. As a result, he had become a constant source of irritation to T. He took a certain delight in ferreting out what he considered laziness and sloth. It seemed a better exercise than actually doing the work.

"You mind yo' own damn business, and I'll mind mine and not notice I plant three rows for yo' every one," T answered back.

"See, that's why nobody be talkin' to you. Ain't nothin' I said make you cross with me."

"Ain't nobody cross with you, jus' stay in yo' own business," and T turned back to his row.

Planting turnips was not simply a matter of dropping seeds in the ground, and the care and preparation was one of T's special talents. Earlier that morning, he had taken the seedlings that had been soaking overnight in rainwater with a sprinkle of lime and gently rolled them in ash for a quick dry. The fragile seedlings now rested in a tin at his side. This process, which T approached with the acumen of a surgeon, protected the plants from the voracious root maggot which could devastate the entire crop before any shoots could sprout. The lime was the key by making the seedlings unappetizing to predators.

He created a hole about an inch deep in the loamy soil, then placed three seedlings in each hole before gently covering them back up. The planting ritual was repetitious and a torment on the neck and back, and even with his forced tolerance for pain, T was careful to pace himself. Which still put him several yards ahead of his nemesis.

He straightened and wiped away the mid-morning sweat. He had been distracted. The memory of a recent experience continued to leave him more shaken than he cared to admit. His agitation made him even more of a man not to be trifled with this morning. The experience had the sense of unfinished business or maybe business that could not be finished because of his life and times. It was one of those unchangeable facts that he could not fix that he would typically file, forget and move on.

Kincaid was making his bi-monthly trip to Owenton for supplies. He usually went alone but needed T to join him on this trip as he had planned on picking up equipment that needed more muscle than his own. They were loading the wagon for the return when T caught a glimpse of a slave woman scuttling past. This was not an unusual sight, but this woman caught his eye. She had broad, sturdy shoulders and a presence that seemed familiar. She was gripping the hand of a boy who looked to be six or seven and with her free arm, she held a woven splint market basket that was full with produce covered with a red gingham cloth.

While being pulled along, the boy himself was pulling a metal cart with a missing wheel at the rear. T could not turn away. All other distractions vanished. She stopped at the corner, adjusted her basket, and blasted four inaudible words at the boy, who looked up at her and turned away sulking and resentful. T was close to hyperventilating and had to grab hold of the Wagons jockey box to steady himself.

"You know those folks?" Kincaid noticed T's reaction to the woman and the boy.

"No, it be hot today and guess I rose up too fast," he answered and grabbed his water jug and turned it up to his mouth and emptied it with one long swallow. "We gon' need some water before we head back, Mr. Kincaid."

"Guess we will now," he said, annoyed at T's greed. "Go on then but make it quick."

"Yes sir." T jogged to a well that rose near the corner where the slave woman had paused to scold her boy. He looked for them. They had vanished. This was Clay Street, which was the main street in Owenton and there were any number of shops and businesses that could have served as cover.

Then they caught sight of each other, she gasped and spilled several parakeet green apples. T watched her and the boy pick them up with the urgency of being on the run then disappear around a corner.

T's eyes shot down Clay Street past a freshly constructed two-story schoolhouse for any sign of the duo but saw nothing. There was no time to search the entire block.

As he headed back to the wagon, he remembered the two of them, pressed together in a stifling barn while a sadistic overseer leered from the shadows and took his own pleasure. He had wanted to study that face with eyes as big and brown as his own and a nose and mouth that looked to be his exact miniatures, but they had vanished.

He leaned on his hoe, now for honest support, as the memory continued to vex him. He was drenched like someone who'd been shaken awake from a fever. There were so many things that fell into the category of the unfixable, the unchangeable and for the most part he let those things be and lived on. He also knew he had children, probably lots of them. After all, that was the purpose of those forced unions. They had for the most part been mindless and without affection and he never thought about the outcome. Simply, when one was treated like an animal those are the thoughts and behavior that followed, and so it was with T.

This odd, visceral reaction to seeing that mother and son was unnerving, but not surprising. He never saw the offspring from those unions grow much past a year before he or mother and child were sold off. This little man was old enough to reveal his lineage, and he was T's little man. Every fiber of his being confirmed it and it was revelatory and unexpectedly painful. He inhaled deeply to try to clear his mind and reseal that steel door that kept the desire to be connected to his own, firmly out of reach.

His hoe met the soil with lackluster commitment as these thoughts continued to unnerve him. He found a worker he could trust and asked him to keep an eye out while he relieved himself. He didn't need to, but he needed to move, to get away and try to regain his bearing. He walked past the designated area and kept going. If Kincaid showed up and saw him missing, he would claim he needed to go be sick. Even if he didn't show up, that nosy little rodent would be in Mr. Kincaid's ear with a breathless report. So be it. He needed to walk, and he knew just where to go.

He strode out of the plowed acreage and onto an untended path that ran alongside it. After a couple hundred yards, he stopped and played at kicking up some loose gravel while keeping a keen eye out. Satisfied that he was alone, he made a sharp left into a thicket of flowering dogwood. This part of the plantation was a mass of unruly trees and bushes, thick, impenetrable and inviting to thieves. Since his intent was to go unwatched, it provided the ideal hideout.

He found his claim of ropy shrubs, which were easy for him to part. Big yellow poplar trees conspired with an occasional bald cypress to block out much of the unyielding sun. Lilting calls of the black-throated warbler and other forest orchestra kept him company. He became a bloodhound chasing a scent. He pressed forward, tearing aside more dogwood and the occasional brilliant oak leaf hydrangea, which though white, would turn the deepest burgundy in mere days.

He was soon deep in the forest. Splashes of hot, golden rays cut through the foliage as he came upon a clearing guarded by a tangle of ripe blackberries. They were gorgeously plumb and wondrously all his. "The Devil won't piss on these babies until October," he said to himself as he gently lifted one from its vine. It had taken the vines a couple of years to reach their present magnificence, since those first pilfered seeds he dropped in the ground. He was gambling that the sun would reach her hand down and hold them long enough to grow.

This bounty, his bounty, made him proud as the richest landowner in Louisa. He approached them with the gentle caution of a grateful lover. Dazzled by the perfection of one simply resting in his hand, he bestowed his own form of prayer before putting it in his mouth and letting the burgundy sweetness overtake his nose and throat.

He was reaching for a second helping but stopped midway when he heard splashing. The fields were close enough to pick up distant echoes of the terrified screams and joyful shouts that made up a day at the falls, but it was unusual for anyone to be there this early. It was most likely a group of kids that thought it better to be in that frigid pool than to sit in a stifling classroom sharing each other's misery, he figured. *"Good for them,"* he thought and continued to feast on his bounty and enjoy his solitude. He was fortunate to have an active, intelligent inner life that was the only company he needed, most of the time, which worked out well since no other company much came his way.

T's range of topics were extensive, a song here, a phrase he heard there. God's failings. Food. His blackberry sanctuary. This vibrant inner life would occasionally break free and include two-way conversations that did not always stay in his head. Today was a perfect example. His memory of the incident in Owenton was so authentic that someone close enough to hear might have heard him talking to some invisible companion.

As he gave himself over to the shaded sunlight, the tart sweetness of his largess and the tranquil security of his lush surroundings, even though it was still mid-morning, he yawned and stretched, fully ready to take a nap as if he didn't have to get back to the fields. Then a breeze, quite possibly pushed further along by the whoosh and the whisk of fans moving across the weathered faces of our old ones, connected like a live wire. It passed over him, as light as gossamer, then faded quickly, but not before echoing a very distinctive "help" to ears that were always tuned to foreboding. He was off like a rocket.

CHAPTER 7

He got to the falls in time to witness the branch bludgeon Rabbit and send him spinning toward the drop and Tommie disappear from view. He plunged in, mindless of the cold and the current, and propelled himself forward praying for the same echolocation or magic that drove dolphins toward their targets.

He pulled and kicked and grabbed but the cold would not be denied, and he became shockingly aware of the steep drop in temperature just below the surface that now seized his fighting limbs and sent his blood pressure rocketing and booming into his head. Despite his heroism he was being dragged toward the falls with merciless accuracy and realized that if he was this close to the drop Tommie and Rabbit had certainly gone down the falls.

He yanked and tugged in the direction where he thought he last saw Tommie and Rabbit but the crashing in his ears and near oxygen depletion made his accuracy nothing more than a prayer. If he stopped moving for a second the cold stabbed into him unmercifully, so he didn't stop. The oxygen depletion started to have its effect and without warning he thought he heard the screams of whippings and flesh being torn off backs then the wretched cries of the mulatto sisters being split apart and, as suddenly, the face of the boy he had taken to be his son.

A floating piece of debris struck his leg and brought him back to the present. It was a small tree limb and in the darkness, he thought it might be Tommie before it swept past. His clothes flapped against his arms and legs like sheets of lead. He kicked and pulled against them and was barely able to thrust his way back up. He broke the surface and gulped in air with such force it would almost not go in. He performed a wild scan of the shoreline. His good eye wasn't focusing fast enough, but what he could see did not include any sign of Tommie.

He willed breath deep into his belly and dove back under. When he opened his eyes in the frigid darkness, the water felt like twin anvils pounding him with its cold and muck and fear. His hands opened and closed in wild grasping movements, vainly trying to latch on to anything that resembled a limb or hair or clothing. He was rewarded with nothing as he moved deeper into the liquid purgatory.

The noise grew muffled, its intensity seeming to modulate with the ebb and flow of the throbbing in his inner ear. Mrs. Kincaid's warning flashed forward. She told Tommie to stay away from this place unless he was with her, and he was right there outside the open door to hear her say it. Her daddy said so too. *What could have put this fool thought in her mind!? So what it's hot. Wasn't no different from morning till night every day in August. What happened today?* He wondered in desperate frustration. She knew he would always come with her if she asked so long as it was okay with her mama and daddy. Despite the chill, an even colder sense of dread seized him at the thought of what would've happened had he not ditched the turnips in favor of his precious blackberries, but tragedy was still just at his fingertips.

He knew that even if he were able to achieve the unbelievable and save Tommie, there would be a phalanx of onlookers ready to take this opportunity for "justice." His relationship with Tommie was a powder keg in the county. It was considered "unnatural" by many who would gladly take this opportunity to invent

44

lies that turned his heroics into evidence of something evil.

If the unthinkable happened and Tommie didn't survive there would be, without question, a twisted retelling of events culminating in a bloodlust for vengeance that even Kincaid might be helpless to stop. He knew too many to name that went to their deaths or lost limbs based on false accusations by white men, women, and children. One of the first was Ol' Pete. He had to make do with three fingers on his left hand after being snatched out of his quarters one night by an overseer, ax in hand and taken to a coppering shed where he was questioned about antics surrounding a pit school in the woods. He confessed to the truth, that he knew nothing about no pit school. And he kept confessing to the only truth he knew even as the ax came down on his fingers as a warning to any nigger that might think about starting or attending one of those "schools" hidden deep in the woods. The overseer didn't take the entire hand or dangle him from a tree limb "'cause we a little short on you niggers right now."

These thoughts took seconds when a glint of light invaded his delirium. It was different from the other images: brighter, more luminous, more discernibly out of place. Like a powerful magnet, his instincts torpedoed him toward it, mindless of the depth and his near oxygen depletion.

As he got closer to the reflection, he was able to make out a listless figure that seemed to be offered up by a pair of unsteady, invisible hands. The object swayed with the rocking of the water and was pressed against the shale perimeter as pliably as any random piece of floating debris. Tommie had a necklace made from gold ring and cork and there it was, swaying with the current and intermittently reflecting the sun. She was bent so far forward that the necklace would have fallen off were it not for the tangle of blond hair that caught it at the very last minute. Had it been lost to the current, he might have never found her. He tore her shift from the rock that had stopped her plunge toward the falls and the water grew cloudy with blood where the shift had been snagged. Her inert body was buoyant and weighed nothing. He took her by the waist and started up.

Unconsciousness began an insipid competition with his scant reserves. He clamped down on his jaw and gripped the rocks to use them as steps. He endeavored to stay out the current while he pulled himself up with his free arm. For the first time since hitting the water, he was glad he hadn't lost his boots because they saved his feet from the jagged, cutting surfaces. He was not yet conscious of his left hand which, sliced like peach pulp on the palm, bled mere inches from his nose. The current was more rapid, and he made a vise of his arm, lest she be snatched away in a heartbeat. When his hand broke the surface, he refused to believe it and waved it wildly around to be certain, then hauled them onto the blessed, flat, sandstone shelf.

He lay next to her, his chest like a piston as it grabbed in air then blew it out with enough force to rattle his whole body. He turned his head to Tommie and saw her blue pallor and was barely able to sputter out a disbelieving, "No!" Then with teeth chattering he cried out again, "No! Sweet Jesus, No!" He pleaded to the same God he cursed. He tried to stand but his knees buckled. He fell onto his elbows which stopped his body from crushing hers. "Breathe!" he commanded, shaking her with dangerous force.

He abruptly stopped as a memory surfaced that offered Tommie a chance, most likely, her only chance. He shakily brought himself up on one knee and with

46

arms preternaturally steady lifted her up and gently draped her over the thigh of his other leg so that her stomach was pressed against it and her head was down. He had to tighten his calf to stop the spasms that were causing his leg to bounce uncontrollably. The movement was what he wanted but he needed to control it.

Blood was spilling from the wound on his palm. He ignored this and focused on his task. Her linen shift was ripped and red from their respective injuries. Her back, still warm from the heat of the rock, was rapidly turning to cold blue.

When he was a boy, he had seen a drowned slave named Fountain Hughes tossed over the back of a dray horse which was then set to trot. The bouncing movement had forced water out of the dying victim's lungs and saved his life. This bouncing movement was what he was now trying to replicate.

The knee that was on the rock had been scraping across its rough surface with every bounce and now he saw and felt the rush of warm, fresh blood soaking through his pant leg and painting the light stone red. He wondered when the pain would come. Nor was there pain where the rocks had slashed his palm. There was just blood, and it seemed to be everywhere.

She was still cold. So cold. He had the disquieting thought that if she were this cold all the way through…but he kept up his gentle, rhythmic bouncing. He had not been aware of the throbbing in his bad eye, but now it pulsed and vibrated with painful insistence. Since the injury, it had never been the same. It was sensitive to the seasons and fluctuations in temperature and was now pulsating with his heartbeat.

Tommie was small for her age and even his gentle bouncing caused her extremities to dance and flop like a rag doll and he had to look away. That's when he noticed there was no sound and it had the same effect of a gunshot in its shocking surprise. No bird calls, no sounds of leaves rustling, not even the air seemed to move. There seemed to be a suspension of time as if nature was standing by for an outcome.

He started pressing on the space between her scapulae. He had never seen this done before, he only knew that the water had to come out and he thought that maybe if he pressed... He tried to think of one of the many prayers that had been drummed into him as a boy. But he had no luck summoning spirits that were as faceless to him as his unknown dead ancestors.

The rustling stopped everything. It came from behind him where a thicket of birch trees lined the perimeter. He became rigid as the stone beneath him. The impossible tableau he and Tommie presented could lead to a not swift and very painful death for him. Time stopped until the suspect squirrel came into view and quickly disappeared with his prized pawpaw. His heart did not slow immediately.

"Don't you die. You hear me, Tommie? Don't you dare die on T," he whispered as if it were the prayer he sought and it released his tears, a frustrating apogee to all his useless heroics. He didn't stop to wipe them away and the warm droplets pooled on the small of her back, which reacted with an involuntary flinch too small for him to notice. He kept up the bouncing and the pressing and the keening, and the water continued to drip from her hair and clothes and onto his worn boot. He looked for the return of color to her fingers, to the tips of her ears, the nape of her neck and saw no life.

Miss Kincaid would lose herself for sure. He'd seen it happen before with the enslaved and white women alike. The steady and sure descent into a listless

48

fog from which there would be no return. Rabbit would be mourned and forgotten but Tommie would always be just around the next corner and always just out of reach. "Of all the fool things, why this? Why this one, Tommie?" he pleaded as he shook his head in frustration. One time he caught her tossing rocks at a beehive which resulted in her staying out of school for a week as her mama tended to the angry, painful welts that rewarded her curiosity. Tommie did those kinds of things, things for which sometimes they both paid a price.

"Hey, you, nigger!" T whirled around. "What are you doing there with Tommie? Let her go." Stanley Mitchell was holding a rock he looked ready to launch. Wide eyed with disbelief he hollered, "You killed her. Sweet Jesus. You killed, Tommie."

"You know me, Massa Stan. You know I ain't killed nobody. I pull her out the falls."

"Oh, I know you, all right." He dropped the rock and cupped his hands and let loose a scream, "Help! Help! He killed her! This nigger killed Tommie!" It echoed off the rocks like a clarion call to the Devil himself. He retrieved his rock and launched it at T and it thudded off his shoulder. T only flinched and continued trying to bring life into Tommie. Stanley, who looked younger and smaller than Tommie, reacted as if dared. "I told you, nigger, let her go!" He advanced on T's back, now with a stick in hand.

T looked over his shoulder and Stanley stopped in his tracks. Whatever privilege he felt, T's undeniable presence gave Stanley pause. T could crush him like a bug even though he never knew a nigger to raise his hand against a white child, still… T noted that the switch Stanley carried would not inflict serious injury and blotted him out as he returned his focus to Tommie.

49

This insult went right to Stanley's biblical belief in his superiority, and he fell on T, beating him with all the force of his righteous nine-year-old anger.

T made no attempt to shield himself or to consider the very real possibility that those blows, the sun and the weight of Tommie on his knee would be his last earthly memories. He shifted and Stanley jumped back. "I won't touch you, Massa Stan. You don't be afraid of me."

"Damn right you won't touch me," Stanley squeaked out.

The mob would be here soon with their rocks, their sticks and their ropes. They would take Tommie then descend on T. Whatever was left after they took their souvenirs would be hoisted up and left as a reminder of how the world worked in these southern United States. Whatever happened today would bring peace, final and rewarding. T had concluded some time ago that since death made the pain stop, there was really no need for heaven, and he was ready for the pain to stop. As if in answer to his silent prayer, voices started making their way through the noise of the falls. "Over here!" Stanley shouted, "The nigger killed Tommie and tried to kill me too!" The crowd noise grew angrier as the first of the mob appeared.

"I see 'em" someone shouted as the outrage grew louder. T didn't look up as they started moving up the rocks. *It will be soon now,* he thought, and once started, would be closer to ending. His breathing was steady and without fear.

A shot echoed off the rocks with the magnitude of a canon. Screams rang out and several people took cover. The crowd stopped advancing in a desperate search for the source.

"The next one of you that makes a move toward T will meet the business end of this gun,"

50

shouted Kincaid, almost frothing with fear and anger. Nobody moved except to clear his way to where T sat with his lifeless daughter.

He met T's eyes. They were blank with grief too monumental to let escape. His face was a painful, twisted history of all that had transpired. Kincaid searched T's eyes for the impossible not to be true, and when T looked down with the whisper of a head shake, Kincaid moved toward them as if disembodied. There could be no world where this was possible, then Tommie coughed.

CHAPTER 8

The room had always been familiar and comforting. From the yellow lace curtains that covered the window opposite the iron bed frame and cotton mattress where Tommie lay, to the chair where her mother now sat. But all was unfamiliar to Grace now. The chair still held her, as it always had, steadfast and solid, but its deeper meaning, its reminder of all things normal and untroubled, abandoned her as she stared down at her sleeping daughter. Nights in this chair, in this room, at Tommie's bedside, sharing nightly prayers and sweet secrets had been the best part of her existence.

The door opened slowly, and Kincaid quietly beckoned her out. Once outside, she searched her husband's face, he slowly shook his head. "Oh no," she said, "Are you sure?"

"T stayed in the water for a long time, then walked the banks and couldn't find him. He may have gone over the falls."

"Roland, that dog was everything to her. She'll be heartbroken." Kincaid held her as she quietly wept.

"We'll keep looking," was all he could offer. She broke from the embrace and returned to Tommie's bedside where she would remain vigilant for the rest of the night. She needed to be the first person Tommie saw when she awoke. And to absorb the tonic of her daughter's living, breathing presence, to help her stay on the right side of sanity. But now all was unfamiliar. When her eyes settled on an object it was as if she was staring through it, a solid that misted into something else then back again.

After getting Tommie out of her wet clothes, dressing her wounds and putting her to bed, the truth of what could have happened caused her world to tilt. Roland had to help her to where she now sat. She asked to be alone with her daughter but was now fearful that she would be overcome as she imagined the unthinkable.

She had almost lost her only child today, and there would be no conceivable world without her in it. The silence was broken by the grandfather clock in the main room. This ticking. This quietly insistent, familiar and steady reminder of the day passing, invaded her fog and acted as an additional anchor to what was real.

She reclaimed her tentative grip on the present and took several deep breaths, determined that Tommie not see how close she had come to losing herself. She smoothed a few wisps of hair from Tommie's damp forehead. As she softly rubbed her moist fingers together and as the stillness absorbed her, she was reminded again of her failure to give Roland the family they assumed was their birthright.

Tommie was a miracle baby, surprising no one more than the doctors who told her something about her womb not being strong enough after a series of miscarriages. She treated this news as a scarlet letter and took to bed for several days in a dark depression. Their dream was too big, too real to be snatched away because she was not woman enough to make it come true. She was a failure at her most precious responsibility as a wife and no amount of gentle, supportive reasoning from her husband could disabuse her of this belief.

He offered a stoic and uncomplaining shoulder with no insight into his own shattered dreams. This masculine instinct of denial only served to magnify the blow. He was ill-equipped to recognize the damage of his well-intentioned dishonesty. She needed to comfort, to be taken out of her own center of pain and join him in his. His refusal to lay open his own wounds, in her eyes, diminished his efforts. This all happened before Rabbit entered their lives, so there was nothing to distract from the quiet hopelessness that pervaded their lives. Their fleeting moments of happiness could not escape the pall of sadness that clung like a second skin.

The news came on a Tuesday. That Sunday they felt well enough to attend church services. They were perfunctory Christians, attending church so they could not be accused of not attending, and prayed out of habit. Both done with the same mindless regularity as making the morning coffee. But this morning they were hoping for nothing less than divine intervention, grasping at anything that might help them understand and cope with the impossible.

As soon as they stepped through the doors of the church, Grace regretted their decision. There was no way to hide the effects of days in bed with minimal nourishment, and the whispers and side glances nearly erased any confidence she had been able to muster.

"My brothers and sisters," the minister began, "as I was reflecting on my message this morning, I did what I always do. I opened the precious good book to a passage guided by the hand of the Lord, and He led me to Proverbs 3 verses 5 through 6." He put on reading glasses. "Trust in the Lord with all thine heart and lean not unto thine own understanding. In all thy ways acknowledge Him, and He shall direct thy paths." He took off his glasses, and using them as a pointer continued, "Now, why He lead me there, I was not immediately privy to and then I thought, "lean not unto thine OWN understanding" but is it really just your own understanding you have to question? What about the understanding of someone else? The other man that tells you you can't, when God might tell you you can? Are you going to believe God or another man? How will you know you can't until you have a talk with our Lord in heaven? Brothers and sisters, it seems like there is always someone out there trying to break our sprits by telling us our dreams are impossible."

There was little chance that Grace would not be deeply affected by any message, given her fragile state. But this one had her transfixed.

"My dear brethren I'm here to tell you that nothing, let me be clear about that, nothing is impossible through the grace of our Lord Jesus. Say amen if you believe that." She added her voice to the chorus of amens and walked out of those church doors confident there would be a miracle in store for them.

Kincaid was less convinced. He thought it was more coincidence than divinity. He worried more that the message would aggravate his wife's already fragile state, and his concern proved prescient. A night did not go by without Grace praying for the miracle baby they were promised and nothing Kincaid said could convince her otherwise.

After several months he pleaded with their doctors to intervene. She was prescribed a small amount of bromide salts, which helped them through those difficult months of unanswered prayers. Slowly, with great care and a loving patience that moved her to a profoundly deeper love for her husband, she began to improve. Through it all he remained her stalwart and opened the door only to the entrance, and no further, to his own profound, sense of loss and disappointment.

The demands of farm life proved to be its own therapeutic distraction, and after several months they were on their way to a new kind of normalcy.

About six months after she stopped taking the bromide salts and the lethargic side effects had long vanished, she was gripped with a bout of unshakable fatigue. Kincaid prepared a ginger infused tea that Miss

Edna, a well know slave "healer," had recommended. But it didn't help. She still found she could barely keep her eyes open past noon. Shortly after the fatigue set in, she thought she might cheer herself up one morning by slipping into one of her fancy dresses she brought with her from Owenton, most of which hung in her closet, unsuitable for the work of a farmer's wife.

The one she chose was a favorite party frock with a delicate floral pattern and a high neck and long sleeves. She had spent a few luxuriant moments admiring herself in it not even a month ago to the delight of Roland who appreciated the distraction and wisely joined in with an invitation to the "ball." After a dance or two she was transported back to Owenton and a past as different from her present as almost never to have existed. A past that included escaping from a penguin of a man that had been her betrothed.

Now, even before she called in Roland to help with the hooks and eyes, she could tell the back wouldn't close. Her diet hadn't changed, and she was as active around the plantation as she had been before that fateful doctor's visit. She was worried she might be ill but said nothing to her husband because they could not afford to waste money on a useless doctor's visit. She put the dress away with a commitment for one less slice of cheese and maybe one piece of toast instead of three.

A few weeks after that she was putting away laundry, when her eyes fell on the contents of the drawer that held her feminine supplies. With a start, she realized she was several weeks late. There was no exact timetable for these things, but she was well beyond the furthest she had ever gone. She had no expectations of pregnancy so she hadn't paid no attention. Now, as she stared into the drawer, she had to grab onto to its sides to steady herself.

When her head cleared, she collapsed into a chair, legs splayed and arms flopped over the sides in wonderment. After thanking Jesus for His delayed response, she thought about what to say, if anything, to her husband. If she were truly pregnant it was so early it might not take. Just as the others hadn't. In the end she decided to wait through those terrifying first few months. If this were not to be, she would bear it alone and pray for her sanity. She reasoned that one shattered soul was preferable to two.

The first month of waiting was followed by a second and finally, miraculously, that was followed by a third month with her baby intact. She was contemplating how to tell him one afternoon when he playfully tapped her on the rump and commented on how she seemed to be getting a little thick. "Well, I certainly hope so!" she responded with such enthusiasm that Kincaid wrinkled his brow in confusion. She didn't say anything else but held his gaze, smiling and waiting. Fortunately, Kincaid was quicker than most men. An astonished, "Oh, No. Oh My Lord," came rushing out as he grabbed her. "You sure, Grace, are you sure?!

"Yes," she responded through tears. "Roland, we're going to have a baby." He went to hoist her up in his enthusiasm. She put her hands on this chest to stop him. "We must be careful, my darling." She placed her hands on her belly. "Our little one will need some extra care."

She remembered those pregnancy months as a kind of nirvana, apart from morning sickness, which seemed like a cruel joke in an otherwise miraculous process. Roland was the picture of a nervous father to be, never letting her lift a hand and jumping at every groan and complaint, ready to fix it, and most often having no idea how. Then Tommie arrived, and they both knew there would be no greater love, and today she almost lost her. But God had granted them another miracle.

CHAPTER 9

K incaid paused, straining to catch the hint of a sob or cry. He was reluctantly carving a path under one of the many large oaks that made up the property and shaded him from the afternoon sun. This one was close enough to Tommie's window, but the proximity was barely able to assuage his feelings of guilt for abandoning his wife when she had asked to be alone with her own noisy panic. She seemed to be drawing strength and calm from the solid, breathing presence of her only child and he prayed this would bat away the near madness that threatened to take hold. But if her courage flagged, he would be there in an instant.

He had been outside for several hours and he hoped he had given her the solitude she needed. He entered Tommie's bedroom with the quiet and reverence of entering a chapel. His wife looked up at him with a face drawn in grief and exhaustion, but he knew she would stay in that chair all night and made no attempt to coax her to their bed. *"She is where she needs to be,"* he thought, and he gently kissed the top of her head. "I'm gonna go see T and I'll be right back." She was asleep almost before he closed the bedroom door.

T was out back, and Kincaid was heading that way when he heard a wagon approaching from the front. He opened the front door just as a buckboard pulled up, weighted down by the generous spread of Mrs. Gloadstone, the resident schoolmarm, accompanied by her cadaverous husband who wore a perpetual look of astonishment. It was clearly not his idea to drop by. As Kincaid descended the porch, he took advantage of the placement of the wagon to block out the sun. With the cloth required to keep her girth in a state of decency, Mrs. Gloadstone might have shaded the entire house herself. The dress had sleeves puffy enough to risk sending the buckboard airborne if a breeze were to swoop down and fill them.

Kincaid approached them warily as Mrs. Gloadstone had been outspoken about her disdain for Tommie's relationship with T. Her nearly vanishing husband held onto the reins with thin hands that looked almost insulted by the long, boney fingers they were forced to support. His linen shirt draped over his skeleton more like a death shroud and was cut by a black woolen vest that on most men would add a touch of elegance and volume. Failing on both counts, it hung off the linen as if trying to get away. His gaunt face with its sunken eyes, lips so thin as to be non-existent and nose sharp as a razor, completed the impression of an undertaker accompanying a florid beast through purgatory. Kincaid was not put off by the undertaker's opinions, because he had none. He greeted them.

"Mr. Gloadstone, Mrs. Gloadstone."

"My Billy and me were just on our way to town and thought we'd check up on you. We heard about Tommie and wanted to offer our thoughts and prayers."

"Thank you. I'll pass them onto the missus."

"Oh, you think I might have a word? Sometimes an understanding womanly presence can be such a comfort when this sort of thing happens."

"That's good to know, Mrs. Gloadstone, but I wouldn't want to keep you from your day. You were generous just to stop by."

"It's no bother, really. Tommie is such an inquisitive child. I'm so glad that she is safe."

"You can thank T for that, you know, the nigger."

"Hmm, well, are you sure I can't offer some comfort to Mrs. Kincaid?"

60

"Absolutely."

"Well, that was definitive."

"Indeed. Good day to you both," Kincaid turned away without waiting for a reply.

T was sitting on a worn stump in the Kincaid backyard. He was awkwardly holding a small oak branch, when he heard a wagon approach. He recognized the voice of Gloadstone. She had been candid with Tommie about her mistrust of him, going so far as to warn her parents about the dangers of "putting your child in the trust of that mean-looking nigger." Mrs. Kincaid promised that she wouldn't tell her how to teach her classes and Gloadstone shouldn't presume to tell her how to raise her daughter, especially since she had no children of her own. One day T had the revelation that she looked like she sucked in a lot of air then couldn't get it out. Tommie proclaimed that she would be known to them as "Pig Gloadstone" from that day forward.

T held the oak branch in one bandaged hand while trying to shape it into something with his favorite knife in the other, a knife he had kept a secret until Kincaid witnessed his artistry. He also figured that if T wanted to kill him, he could do it just as easily with a rock as with a knife. While he could whittle a corn pipe out of a cob like thousands of others, it was with the right piece of pliable wood that T displayed his true gifts. A shelf in Tommie's bedroom held a startlingly detailed menagerie of animals as a testament.

Today things were not going well. If he applied too much pressure to the wood or turned it to get at a particular angle, he was rewarded with a shooting pain through his bandaged hand. After struggling with the knot of wood for a few more minutes, he threw it over his shoulder in frustration and put his knife back in his pocket, still marveling that it wasn't lost in the water.

He had settled in the backyard after carrying Tommie into the house and carefully putting her on the sofa. Mrs. Kincaid had the wisdom to choose the sofa in order to keep her bed dry. He wanted to stay close in case he was needed, at least until sundown. Mr. Kincaid came out of the back door with a couple of glasses of water.

"Here, you can probably use this." T took one big gulp.

"Much obliged. How Tommie be?"

"She's resting. I imagine she'll sleep through the night. Besides a few cuts and scrapes on her back, she should be good as new thanks to you."

"Wasn't nothin' nobody else wouldn't do."

"I can't speak for nobody else 'cept you, T, and God bless you." They didn't speak for a few minutes. "Never told you about what happened up at those falls when I was boy, did I?" he continued.

"No sir."

"Wasn't anything that I'm proud of and it will follow me till the day I die. After what you did today, I think you deserve to know."

"That be yo' business, Mista Kincaid, ain't nothin' you owe me to tell."

"You're right. But maybe I need you to listen. Been having a heavy heart for a very long time, T, and you do me a service if you let me just get it out." T shrugged. "Was about 15, I think, when it happened. See, my daddy and me didn't see eye to eye on this place. Even then I saw the injustice of one man owning another and did not want to spend the rest of my life on a plantation.

But he saw me as the only one that could keep it going because my older brother, Leon, was reckless and had started in on drinking that same summer. Some people take to this life naturally and I was not one of

62

those people. I was into my books and saw myself living in a big city wearing suits and working in an office, and I was pig-headed about it.

That summer my uncle paid us a visit and told my daddy that a solicitor friend of his was looking for an apprentice for the summer in Frankfort. It was a dream come true for me, but my daddy said there was no way that he was gonna let me go. We got into a big fight about it, the worst one we ever had, and I ran out of the house. Didn't know where I was going, just needed to run away from him always telling me no. Wasn't gonna get too far, though, since I only had the clothes on my back.

Anyway, I got tired and fell asleep against an old birch tree that was close to the falls. I remember thinking I had never seen so many stars before and, to tell you the truth, I never saw a sky like that ever again. So, I'm asleep and think I'm dreaming 'cause I heard these voices. Turns out there were some boys at the falls in the middle of the night, which didn't make sense. It was too dark to swim, and you could hurt yourself bad on those rocks.

Then I heard a girl scream and I jumped up to go see what was happening, but before I got there, I heard a splash and the boys came running my way. I could hear them arguing with each other, so I decided to hide behind some bushes because they sounded scared and angry, and it was three of them and one of me.

When they got closer, I heard them say something about how Judge Whiteside was gonna kill them. One of the boys was the son of a rich landowner named Wallace and just about everybody in town, including my daddy, had to do business with that family because it seemed like they owned some of everything. So, the son, they called him Jr. Wallace, told the other two, George Watson and Jonny Pitt, that his family would destroy their families if they told what happened. He said no one would believe them anyway because he was rich, and they were poor.

I didn't know if he could really do that, but I was young and scared and I believed him just like those other two boys did. A couple of days later when I was coming home from school, I noticed a lot of people going toward the falls. Turns out they found Judge Whiteside's daughter downstream. I'll never forget the sound of The Widow Whiteside's screams. I could hear her all the way from where I was at the bottom of the mountain. It was like something I never heard, and I ran home and closed myself up in my bedroom."

Kincaid stopped speaking for a moment, lost in the memory. "Her name was Jesse and you see, T, I never told anybody that I knew what happened to that girl. Someone claimed to see some black boy talking to her earlier that day and I still have nightmares over what they did to him on account of me being a coward. That boy could have been you."

"You don't come when you do today, I be that boy," agreed T. "You ain't told nobody what you know?"

"Just my wife. She wanted me to tell the sheriff, but what could I prove now? Just because I said it happened doesn't mean anybody would believe me and the Wallace's are still a powerful family."

T had heard of the legendary Wallaces and said, "So that be why you and the missus be beside yo'selves 'bout the falls."

"That's right. Ain't something we would ever tell Tommie, but we think about it every time she ask us to go there."

"Seems to me you be right, Mista Kincaid. You bring nothin' but trouble to yo' family, you talk 'bout it now. Besides, you ain't the one done it."

"That doesn't matter, T. That girl was somebody's daughter. They say that Judge Whiteside went to an early grave grieving over that child. I'm the only one that could've let him die knowing the truth, even as horrible as it was."

"That be why you like this, ain't it?"

"What do you mean?"

"Why you treat us like you do."

"That's part of it. I am hoping for some grace come judgment day, but it's also the right thing to do. I believe what I say about you and me."

"So, what happened to them other boys?"

"They all left Louisa and I heard one of them was killed in a fight. Think it was George Watson. Folks say Jr. Wallace was sent somewhere to keep him from tarnishing the family name. He just started getting into more and more trouble. I don't know, T, when I think about what could have happened today if you hadn't been there to save Tommie, it's like God is still trying to make me pay."

"Can't say nothin' 'bout that. Yo' God ain't never been right by me, but can't you say he put me there to save Tommie?"

"That's true," admitted Kincaid. "I will be saying a prayer of forgiveness and one of thanks this evening."

CHAPTER 10

Prayers of thanks and forgiveness also weaved in and out of Rev. Clyde's service a few days after Kincaid's confession to T. He was facing a rapt group of black faces in a small room on one of the largest plantations in Kentucky. The Wallace plantation was owned by the father of the threatening teen in Kincaid's tale and today the Rev. held his audience spellbound as he spoke of obedience.

"And not just to the Lord above, my children, but to those good massas that give you food and shelter. For they are sent from God to keep us from sin and show us the way to the kingdom, and it is a glorious kingdom. Who walks with our Jesus this morning?" He shouted out. Shouts rang back in response. Even louder, he shouted, "Who BELIEVES Jesus died so we can see the glory." The room erupted once more, except for his son, Raymond, who sat on a stump off to the side.

The proclamation that God ordained blind obedience to The Massa was required if these meetings were to take place, but it was one that Raymond would never deliver from his pulpit. He was heir apparent to his father's legacy and wanted to jump up and shout, NO! whenever he heard his father deliver this edict with the same passion as he delivered the Lord's prayer. Blind obedience in the face of unspeakable cruelty would strip away the last vestiges of self-respect his enslaved brothers and sisters might have, and he would have no part of it.

Massa almost never showed up at these meetings so he would never know. His father knew this too but was too much in love with his vaunted position to put it at risk. Raymond accused him of delivering the congregation into the hands of the Devil and this led to some of their most heated arguments.

Everyone agreed Rev. Clyde could land a phrase with fire and passion but, thought Raymond, not with much insight. His goal was to make the congregation feel good and little else. He often told his son, "Ain't no need to go too deep into scripture since they won't understand. Yo' job is to make them forget all they pain." This was not good enough for Raymond who felt that it was possible to make the scripture interesting and accessible to anyone, you just had to want to do it.

He glanced over at his father and noticed that he was sweating a little more profusely than he usually did then, just as he was about to launch into his next call and respond exercise, he suddenly hunched over and collapsed.

***

"You been takin' the medicine Miss Edna give you?" Raymond asked. His father was laying on a straw bed in the quarters they shared. It reflected their hierarchy on the plantation and was nicer than the typical slave shack. It also held a small table and chairs.

"I been prayin' for a healing. That woman claims to believe in our Lord, but I also know she bring back strange voodoo from where come from."

"But it work, Daddy. You say it make the pain go away."

"It be the prayer that take the pain away."

"Well, take some now and we pray too," he said as he poured some of the elixir in a cup and his father drank. Then they proceeded to pray the pain away. Soon, because of the medicine or prayer or both, Rev. Clyde settled. Raymond started to prepare dinner.

"Sista Maxine girl look pretty today. What's her name? Sheila?" his father asked.

"She ain't the one I take for a wife. I told you that."

"Don't know why you need to be so particular. Plenty of good women out there. And I told you it might even be a healin' for me when you find one."

"I ain't stop looking, I promise."

"Don't take too long. Like I tell you, people can start thinkin' evil, filthy things 'bout a man who take too long to find a woman. You need to know that too, son."

This was not the first time Raymond had heard this, and it always left him with an undefined sense of guilt. It was as if Rev. Clyde thought that his slight, studious son might be at risk for this particular kind of evil. Through his passionate readings of The Book of Leviticus with his son, it was clear that the thought filled Rev. Clyde with a deep sense of shame and fear. "You ain't need to say that to me, Daddy. Jus' ain't found nobody that's all," said Raymond.

He ate his dinner while his father slept. He was 19 and there were men at his age that had "jumped the broom" with or without their massa's consent. Massa Wallace had allowed Raymond's father and mother to have the ceremony and would probably allow Raymond as well, but he wasn't interested.

There had been no one that captured his heart more than the scriptures. He felt a calling to minister to his enslaved brethren, to teach them the lessons of the Bible in a way that was more personal and relevant than the uniformed lessons his father fed to the congregation.

But it was those times when his father would talk about the love he had for his wife, that Raymond truly felt on unsteady ground. The reminiscence often ended with his father in tears even though she had passed more then ten years ago.

As devoted as Raymond was to the scriptures and enjoyed the respect and admiration his father's station brought to their lives, it was also isolating. No one reached out just to be a friend. It was as if folks assumed that God provided everything Raymond needed, but He did not. This was brought home with painful clarity when his father would remind him of the beauty of his relationship with his wife. He always ended these reflections expressing a fervent desire that God grant his only son the gift of such a union.

He would never admit how these conversations revealed his profound loneliness, because he didn't have the language. He could not deny a longing for that same intimacy and passion, and frustration that God seemed to not want to bring it into his life.

Rev. Clyde would never see his son jump the broom because he died a month later. Raymond felt unprepared to fill his legendary shoes, but all eyes now looked to him as the voice of God and he would look to that same God for guidance. One day he was ministering to one of the younger enslaved who thanked the "Rev. R" and in time that's who he became to everyone. Now that he was no longer under the huge shadow cast by his father, he struggled to find his own voice. He also found that scripture was becoming a less successful surrogate for a loving, physical presence in his life, one that remained out of reach.

CHAPTER 11

"Mama, is T okay?"

Mrs. Kincaid was jolted awake. She thought she had just closed her eyes, but sunlight was streaming through the window. She took Tommie's hands. "He's fine, Honey," she said.

"Where's Rabbit?"

"We're still looking for him. I'm sure he'll turn up. T went to look for him this morning."

Tommie burst into tears. "He tried to save me, Mama. He tried so hard to save me," she repeated through racking sobs as her mother held her.

"I'm sure he did, sweetheart, and we won't stop looking for him, don't you worry." But Grace had no expectation they would ever see Rabbit again.

With her head still in her mother's lap she said, "I'm so, so sorry, Mama. I know you and daddy are really mad, but I promise, I mean, I really promise, I won't ever do that again."

Mrs. Kincaid was glad her daughter couldn't see the tears in her eyes. "Well, you shouldn't have done that fool thing, that's true," she said with painfully gentle reproach as she stroked Tommie's hair. "But the Lord brought you back to us and we think He considers what you've been through payment enough, just like me and your daddy." Tommie squeezed her mother tighter as she quieted down.

She ate sporadically and would spontaneously burst into tears over the next several days. Sleep offered a unique challenge as her scarred back tried to heal and she would wake from a turbulent night, moody and emotionally fragile. The doctor assured them that other than the visible scars there was nothing physically wrong with her, but the shock of losing Rabbit would keep her in a fragile state for a little while. He advised them to make sure she ate, got plenty of rest and remained calm. Mrs. Kincaid prepared her favorite dishes only to have them nibbled at then pushed aside. Her father was no more successful with his promises of fishing trips and other adventures. They began to worry that she was descending into a dangerously brittle state.

T paid her a visit about three days later. As he sat by her bed, he pulled out a carving. "Look what I find on the porch," and presented her with an uncanny likeness of Rabbit carved out of oak.

Tommie burst into tears and hugged T with all the ferocity her ten-year-old frame could muster. He uncomfortably returned the embrace. "Thank you, T! It looks just like him!"

"You welcome. Maybe one day we figure who be leaving these on yo' porch. I jus' be vexed, like always."

"Oh, T. I know it's you, I know it!" She hugged him even tighter, tearful and smiling at the same time. It was the first time she had genuinely smiled since the accident.

"And I keep tellin' you I ain't even know what a knife look like," he said through a half smile. "Where you think to put him? Got to make sure it ain't close to no squirrel, else they won't stand no chance if he gets hungry."

She got out of bed with surprising energy and walked over to her menagerie. "I know! I'll put him next to the horse, 'cause he likes to play with the horses."

"That a fine idea, Tommie." She placed him next to a horse and lingered as her hand traced the lines of his coat, then she quietly returned to bed, the somber mood returning.

"When you think you come back out, Tommie?"

"I don't know. Ain't felt like doin' nothin'." Suddenly she grabbed his shirt sleeve "Oh T, I had a really bad dream 'bout you! You got to promise me, you stay far away from the Crazy McKinney house! You got to promise me, please T, promise me!"

"Okay, Tommie, I promise. I ain't never been there and got no reason to go." He patted her hand trying to calm her.

"Okay. You just stay away from that Devil place!"

"Don't you worry 'bout that, you got my word. Now, you jus' calm yo'self and get some rest, 'cause I really need you to come visit me. I take to talkin' to trees since you ain't come out and people lookin' at me even funnier than they always do." She grinned at this. "But I know you come out when you ready, jus' hope it don't be too long." He got up. "You get yo' rest now."

"You be careful, T."

"I been takin' care of myself for a long time and it's been workin' pretty good so far. You come to see me soon as you can." He left her to rest, distracted and out of sorts by her passionate and unexpected warning.

That night was proving to be another restless one for Tommie as she contemplated her shelf of wild miniatures. Light from a full moon shone through her window and illuminated Rabbit in eerie shadows such that Tommie could not take her eyes off him. She could almost believe that if she stared long enough, he might start moving, but soon enough her breathing slowed and, gratefully, her world blurred and just as quickly she was at the schoolhouse with Pig Gloadstone calling her name.

"Tommie, would you be so kind as to tell us what 12x9 equals." All eyes shifted to her. Pig

72

Gloadstone knew Tommie was not good with her multiplication tables and there was a smile of snarky triumph as she anticipated her failure. Tommie looked around at the faces of her classmates who were also clearly relishing her impending fall. Then with a shock she noticed Rabbit on the floor beside Gloadstone's desk.

"Rabbit!" she shouted and tried to get up to go toward him, but something kept her pinned to her seat and she couldn't move. Rabbit casually looked up at Gloadstone as if waiting for instruction.

"Oh, he's mine now Tommie," she said with smug satisfaction. "You think he wants to be with you after you and that nigger let him drown?"

"I didn't let him drown! You're a liar!" she heard herself scream. Rabbit started whimpering.

"How dare you raise your voice at me! Come up here this minute, young lady!" She took a ruler out of her desk drawer ready to deliver punishment. Tommie dropped her head and this time she was able to slowly rise from her desk chair and shuffle forward. Rabbit's moans became more intense, seeming to block out the other noise in the room as she continued her slog toward Pig Gloadstone, who oddly seemed to be moving further away. Then suddenly Rabbit stood up and barked.

She sprang up in bed with a start. Her moonlit menagerie was the first thing to fill her vision and ground her to the present. This was not her first dream about Rabbit, and she lay back in bed newly enveloped in the pain of his loss. Then she realized she must still be dreaming because there was that whimpering again, but this time she was in her own room and it was still night and the moon was just the same. *Please God not a nightmare about Rabbit,* she prayed and squeezed her dream eyes tight, but it wasn't working and in fact the whimpering grew louder and this time it was followed by scratching. She leapt out of bed as if shocked by a thunderclap and ran to her window and there, below it, thin and with blood caked on one side of his head but with eyes full of love and gratitude, was her Rabbit.

There was no more sleep that night. After the initial shock of his heroic arrival Kincaid went to get T. A closer examination revealed an injured leg in addition to the scar on his head. T brought in water and Mrs. Kincaid heated it and gently cleaned and treated his wounds while he gratefully licked her hand as often as he could get to it. After all was done, they gathered outside to catch any stray breeze offered up on an August night. Rabbit lay at Tommie's feet snoring loudly.

"I figure the leg got hurt when he went over the falls." T said.

"And he was able to survive that? Always knew he was a strong beast," offered Mrs. Kincaid. Rabbit chuffed, never one to ignore a compliment even in sleep. "But you looked everywhere, T, and couldn't find him."

"He must have held on to that branch somethin' fierce and got dragged down the river," he concluded.

"Animals know their homes," added Kincaid. "No matter how far Rabbit was taken down that river, long as he could walk, he would have found his way back. It's like a man can be asleep on the back of a horse, which was often the case with my brother, and that horse always walked him right up to our front door."

"Well, I ain't never goin' back to those falls again," concluded Tommie.

Over the next several weeks Rabbit made it clear that this was his moment in the sun. He limped a little more than he needed to and got more ear scratches than he ever would otherwise. He would plop his massive head on any unoccupied lap to drive that point home. His leg got marginally better as the weeks passed and he was able to put some weight on it, but he would always have a limp.

Tommie was reborn. Almost overnight, the joy, enthusiasm and exasperating curiosity that had vanished came back in full force. She and Rabbit were a tonic for each other, and their improvements were quick and dramatic.

75

CHAPTER 12

The summer threw it's fireball across the sky, the fall harvest was strong, and the winter had melted its way to a glorious day in May, when Grace announced one morning, "My sister invited us out to Bardstown to see the new baby in a couple of months."

"You sure she means 'us' That would be a change," offered Kincaid, as he took his seat at the kitchen table. Her family still struggled with the broken engagement to a man that would have put her at the top of society. She assured them she would never "learn" to love that arrogant penguin and remained dispassionate about the arrangement even before she met Kincaid. Her family had been chilly toward him ever since.

When Tommie heard, she was thrilled. She had seen her cousin only once before and after that week they considered each other "play" sisters. Her aunt's house was a classic Antebellum in the Greek Revival Style with the typical pilasters, columns and a grand front porch entry. Tommie and her cousin, Laura, had the run of the place on that first visit. Tommie didn't need to pretend she was staying in a mansion, compared to her own simple clapboard structure.

"If we keep avoiding them, they won't ever come around," reasoned Grace.

"Let them work on their coming around without me. It's not something I enjoy watching."

"Oh Roland, they extended the invitation. We can at least be civil. These are Tommie's relations, and she had such a good time on the last visit."

"She should get to know her relations, I don't have a problem with that, and I'll go. But I won't stay in that house and be insulted."

"This really needs to be a family trip, Roland. They shouldn't think we're at odds."

"You and me are not at odds, and that's what they'll see. It's them I'm at odds with, and that's also what they'll see. In all these years your family still can't look me straight in the eye, especially that sister of yours. You weren't married yet and you changed your mind. Won't be the first or last time that happens. I get sick of having to pretend to be nice when it's clear they think you made a mistake. I don't consider myself a mistake."

"Well, the jury is still out in my mind."

He burst out laughing then got up and grabbed her. "That so?" he whispered into her ear.

She turned around and put her arms around his neck. "There may be one or two good things."

"That's a start."

"You are a stubborn one, Kincaid."

"Look sweetheart, I'll tell them that I have some business I need to tend to in town. Okay? I promise to be very good."

"I can tell," she said a little breathless as he pressed against her.

They left breakfast on the table.

Tommie would not stop talking about the trip. One night as they lay in bed Grace turned on her side and said, "You have one excited little girl."

"Yeah, I know. Tommie's excited too," he answered, and she laughed.

"I really am excited to see that new baby."

"Then why do you still look so worried?"

"Oh, just hoping it all works out and Tommie has a good time."

"It's probably a good thing this is happening now. It'll put the accident even further behind her. Now, when your sister asks about my suspicious absence, you make sure to tell her how sorry I am that I couldn't be there. That I'm absolutely heartbroken."

"I'll be sure to use those exact words."

"Please. 'Cause I know she'll be just as devastated. But ask her to struggle through." She poked him in the side.

"What was that for?"

"She's not that horrible."

"I agree. She's not that horrible. Only a little," he said.

Grace parried back, "Her sentiments exactly."

"But see, that's where she would be wrong. Right?" In answer, Grace silently turned her back to him. He laughed and pulled her to him. "I love you, Grace Kincaid."

"Well, at least you still have some sense," she reasoned

That night as he snored softly, she remained wide-awake. *That man has an uncanny sense of me,* she thought and was grateful he didn't pursue his suspicions. She was fragile enough to have confessed. A few nights ago, as she bathed, she noticed a tiny lump on her left breast. Maybe it was the angle she held the cloth this time, but she hadn't noticed the lump before. She put the cloth down to further investigate and felt a distinctive growth. There had been similar inconsistencies with her breasts through the years and these small growths always seemed to disappear.

She had no intention of worrying her husband over what was probably nothing, probably, but as she lingered over the area there was something different about this one. It felt harder than the previous growths and deeper. Still, she felt there was no reason to share this news based on her previous experience.

She would never forgive herself if they called in a doctor only to find out it was nothing. Just because her mother and an aunt were victims of breast cancer didn't mean that was to be her destiny. She could point to several other aunts and women in her family that lived long, healthy lives. If asked, Grace was sure they would reveal similar scares on their journey to old age. She fell into a fitful sleep.

Tommie's enthusiasm was like a tonic, and it was one of the few things that was able to penetrate Grace's morose preoccupation. Every day she seemed to remember more about the last trip and would pepper her mother with recollections at all hours of the day: "Oh, Mama, do you remember when..?" seemed to be on a recorded loop and Grace would add a detail here and there until she found herself fully immersed in the memory. She would stop whatever she was doing and engage Tommy, who could not know that reliving those memories was one of the few things keeping her mother from debilitating anxiety. For his part, Kincaid was affectionate and reassuring about the "little cold" she felt.

As the days passed, Grace became cautiously optimistic. There had been no change in the growth, and it did appear that this might go the way of the other scares. It was still too early, to be sure, but her relief was overwhelming and lifted the shroud of foreboding. She reengaged with the passion of someone granted a pardon to the delight of her confused and grateful family.

The days that followed had her out of bed early with breakfast on the table and an energetic agenda, as the trip loomed near. She even conceded that Kincaid was not completely off-base in his assessment of her sister, who was not shy about delivering the insult that, "she only had Grace's best interest in mind." Grace was in a quandary. Would this be the time to have it out with her? *It would all be so messy,* she thought. It would also be unfair to poison the trip after what Tommie had been through. She decided this would not be the time, and that it would happen.

Her enthusiasm must have been driving her beyond her limits, she surmised, and was the reason that she began to tire easily. She found herself more and more looking forward to an unusual afternoon nap. If Kincaid or Tommie commented on seeing her resting on the couch mid-day, she was quick to assure them, "I just need to put my feet up for a bit."

Her herculean effort to deny the truth was shattered one evening when she noticed that the growth had changed. It felt different and was a little bigger. There also seemed to be edges on one side that she must have missed before, which was surprising as she considered herself thorough with this process. Still, she was loath to tell her husband because the money for an unnecessary doctor's visit would put an additional strain on their finances, when they were already spending so much on the trip.

Something was not right. Kincaid saw through his wife's brave attempt at normalcy. At first, he put it off to the excitement of the trip but now sensed something else was at the root of her unusual behavior. They were blessed to have a union with very few secrets between them, so this recent change behavior had him on high alert. What's more, the problem persisted in their bedroom where any attempts at intimacy were met with kind but firm protestations of fatigue and excuses about the mountain of work that awaited them in the morning. It was her afternoon naps, though, that disturbed him most because they hinted at something other than a "little cold". His suspicions were confirmed when he came home one afternoon and overheard her weeping in the bathroom. Fortunately, Tommie was still in school. He knocked on the door, "Grace. Grace! Are you alright?" he called out.

"Oh, Roland," she replied through tears that pleaded for him to enter. He walked in and found her standing in front of the mirror with her arms shielding her bare breasts. She let them fall then gently cradled her left breast with both hands. "It's diseased Roland, like my mother's was before she died." Kincaid could only stare in disbelief. He knew her mother died of cancer, but they rarely talked about it.

"Grace, you can't be sure." But even as he said it, he could see that, indeed, there was an unusual growth visible on her left breast that caused a chill to creep down his spine. "We'll call for the doctor today, right now. Don't you worry." Then he gently embraced her, and she fell into his arms, the need for his strong, physical presence almost overwhelming her. He held her to make clear that he would love her through whatever their journey might be and that her body could never make him turn away.

Upon examining her, the only doctor in Louisa declared her condition one that was beyond his field of expertise and recommended a cancer specialist from a nearby town. He gave her a small amount of morphine for the pain and promised to contact the doctor himself with an urgent request. Still, it took several agonizing weeks to get a specialist to the house. By the time he arrived Grace was losing her appetite and growing weaker by the day. She was also running dangerously low on her morphine, as she had to increase her dose to keep the pain at bay.

"Well, let's take a look, shall we?" The doctor proceeded to gingerly open her blouse. When her breasts were exposed, he involuntarily raised an eyebrow that Grace didn't miss. She had already guessed what his face betrayed.

"Are you in any pain at the moment, Mrs. Kincaid?"

"I, I don't think so, no, not really," she managed to get out through the haze of the morphine. "Am I going to die?"

"Oh, now, don't you worry about such things, Mrs. Kincaid. I'm going to close you up and you just lay right back down and try to get some rest." She was in too much of a fog to protest and did as she was instructed. Kincaid had been anxiously observing the examination and the doctor signaled for him to join him in the hallway.

"I'm so very sorry, Mr. Kincaid," he said as Kincaid dropped his head. The doctor put his hand on his shoulder as he delivered the rest. "There is really nothing left to do at this point other than to make her comfortable. There is a surgical option that has been used but in your wife's case she would be too weak, and her illness is too far along to consider it viable. I'm going to leave you some more morphine and you might want to keep a cold compress handy if she starts a fever." As the doctor left, he walked past Tommie sitting on the steps with Rabbit at her feet.

"My mama gonna die?"

"No one but God knows that child. Do you say your prayers?"

"Every night, with my mama."

"Well, she may not be feeling well enough to join you, but you and your daddy say a prayer for her every night. Can you do that?" Tommie nodded as she wiped tears away.

As her illness progressed Kincaid gave Grace the bedroom and he took the couch. He would stay with her until she fell asleep before he quietly made his way to the front room. In the living room he could be near her while giving her the privacy and dignity that she needed and deserved. The door stayed open so he would be sure to hear her moaning so he could rush in and give her more morphine as the cancer progressed. Tommie tried to be a comfort, putting on a brave face as she tended to her mother. But Mrs. Kincaid would only have to take Tommie's hands and put them to her cheek, one of her favorite gestures now that hugging was too painful, and Tommie's resolve would vanish.

CHAPTER 13

Owenton, KY was a couple of hours from Louisa, and the next largest town that drew landowners from several miles. Here, plantation owners replenished their supplies and argued the Farmer's Almanac at the two small saloons. The medicinal mysteries of Kentucky's various roots, trees and barks were teased into potions and salves by a healer/shaman/witch who was known as Miss Edna and sold to the likes of Kincaid, who had witnessed examples of her talent on his own plantation.

She came from the Augustus Plantation, a considerably larger one than Kincaid's. And while Augustus was not quite as revolutionary as Kincaid, he was also not sadistic, nor was he insecure. He considered his slaves more than simple property but less than himself and he and Kincaid considered each other a bit more than acquaintances.

Miss Edna had earned the reputation among her fellow enslaved of being able to work miracles with all that the surrounding forest had to offer. The mystery surrounding her alchemy had the folks she cared for keeping a respectful distance when not in need of her talents. She asked for, and got, an isolated cabin where she could do her conjuring in private. Besides her plant-based ingredients, she also had a bag of human bones, origins unknown, that could be ground up and added whenever necessary.

If asked, she was happy to sing the praises of the plant kingdom, explaining how the bark of a coffee tree would keep things moving along or of the endless possibilities of ginseng, while keeping any mention of a femur or scapulae out of the conversation. Having seen examples of her handy work with his own enslaved, Kincaid was hoping for a miracle of his own today. He watched Augustus hitch his wagon to a post and headed over. "Afternoon, Augustus."

"And to you sir." While they were greeting each other, a customer walked to the back of the wagon and started a transaction with Miss Edna. "Glad to see you today, Kincaid. Got something I'd like to run by you."

"Yes."

"One of my best was kicked in the leg but should heal fine. In the meantime, I have a barn that is in need of repair before harvest. I was wondering if you might be able to spare one of your slaves, oh, forgive me 'workers' for a week or two. I would be willing to pay of course."

Most of his peers knew about Kincaid's unusual arrangement and did not approve. He was paying for labor that could have easily been his for free. "I just might be able to help you out. Unfortunately, my wife has taken ill, so we had to cancel a trip Bardstown. I'm sure we can work out some arrangement." He did not feel compelled to mention that his wife's illness put a severe financial strain on him, and this offer could not have come at a better time.

"I'm sorry to hear about your wife and I'll be sure to keep her in my prayers and I thank you kindly for the help."

"Let me know when you need him."

"Much obliged. Let's go get you what you need, and you can consider it on me today." They headed to the back of the wagon. Augustus took a bench in view of the wagon where he would stay and collect payment.

"Well, good day to you Mista' Kincaid," she said over the shoulder of a customer who was just finishing his business with her. When the buyer turned and saw that it was a white man that she was so familiar with, he looked from one to the other and turned on his heels.

"That's right. You mind your business, sir," Kincaid called after him.

"I thank you, kindly. What is it I do for you today, Mista Kincaid?"

"It's my wife, Miss Edna, she got the cancer throughout her whole body, and the doctors say there's nothing they can do. Can you please help me?"

Her pause confirmed his worst fears. She answered slowly, quietly, "I so sorry for you, Mista' Kincaid, but ain't nothin' I got can take that away. Most be done now is keep the pain away."

He was not surprised. This was a last, desperate attempt he prayed might work, but knew most likely wouldn't. "Whatever you have, please," he was barely able to get out.

She went to a box that was about six feet long and four feet wide and took out several items. After instructing him she said, "I be prayin' for the missus. God do miracles for his children, and we gon pray for one now."

"God bless you, Miss Edna."

After the last customer left, Augustus instructed Miss Edna to wait in the wagon while he tended to some business. He gave a stern warning that there would be no transactions while he was gone. He hurried off with the determination of a man who would not be kept from his purpose as he absentmindedly played with a locket in his jacket pocket. He headed straight to the local bank and was greeted with condescending familiarity by one of the staff.

"So nice to see you again, Mr. Augustus."

"Any luck?" He got right to the point.

"As a matter of fact, this may be your day. There was just someone in who is returning from

Europe and is interested in relocating here. I told him about your property, including your slave count. That witch was an added bonus. He said he might be interested."

"Can he meet my price?"

"With this gentleman that really wouldn't be an issue."

"When would he be ready?" Augustus asked, too enthusiastically.

"One step at a time Mr. Augustus. Let's see if we get a bite first."

Augustus had been trying to unload the plantation for several months with no luck even after several price reductions. He was desperate to leave Louisa because of the contents of that Locket he so tenderly fingered. It held the blurry visage of the woman that destiny had created only for him.

That she lived in Paris was an inconvenience he intended to remedy soon as the sale closed. Prior to inheriting the Plantation and settling in Owenton he had spent time as a merchant marine, usually embarking from New Orleans to parts around the globe. It was on one of these business trips to Paris that he met Rimona.

She was sitting alone with a book and a demitasse at one of the many cafes that were as ubiquitous as romance in Paris. She caught his eye and looked away just a bit too slowly and they proceeded with a courtship that was thunderous. After a few weeks he professed his life to be meaningless unless they were together for all time and left her with a promise to return as soon as possible to start their new life.

Rimona was indulgent at best and assured him that she would be waiting for him more out of a desire to not crush his fragile sensibilities than out of love. His arrogance would never let him imagine she didn't feel as he did. A month or so after he returned, he received an alarming letter in which she described an unfortunate accident that left her father unable to work and support the family. She painfully explained that her parents begged her not to write and understood if this shameful lack of pride would forever put him off, but she was simply unable to stand idle while her dear parents suffered so.

This allowed Augustus to become the hero he imagined himself to be, and he promptly began sending her a monthly allowance. Over the next year several unpredictable events occurred that required him to send more than the original stipend and he did not hesitate. His poor Rimona seemed cursed by the fates. Thank goodness he was able to be her safe harbor. Even as the impact on his finances became more pronounced, he continued to shower her with gifts. He was confident that once he arrived in Paris, she would have no doubt about his love, and he would have won his prize.

"He plans on returning in a few days, Mr. Augustus, to let us know his decision. It might be wise for you to be here. That would speed up any potential transaction."

"I'll plan on being here."

"Good. By the way he comes from a well-established family in the area, the Wallaces. This would be one of the sons, Jr. Wallace."

***

Grace died a few days after Kincaid's visit to Miss Edna. It was not a peaceful passing. There didn't seem to be enough morphine to compete with the relentless march of her illness. As a result, even as overwhelming sadness marked the event, there was gratitude that she was no longer in the agony that marked her last days. Her service was well attended, and she was laid to rest in the Kincaid family plot.

Later that week Kincaid sat at his desk and reviewed receipts from the doctor visits and the medications, primarily morphine, that had been prescribed for Grace. The results were not encouraging. He then examined the ledger book and added up what his workers were being paid. These figures were deducted from what was owed to run the plantation and they were always left with just enough to survie. He saw these figures as confirmation of Grace's accusations of his misguided morality.

How much had she gone without? he wondered. He was under no illusion that had she not taken ill, the money would have gone toward his grand scheme for his workers and he would have continued to treat her meager requests with condescension and arrogance. *He was no husband that loved his wife,* he thought. She had only asked for some small demonstration that she was in his thoughts, that she held a special place above his noble plan, and he had responded like some misguided zealot, shaming her for wanting to bring some small elements of refinement into their lives.

She was living his life, not hers and she did it lovingly. Her occasional complaints took nothing away from her sacrifice. She delivered herself to his cause and treated the workers and the enslaved with the same respect he did, and he could not even give her the few vestiges of the life she willingly abandoned. A tear fell onto the ledger book. Now it was too late. Too late to surprise her with something that she thought was out of reach, and to tell her that his life was her life, that he became the man she loved because she was the woman beside him.

Now all eyes were on Tommie. To have suffered a loss of this magnitude so soon after her own trauma had Kincaid, T and Rabbit watchful for signs that she might be overwhelmed.

For his part, Rabbit was sure to be the first face she saw when she woke and the last one she saw at bedtime. After prayers with her daddy, he would move quietly up to her bed and sit so she could stare into his deeply sensitive eyes and pet him if she needed to. He would gently lick her hand. It wasn't the hyper, excited lapping of a greeting but one that acknowledged and empathized with the gravity of her emotional state as only pets can.

Even Gloadstone felt compelled to show uncharacteristic sensitivity. She offered to prepare lesson plans that Tommie could do from home and applied no pressure to return to school until she was ready. And slowly Tommie became ready. The sun rose and set and moved the tragedy further into memory, and the tasks and mundane rhythms of a day were the unique balm that they have been since creation. When Tommie was able to return to school, Kincaid went about his business and Rabbit oversaw it all. A new normalcy replaced what had been.

Augustus was due to show up about a week after Grace's passing to claim the slave promised him by Kincaid. Kincaid had thought he might lend out T but that was now out of the question. Tommie took solace from his presence and allowed Kincaid to worry less while he focused on the business of running the Plantation. To lose him now would threaten her already fragile state. Instead, he decided to approach Warren, another of the freed enslaved that stayed on as a worker. Though not as tall or as strong as T he was a hard worker and Augustus would be able to get done what he needed.

This did not sit well with Warren who, with barely an exception for Kincaid, held an intrinsic mistrust of all white men. He and his contemporaries considered Kincaid as something akin to a unicorn. They knew they would most likely never find another like him and the thought of leaving for even a few weeks, amounted to stepping off a cliff. Warren felt like he was looking over the edge of that cliff with Kincaid's encouraging hands on his back. Even after Kincaid explained his relationship to Augustus and their similar views on the trade, Warren felt no different. In his mind there could be quite a distance between similar and the same. Kincaid was also candid about needing the extra money Augustus offered.

"Sounds like you sellin' me, Mista Kincaid. Thought you said you never do that," challenged Warren.

"I'm not selling you, Warren. You're coming back, I promise. He's only paying to use you for a few weeks and, frankly, I might have expected you could show more gratitude. The missus and I have been as respectable to you people as anyone I know."

Warren was thinking Kincaid seemed different, like he didn't care like he used to, but he spoke the truth. "You right Mista Kincaid. Don't matter that it don't sit right with me. I do this for you and the missus."

On the appointed day Augustus pulled into The Kincaid Plantation. He took in the visible hostility on the faces as he scanned the crowd that had gathered to see Warren off. "Good day to you, Mr. Kincaid."

"Mr. Augustus," Kincaid tipped his hat.

Augustus reached into his saddlebag and pulled out a small bag of coins and handed it to him. "As promised and I thank you again for this small favor."

Kincaid took the bag. "This helps us both and I'm glad to be able to do it."

"So, which one will it be, and I can be on my way."

"That be me, massa," Warren said and made his way forward. At that moment Rabbit saw one of his furry namesakes scurry past and immediately gave chase which put him on a collision course with Warren who was knocked off his feet.

"Rabbit!" shouted Tommie but he was gone, and she secretly hoped he would return with that rabbit.

As the other enslaved rushed to his aid, Warren put up his hand to stop them. "I be fine. Don't need no help. That dog do like his rabbits," he joked as he brought himself to his feet, clearly in pain.

Everyone was silent as they watched him limp toward the wagon. It was clear his foot was no longer in working order.

"Hold on there, boy," said Augustus. "I appreciate your spirit but I'm afraid that foot won't allow you to do the work I need." To Kincaid he said, "Too bad that dog can't work in his place after takin' away a good-lookin' nigger like this one. Guess this couldn't be predicted and I'm sorry for you, Kincaid." Several of the male slaves helped Warren to the porch.

"Not your fault, Mr. Augustus. Sorry your trip was wasted." He went to hand him back his money then noticed that Augustus was looking past him. Kincaid turned to see T approaching.

"No!" shouted Tommie, as she ran to the wagon.

"Well, this one looks like he'll do just fine, Mr. Kincaid. But I see your little girl might have a problem."

"You can't take him, you can't! Daddy do something!" she demanded.

"I be back real soon, Tommie. I promise. It be like yo' daddy say. He doin' what he got to for us all,"

T said before Kincaid could answer. Tommie wrapped her arms around his waist as Augustus watched with shocked amusement.

"But the dream, T. Somethin' bad gonna happen, I know it."

"I told you I be extra careful, and this be a friend of yo' daddy, so I be safe." He responded as a chill rippled through him at the mention of the dream.

"Sorry, Mr. Augustus but I can't let this one go," Kincaid said. "He's my Foreman and you can see he's important to my little girl, as well."

"I see." Augustus had never seen a little white girl so unnaturally attached to a nigger.

Kincaid again went to hand him the money and this time T put his hand on Kincaid's arm. "Mista Kincaid, I do this for the missus too. She want to see you have a better time and this help you." He looked down at Tommie. "You know how fast a few weeks go by? You go to sleep, and you wake up a few times and I be back. I promise it be jus' like that."

One of the older females walked up and coaxed Tommie away as she sniffled and wiped her face.

"Hold on a minute," Kincaid said, "there's something I need get from the house." He left and returned a few minutes later with some papers. "You know most of the men and women on my plantation are free. I'm gonna give T his papers just in case he needs proof."

"That's fine, if you like. But I can't see cause for him needing to prove that," responded Augustus.

"Maybe not but there's no harm in being sure." He handed the papers to T. "You be real careful with these, T. You worked hard for your papers."

"Thank you, Mista Kincaid. I never let these outta my sight."

The Old Ones

CHAPTER 14

With its 12,000 square foot Greek Revival mansion, the Wallace Plantation on Frankfort Rd. in Georgetown, Kentucky was the largest in the state. Constructed in 1823 by Julius Richard Wallace, it featured 27-foot-high fluted Corinthian columns that might have had some visitors expecting a robed and sandaled senator to come sweeping out to greet them. Julius came from a political and economic dynasty dating back several generations. His unique stamp on the bloodline was to amass the second largest slave holding in the county, behind the legendary Stephen Duncan.

His progeny consisted of three children. The youngest, Charmaine, was to be married off to a good family in the coming months. Of the two boys, Ira, the middle child, was a gifted painter whose work hung in galleries around the world. Julius and his wife had concerns about Ira's lack of interest in marriage. His striking good looks and artistic sensibilities had one ingénue after another parading themselves through the house to no avail. Julius joked that he expected to see some desperate debutant stroll naked through the hallways just to get his attention.

The eldest son or "Jr. Wallace" was the embodiment of Newton's third law that stated for every action there is an equal and opposite reaction. For every success of his siblings, Jr. Wallace's life had been a series of equally consistent failures that were mostly self-inflicted and could generally be traced back to his unyielding love of a good, or bad, glass of gin. Now aging, bloated, in a difficult marriage and close to penniless, he sat in the musty library of his family home with his literal hat in hand. He shifted uncomfortably in a chair that seemed designed for just that purpose. His father sat behind a magnificent oak desk, arms folded and tight lipped.

"So, um, Papa, you see I ain't doin' this just for me. I want to do better by the family and show them that I ain't the same man I used to be."

"You will always be that man, Jr. You are the man that God has chosen to pay for the sin of our forefathers. He said He would and now I believe Him. There can be no other explanation for your dismal life. So, perhaps, I should be more sympathetic, but I struggle. There is nothing you lacked to make you successful except your own personal failings. Now here you are again, like some mangy street dog come in from the cold to, once again, dip your cup into the well." Jr. Wallace was crimson.

"Then you see it ain't my fault. If God want to make me unlucky nothin' I can do about that."

"Why don't you try not being the jackass that falls for every hair-brained scheme that comes your way and then the idiot that drowns his regrets in a goddamn bottle! But I need to calm myself. I'm not going to let your useless life cut mine short. Against my better judgment I'll fund this land grab you propose. Consider it a onetime only welcome back to America gift after your failure overseas. But only half. The other half you'll have to find a bank foolish enough to trust you because I will not be backing any loan.

Also, do not sell a single nigger you pick up from this transaction. My man will identify each one and I will check and I will know if any go missing. There will be no repeat of that shameful stunt." Jr. Wallace flushed at this memory. He had sold one of his father's slaves to satisfy a gambling debt. "Look at me." Jr. looked up. "If I get wind that you've also gone to your mother for money I will find a way to ensure

96

you find yourself and that harpy of a wife of yours on the street the very next day. Am I clear?"

"You ain't got to be so mean about my wife."

"My boy, I was being kind. Believe me. By the way remind me again where I'm throwing away my money."

"It's called the Augustus Plantation."

CHAPTER 15

"You the one that belong to Mista' Kincaid, ain't you?" Miss Edna had walked up behind T as he was on his way to continue the barn repair. "I see you sometimes at the market. How you be here?"

"I don't belong to nobody and don't see how that be yo' business."

"You talk to yo' elders that way? Wherever you from ain't teach you no respect?"

"Don't mean nothin' by it. It jus' be somethin' that you ask massa, it be so much to you."

She took him in. "What they call you anyway? Maybe I need to ask massa that too."

Despite himself he was barely able to suppress a grin. "T."

"What?"

"T."

"What fool massa give you that name?"

"I give it myself."

"Oh."

"And I ain't no fool."

"No, you don't seem nowhere near that to me. You can call me Miss Edna."

"I know who you be."

"Well, if you got somethin' strange that even you don't know 'bout you come see me, Mister T."

"Jus' T." He started to walk on then they both turned toward the sound of a wagon approaching the main house. They watched as a squat, balding man and a woman that was most likely his wife exited the cabin. They were close enough to hear Augustus say,

"It's a pleasure to finally make your acquaintance, Mrs. Wallace. May I offer you and Mr.

98

Wallace some refreshments before you take a look
around?"

"Let's get on with it," she replied curtly.

"Well, yes, of course."

"Sweet Jesus, not him," Miss Edna muttered
under her breath. "And her."

Keeping his eyes trained on the activity at the
house, T asked, "You know who they be?"

"That be Jr. Wallace and that mean wife of his.
They never come this way before and you better hope
they go back the way they come, and quick."

"Seem like I hear that name before," T
commented.

"His family big 'round here and got a piece of
almost everybody. That one is the stray that could never
do nothin' for hisself."

As she spoke, T remembered. This was the man
in Kincaid's story about that girl and the falls. Couldn't
be more than one rich Jr. Wallace. His instincts told
him to keep the revelation to himself.

"You say you ain't seen him here before?"

"No, but like I say, those Wallace's got a piece
of everybody."

This scene only added to T's mounting
frustration. What was supposed to have been two
weeks turned into three and this was not his home and
these were not his people.

Augustus had come very close, more than once,
to bringing him to anger he had not visited for a very
long time. Violent, dangerous anger that many thought
came to him as easily as breathing, but in actuality
came only after a deep well of tolerance ran dry. His
well had about a cup left. Augustus was not the fair and
reasonable man Kincaid had professed him to be.

On his first day, as he was unloading lumber,
the overseer was about to raise his whip to put some

speed on him when Augustus appeared at just that instance and stopped him with the following admonition, "Don't want to return you with scars on your back but the next time there's reason for the whip you'll get what's coming to you." This was the climate the entire time. Working in the June sun 'til past dropping, then barely enough food and sleep to follow. But this was the last week. According to his calculations he had five days left.

CHAPTER 16

The pigs, calves and chickens seemed to be born all at once. Kincaid was grateful for the bounty but now there was a plethora of beaks and snouts that gobbled up feed with insatiable appetites. There were also repairs that required additional supplies, so he was headed into Owenton on an unscheduled trip for the second time in a month. T would be returning in a couple of days, and Kincaid was eager to start the work.

Tommie had marked on her calendar when he was supposed to return and when his time was extended, she became morose and difficult.

As Kincaid was loading his wagon another one pulled up across the street in front of a blacksmith shop that would be his next stop. There was a slave chained to a bench in the back that had the disheveled look of a runaway. When he finished loading his wagon, he and the two slaves he brought with him walked over to the shop but stopped mid-way as they recognized T, chained, beaten and staring ahead as if entranced. "T! My God!" shouted Kincaid as he ran over.

Jr. Wallace was coming out of the shop at the same time. "Can I help you?"

"This man works for me. He's a free man! How the hell did this happen to you, T?"

"Isn't this 'bout a strange coincidence? You must be the Kincaid I hear had this nigger before me. He said he was yours and that he's free, before he run off. Never heard nothing like that before. The nigger can't even get a lie straight but no nigger of mine gonna ever run off. Caught up with him this morning and by the time I'm through with him he won't be thinkin' 'bout runnin' ever again."

"He's not yours and he is free. I gave him his papers. I'm going to take him back, now!" Kincaid and his men started to approach the wagon.

Jr. Wallace pulled out a gun. "Don't think so." They all stopped. "And I don't 'preciate you callin' me a thief and a liar. I come by this nigger fair and square by Mr. Augustus. He came with the property that I now own."

"I never sold him. Augustus was supposed to return him to me in a couple of days."

"Can't speak to your dealings with Augustus. Sounds to me like a misunderstanding on your part because this nigger was listed in the sale as part of his property. It was all witnessed and proper when I signed. So, he is most definitely mine. I'd love to stand here and chat, but I need to make my way home and I don't want to have to shoot my way through any of you, but I will."

Kincaid was speechless. He'd known Augustus for years and though they didn't always see eye to eye on the trade, this was unimaginable. "Augustus lied to you. Like this man said, he is free. I pay him to work for me. Why didn't you show him your papers, T?"

"Augustus burn 'em up," he said without looking at Kincaid. His voice sounded hollowed out and dead.

"My God, T. I'm sorry. My dealings with Augustus have always been respectful and honest. I don't know what happened to him, but I promise to get you back." T stared straight ahead without acknowledging this. He registered Kincaid's righteous anger but felt little sympathy. His honest intentions didn't matter now. They were both betrayed but there was only one sitting bloody, beaten and on display and he was sure Kincaid would not offer to take his place. Once again he trusted and once again, he lost. But he knew where to go with these feelings. Now, when anyone looked into those eyes, they would turn away at the cold menace and smoldering danger. Jr. Wallace was like putting on a familiar old coat.

"I also have papers that prove he's mine. Now I'm done with our little conversation. Kindly get the hell out of my way."

"I'll get him back if it's the last thing I do!" Kincaid threatened.

"You keep talkin' or move another muscle toward me and the last thing you do may be today," Jr. Wallace answered coolly and road off.

"Probably don't want to tangle with those Wallace folks. They own everybody," offered a lingering spectator.

"Wallace folks?" Kincaid responded back.

"That was Jr. Wallace, the crazy one. Surprised he ain't dead yet," continued the loiterer before he moved on. This news landed with the force of a gut punch. With a few wisps of gray hair, a sagging gut and alcoholic nose, there was nothing about the man that resembled the teenager he had last seen. He was stunned that that aging sloth could be the same murderous adolescent responsible for the nightmares that haunted him well into adulthood.

He whirled around as if to race after him, knowing he was long gone, but needing to do something, anything to make him feel less helpless. He couldn't imagine a scenario where Jr. Wallace could find out that T knew his secret, but he had no doubt that he would kill him in a heartbeat if ever he did. This news created an urgency that now bordered on panic.

And then there was Tommie. Anticipating her crushing disappointment at finding out there would be no joyous homecoming for T, turned the normally languid ride home into an anguished pilgrimage toward disaster.

They would see each other in court. Kincaid decided that immediately. He had two identical copies of each worker's freedom papers drawn up in anticipation of just such an occurrence. The trade was too lucrative for honest men. T's freedom papers would predate the deed for the property held by Wallace, so there should be no argument. But he had been a lawyer and there was always an argument.

Even a novice lawyer would know to argue that since Wallace had no idea of the arrangement between Kincaid and Augustus, Wallace should not be penalized. Especially when he had ostensibly legitimate documents to prove his ownership. Kincaid knew much would depend on the judge and, because of Kincaid's experience, this did not instill confidence.

"Daddy, you promised me he would be all right, you promised me!" Tommie hurled the accusation at her father through angry sobs.

"I know, Tommie, I know. But I promise you we'll get him back. I trusted the wrong man and I won't rest until he's back with us." He hoped he sounded more confident than he felt. Rabbit sat in a corner whining with confusion. He would be in Tommie's room tonight to comfort her.

"It's just like I told him, Daddy. I said somethin' bad was gonna happen. I saw it all in my dream."

"If it was a scary dream remember what your grandma said about those kinds of dreams, that nightmares was just a way for your mind to take out the trash and get clean."

"Yeah, but just look what happened. I'm real scared for T. You got to get him back real fast, Daddy, you got to!"

***

He only had an hour until departure and Augustus could not leave before posting the letter to his beloved. He could only imagine her delight when she discovered his arrival was imminent. This was destiny, which was the only possible explanation for being able to book the last first-class cabin on the famed Caledonia, one of the four Cunard luxury liners. This was to be its first voyage from New Orleans. After he posted his letter, he sunk into the velvet seat of his coach and dreamed of his new life with his new wife and could almost smell the croissants and demitasse as they strolled the streets of Paris. The coach came to a stop.

"Here we are sir," the driver announced as he stepped down and began unloading the luggage. Augustus stepped out of the coach and was treated to the colorful uniforms of the first-class departure stewards.

One stepped forward, "I'd like to be the first to welcome you on board sir. If you show me your ticket, I'd be glad to escort you to your cabin. Your luggage will follow without delay."

His cabin was steeped in the luxury of the day. The interior was of highly polished cherry. There was a porthole for viewing, a silver wash basin and pitcher, a bed and small desk completed his accommodations. He lay on the bed, not fully able to relax. An undercurrent of anxiety had followed him like a shadow since he started his journey and now every time he heard someone making their way down the hall his eyes never left his door until they passed.

He was only slightly remorseful that he had betrayed Kincaid. He did consider him a friend, but that slave was the linchpin to the sale. Jr. Wallace had been unequivocal; there would be no deal without him.

Stealing T's freedom papers had been a little inconvenient. When T, discovered they were gone, he went on a rampage, and it took his overseer and four more strong men to hold him down so he could be chained up until the sale went through. Augustus included him in his listing of assets with no one the wiser and he was now on his way to the life he deserved.

He did worry, though, that he might be served justice at the final moment. That an outraged Kincaid would come rushing into his cabin with the Sheriff close behind and instead of spending his days in the creamy arms of his grateful Rimona, he would be sitting on the dirt floor of a prison cell avoiding the lustful eye of a grinning, toothless cellmate.

He would not be content until he was surrounded by water. Then, as if on cue, the loud boom of the departure whistle vibrated through the ship. He breathed deeply and reached into a pocket of his coat that was draped over a chair, pulled out a flask filled with the finest Kentucky Bourbon, took several long pulls and fell into a sleep that could only be had by the glide of a magnificent ship through a vast, calm sea.

The Caledonia left New Orleans performing as advertised, cutting through the current like a razor with delighted guests enjoying its splendor and novelty. They had been out to sea for several hours and Augustus was dreaming of a picnic with Rimona who playfully splashed wine on her milky bosom then coyly asked if he would like to help her clean it up. Eager to oblige, his tongue protruded from his lips even in sleep.

Just millimeters from his prize, his head was slammed against the side of his berth with such unexpected force that he thought it was pushed. *My God! They've found me!* was his first confused thought and before he became fully awake, he was thrown off

106

the bed like a child tossing a toy, as the ship lurched up and slammed down as it crested a monstrous wave. The calm seas had suddenly, violently shifted. The wash basin and pitcher came crashing to the floor and the chair tumbled over on top of it all.

His experience as a merchant marine taught him a level of controlled anxiety, not quite calm in these situations and he groggily made his way to the porthole. He cursed as he knocked his shin into a chair leg and was then confronted by sheets of water slapping against the glass obscuring any view the raging sea.

Wiping off the condensation helped just enough for him to make out a wave so high that he first thought the image was a product of his disorientation. Then he was thrown back as if a powerful hand punched through the porthole and sent him flying to the opposite end of his cabin. He remained conscious just long enough to hear and feel the hulking mass of wood and metal lurch onto its side as it made its way to the bottom of the sea.

The Caledonia would never be found, and the storm would later be identified as a "White Squall," a violent windstorm at sea with no black clouds to serve as a warning.

Rimona would receive his letter some weeks later and promptly toss it into the fire, as she cradled her newborn and kissed her husband in the beautiful new cottage paid for by her generous American benefactor.

*T*hey also read the shadows, these same old ones that knew the breezes, the cast of the sun on an oak, speaking volumes about its intentions. Frustration also marked their observations, as every year, the time from the long shadows of winter to the short shadows of summer seemed to shrink, like they were putting back and taking out their summer fans all at once. They held these fans now, in hands with lands and groves and stories to tell, moving stagnant July air past their equally storied faces...to listen...

PART 2

CHAPTER 17

As Jr. Wallace's wagon made its way down the path of his new home, black faces moved, zombie-like, through their daily activities. They paid no attention to the captured runaway, as if to look was to taint their own well-being. There was one who looked like he might be a preacher, but he looked too young. He looked ready to offer some assistance but was wary of the quiet menace that emanated from every pore of this runaway. Still, his calling was to administer to those in need and that included the likes of T. He would wait until the master gave him permission.

T was taking it all in until, without warning, he exploded out of his seat and lunged for the driver, having just enough length in his leg chains to reach him and wrap the chain of his hand shackles around his neck and break it instantly. Jr. Wallace was too shocked and too fat to react in time and howling like the animal of a slave owner's nightmare, T grabbed Wallace's head and snapped his neck in an instant. Then, standing at his full height he lifted the body over his head and flung it out of the wagon where it landed with a thud on several shocked onlookers.

He ripped the bench from its hinges, freeing his legs, and lunged out of the wagon, landing on the overseer before he could get a shot off, then used his heavy shackles to beat the man's head into an unrecognizable pulp. Grabbing a knife from the belt of the overseer, he sprinted up the stairs of the big house, bloody chains clanging and digging through the dirt as he ran. At the top of the stairs, he plunged the blade to its hilt into the milky cleavage of a well-dressed woman who had just appeared on the porch. As she sank to the ground, he dragged the chains over her corpse and ran into the house and, finding a candle, proceeded to set fire to anything that would burn. The slaves continued to look on, expressionless and uninterested.

"Just like I told you, boy preacher, ain't no nigger gonna run away from me." T was violently wrenched from his fever dream and into the present, as Jr. Wallace called out from the wagon bench to the young preacher below.

Rev. R had been the preacher on the Sr. Wallace plantation and was amongst a handful of slaves that Jr. Wallace brought with him. He had recently inherited the position from his deceased father and looked younger than his 23 years, so had to endure the nickname "boy preacher" from time to time. He was still developing the gravitas of his father and was more earnest than confident.

"He look like he be needin' water Massa Wallace. Can I fetch him some?"

"Water the horses first. I'm 'bout to tie him to that tree and show all these niggers what happens if you try to run away from me."

"Just a minute, Wallace." All heads turned to see Lady Wallace. "This one we need healthy with all the work this place needs. Choose another one. Get one of the older ones that eats more than he's worth."

"You sure? I mean we can't let these niggers see this one get away with runnin'. Don't set an example I want."

"Maybe. But they'll see someone get whipped in his place who did nothing. I imagine that will send an equally effective message. At any rate we need the muscle to clean up this place, not that you'd notice, and we don't have many like this one. Find another nigger." She walked back inside leaving Jr. shamefaced in front of those he was supposed to master. He walked up to an elderly slave and kicked him to the ground.

"Leave him Massa Wallace. I go." All eyes turned to T. "I run away so beat me."

Wallace said nothing, only stared at T with renewed interest. Then he addressed the overseer, "Samson, take this old dog to the tree and give him the same 30 that you would give the big one in the wagon. I don't care if he drops, you don't stop until after 30."

"Don't know he last that long Mr. Wallace," warned Samson.

"Only one way to find out, now get on with it." He turned to Rev. R. "Looks like God choose this one today," he indicated T. "Go on and get him some water and only give him a sip. Don't want him getting sick on me."

Cup in hand, Rev. R carefully climbed up spilling as little as possible. He then took it and held the cup to T's lips, keenly aware of his own breathing and the unusual difficulty he was having holding the cup steady. These acts of kindness normally came naturally to him. He had watched his father greet several new arrivals the same way. But there was an explosiveness in the air surrounding T, like he was coiled, ready to strike. It was in his breathing and sideways glances as if he were looking for the closest soft spot. After he took a few sips Rev. R lowered the cup and, as he did, let a little water spill onto T's chest. Rev. R froze hoping this had the intended effect. It did, as T, almost imperceptibly, nodded his thanks.

"You ain't baptizing the nigger," Jr. Wallace shouted. "Give him one more sip so I can put him away." He brought the cup up to T's lips again and said, "God bless you, and welcome."

112

CHAPTER 18

"*What was I thinking?*" Was her usual thought following any interaction with her husband. The little respect Lady Wallace imagined she had for Jr. Wallace was thrown out shortly after they said their misplaced wedding vows. It became clear early on that he found his vices a more engaging spouse. She got early warnings but chose to ignore the faults that her better positioned peers wouldn't. She was in hot pursuit of the Wallace dynasty at all costs. She came from a lower rung with no intention of staying there and made up in ambition what she lacked in status. But this black sheep was no easy target.

The point was driven home in spectacular fashion at one of the first society functions they attended soon after they were married. This was to be a "coming out" in her mind, and she had gone to great lengths with a fall dress of burgundy velvet, and enough combs and sachets for a dormitory of young women. She spent the better part of a month reminding Wallace that this would be a perfect opportunity to demonstrate he wasn't still the drunken cretin of his reputation. After failing to argue her out of her assessment he promised to make her proud and be a paragon of restraint.

The evening started off hopeful as she bragged about fantastical experiences overseas and the challenges of running such a large household. Her cynical audience was too polite to challenge her on both counts. She caught glimpses of Wallace who seemed to be holding court respectfully. There were laughter and an easy camaraderie that flowed from the group. She allowed herself to caution that just maybe this affair would mark a new beginning. Content that all was in order, she continued weaving her fantasies to disbelieving ears.

Willfully or innocently, she missed the scowl on her husband's face before she turned away. One of his comrades had just quipped, "I heard they ran you out of Europe, Wallace. Pretty soon they'll be no place left to kick you out of," to laugher all around.

"Unless daddy buys a country for you," added another to more laughter. Before a third could add to the unfolding roast, a drunken Wallace threw a drink in his face. The man answered with a punch to Wallace's face which sent him toppling over an end table that sent a vase that cost enough to cover the entire affair, crashing to the floor.

The hostess screamed. "Oh no, that's my Ming! What have you done, you drunken fool?" she said looking down at Wallace spread incoherently on the floor. Lady Wallace was there in a flash.

"I am so sorry, Mrs. Hargett. We will, of course, cover the damages."

"I'm sure my insurance company will see to that, Mrs. Wallace." The Lady's face burned at the unmistakable slight of choosing to call her "Mrs. Wallace" rather than "Lady Wallace." "May I suggest that you pick your husband up and be on your way? He obviously is in no condition to remain." To her further humiliation, she struggled with him alone. No one helped as they tittered and whispered their lack of surprise. "And you, sir, may leave as well," indicating the owner of the guilty fist, which cut off his smirk instantly. "Prepare to hear from my solicitor."

"My God! Do you know how long I've been planning for this? Do you?!" The Lady spit venom as they waited for their carriage, "and in ten minutes you, once again, prove you are failure and a fool!"

"They was laughing at us. Sayin' we was kicked out of Europe after our wedding," he slurred in his defense. This caused The Lady to momentarily stop her insults at the realization that they had fallen much further from grace than she had imagined. Before she could find her next poisonous dagger, Wallace turned green and vomited on her lovely burgundy frock then added a little more in her lavishly combed hair.

She had adopted the royal moniker "Lady Wallace" as soon as her vows were complete, certain that a grand life of privilege and opulence awaited. Also, "Gladys Wallace" did not have the gravitas befitting her new position. When questioned about her interesting title, she claimed some distant European royalty, which most did not believe. This move established her pompous, misguided intentions to the class she aspired to, and she was generally shunned as a poser and a fake. Along the way she burned enough bridges to earn the sentiment that her pairing with Jr. Wallace was justice served for them both.

Her current outrage stemmed from their excommunication from England. An uncle of Jr. Wallace had established a profitable shipping business and grudgingly offered to set him up as an associate. When he presented this opportunity to his wife, she would have walked across the Atlantic to make it happen. After so many false starts and humiliations, she would finally get the life she deserved in a country she was certain would respect her roots and treat her like The Lady of her fantasies.

It took him just six months to drain that well of goodwill dry with his debauched and undependable behavior. It took his wife even less time to be found out for the fraud she was. The last generous gesture from the uncle was a one-way ticket back to the states for them both, with an admonishment never to return. Lady

Wallace had gotten the name she coveted at the cost of a loveless, angry union with a man she despised.

Jr. Wallace entered the house after Rev. R watered T and the old slave was being whipped. "That was real smart to whip that old nigger instead of the strong one. Think that put the fear of God in 'em. Bet they speak up now if someone talks about running," he said to The Lady.

"We'll see," she said back.

"You know, you don't need to go announcing to everybody how much you hate this place. Don't make it look good between us."

"So, what should I say? How pleased I am that we had to take the only thing we could afford because we were being evicted from your father's home? That would take too long. So I just say I hate it."

"I know it ain't what you want but can't we try to make something out of it? I mean, it is our home now."

She took a deep breath. "Wallace, we just keep holding on, that's all we do. This is not our house and probably never will be. Half of it belongs to your father the other to that devil Richards that you signed up with."

"This land is good, and he gave us a break for the first few months."

"What happens after that? What happens when you have to pay him at those rates that should be outlawed? The man has no morals and no feeling. He will do to us what he's done to almost everyone else desperate enough to need him. This will be his land before this year is out. Now, I'm going to my room and please do not bother me."

He watched her leave, feeling the familiar sense of dread that was characteristic of most of his conversations with her. He had intended on telling her about his run-in with Kincaid but decided to let her go. She knew nothing about his claim on the nigger and nothing good would come from bringing it up now.

***

The old man's bony scapulae pushed against the thin skin of his back. Samson had trouble securing his hands around the tree because his wrists were so thin. He was finally able to use enough rope to get the job done. The resulting image was of a strangely old child comically tied to a tree with a mountain of rope. The first lash easily tore through the thin flesh and the only mercy in what followed was his death, which happened after the 10th strike. Samson had followed orders and delivered blows with the force meant to tame an animal.

When he was done he ordered the onlookers to untie what was left of the old man and throw him in the section of dirt where the other niggers were buried. T remained chained to the bench and Wallace instructed Samson to keep him there to watch. He claimed a beating was wasted if it wasn't witnessed. Rev. R provided a last act of dignity for the old man with a prayer and a few words. His name was Johnson Alexander Smith. He was born 70 years earlier and died today without dignity, or compassion. But there would be no more pain.

CHAPTER 19

She told him he wasn't no fool and she believed it. Miss Edna also didn't think T was a liar. So when he said he was a free man that worked for Mista Kincaid, she believed that too. When he had run off, she prayed hard for his safe passage to wherever he was headed and her heart sank, along with most of the other slaves, when Jr. Wallace came back with him. She didn't know if he was headed back to Kincaid's or just running. Either way, it was going to be a better life than the one he ran from, she was certain of that.

The way of this new master was on full display today, she thought. The horror of that beating, at the suggestion of The Lady, confirmed what she had heard about that pair, that there was not an ounce of human kindness between the two. She had not had any real concerns for her own well-being for a very long time. She had been around some 55 years and after she learned her medicine, no harm had come to her. On the contrary, most of her masters gave her superior treatment because of her value. A healthy slave was a productive one.

When she was captured and brought over from Senegal as a teen, she was already considered a healer in her village, and she was quick to recognize the healing properties of the local yellow root, yarrow and goldenseal. She quickly mastered formulas for various potions, rubs and poultices and was viewed with equal parts fear and respect. She moved into legendary status when word circulated that she could work wonders with the highly toxic but very useful pokeweed. Unlike the experience of most who tried to work with it, no one died from her pokeweed remedies.

She had assumed the Wallace's would have the same respect she got from other masters, until she witnessed the day's horrible and twisted justice. Needless cruelty was as common as sweat on a hot day, but what happened today reached a new level of darkness. She was friends with that old man and for that to be his death was the closest vision of hell she'd ever hoped to see.

And he died as a result of the unusual new arrival, but she didn't blame T. The runaway had no power. Her friend's blood was on the hands of Wallace and that true witch of a wife of his. There was an unusual confidence about the runaway, she thought. Maybe it was his courage or his intelligence or his sense of self that captivated her, but she found herself feeling unusually protective toward him.

It was probably that she had seen so many others like T, proud young black men that most often had to choose death to remain that way. Whatever it was, this man who declared himself T and could have been the grandson she raised in a different, impossible reality, grabbed her heart and she committed herself to teach him to be smart about a life that was not his doing but could easily be his undoing.

***

I am free. I am a free man. At the end of days that left him in a near delirium from lack of water and heat exhaustion, this became his mantra. It was his north star and became his link to sanity because he knew he would be free again. He believed it like that boy preacher believed in his God.

119

For punishment, Wallace had denied him even the kinder obscenities of the slave quarters. Those tiny wooden structures had straw covered dirt floors and were crammed with up to two families that could include as many as ten people. He was forced to make his bed in the stables where he was chained to a post with just enough room to lay down on bare dirt, the straw being kept underfoot for the horses. He wouldn't freeze, because it was August.

Instead, he would share his suite with all manner of insects and vermin that celebrated the dripping humidity that invited sticky access to any bare skin.

Little Tommie lay heavy on his heart. The love he felt for that child was one of the few truly unfettered emotions he had felt since Ol' Pete died. There was a sense of family with Kincaid that he had never known anywhere else, and with Kincaid, he was free. Miss Edna told him she didn't think he was a fool, and only a fool would stay with Wallace when he had the chance for freedom at Kincaid's, so he ran into the night.

It only took the dogs a day to find him. He was running blindly, using the moon to guide him but with no other plans for the journey. Food, water and a true strategy to avoid capture took a back seat to the immediate and overpowering need to simply flee. His capture was violent and satisfying to his masters, but he did not return a broken man.

If anything, he was even more determined to take back his freedom. He would be smarter next time. In the short time he was on the run he learned what he would need to be successful. If not successful, his freedom was worth dying for. Until then he would give them no reason to raise a whip, but when it came, reason or no, he would not give them the satisfaction of a single tear. There would be no screams for mercy, no begging to end whatever diabolical lesson lay in store.

He stretched out on the dirt summoning up old reserves of cold, dead, detachment that had long been dormant. He would not inhabit his body as much as watch what happened to it, like a disinterested spectator. If death came soon so be it, but every moment he remained under the sadistic boot of Samson, he was becoming less convinced that the death would be his own.

CHAPTER 20

Judge Asher Graham would be hearing Kincaid's case against Wallace. Kincaid had been in his courtroom as a novice lawyer and was cautiously optimistic. Graham had been on the bench for ten years and would never be mistaken for an abolitionist, but he had once expressed being impressed with the young Kincaid and this, possibly, put a plus in his column. With the addition of a few of his like-minded former colleagues, working pro-bono, Kincaid and team entered the courtroom feeling well prepared and hopeful.

Their confidence was cut short when they saw Judge Graham laughing with Jr. Wallace and someone who looked to be Wallace Sr. This was not unusual. The folks that ran the courts and those that could afford to use them often ran in the same circles. But now was not the time to discover that Wallace's legendary influence extended to the judiciary.

The Honorable Graham muttered, "Good afternoon gentlemen," and showed no sign of recognition before he said, "Looks like we can proceed."

Kincaid and his team presented their case with passionate but factual outrage buttressed by an appeal to fairness and the law. Judge Graham sat stone-faced, looking almost insulted, and asked no questions. When they were through, Kincaid wondered why Wallace would waste his time stating his case when it was clearly decided before they walked in the courtroom. Jr. Wallace would keep T.

***

"Hmm, yes." The same banker that negotiated the deal between Augustus and Jr. Wallace was now sitting across from Kincaid examining a list of his assets and liabilities. After his loss in court, Kincaid looked into the possibility of buying T back, however repugnant paying Jr. Wallace might be. The banker said: "I always thought there was something uncomfortably desperate about that one. So sorry to hear about the deception, Mr. Kincaid. I can't say it surprises me but it does appear that the Devil has got his due, as the saying goes."

"Oh?" Kincaid replied curiously.

"You may have heard about the unfortunate fate of the Caledonia?"

"I read about it, yes."

"Well, there was a passenger list released today and it appears our Augustus was one of the unfortunates. Must have been an awful business. One can only pray that it was all over quickly." Kincaid had no response. The banker continued. "Of course, my job is to help you accomplish whatever legal transaction you can afford, but if you don't mind my saying, this is highly unusual. I would ask you again about the wisdom of putting yourself in more serious debt for one nigger."

"Let me ask you this, sir, how much would you pay for your brother, your uncle or your son?

CHAPTER 21

The heat was a thick, physical presence and mosquitos were getting in their eyes and mouths. But the Redcoats sensed victory, so they put on a brave face as cannons exploded and they watched their comrades literally blown out their boots. They had the Bluecoats on the run, about to strike a blow for the crown. They pushed through the heat, fear and enemy gunfire, calling on any last reserves of strength and willpower to finish the job.

Suddenly, an explosion rocked the ground beneath them, followed by two more, and bodies were propelled into the air as if the soles of their boots had springs. When the smoke cleared, body parts littered the landscape, as if hurled from the hand of a giant. Through the moans of the undead, cheers erupted from the Bluecoats. A voice boomed out, "Tommie!"

"OK, Daddy!"

She gathered up the defeated Redcoats and the victorious Bluecoats and put the colorful pieces of pewter in their respective boxes with the care accorded the Crown Jewels. Rabbit was watching, riveted, but from a respectable distance. When she first pulled the soldiers out their cases, he made the mistake of thinking they were chew toys and was swiftly corrected in no uncertain terms.

Tommie had seen an ad for the soldiers and was captivated by the promise of "life-like resemblance and true color detail." It was the first time since T's kidnapping that she had shown an interest in anything, So Kincaid didn't hesitate. This was not the first and surely would not be the last time his high-minded, free-spirited daughter paid no attention to the pink-and-blue rule. The soldiers were made by the premiere toy maker of the day, Field and Francis from Philadelphia. He was able to tap one of his former legal associates to secure the coveted toy.

She took the box and put it on a shelf next to the wooden menagerie of animals. After T's sudden departure, Rabbit would sniff the animals, then look expectantly back at Tommie. She would pet him while he quietly moaned. For several nights, he slept facing them, as if expecting T to materialize out of the lions and the zebras. He would hear T's name and perk up, expecting him to enter suddenly, from anywhere. In time, he got used to his new reality and took on the more pressing task at hand: Tommie.

"Did you see him today?" was the first question Tommie asked when she entered the room. It was the same question asked with the same hopeful cadence whenever he returned from a trip to Owenton.

Rabbit, head cocked in canine curiosity, also fixed his stare on Kincaid. "Not this time, sweetheart, but I'm thinking he'll be there next month."

She silently picked at her meal. Sometimes Tommie accompanied Kincaid on his trips into town. The first time she saw T with Jr. Wallace she raced up to him and wrapped her arms around his waist causing Jr. Wallace to snap. "Get away from my nigger!"

"Come on, Tommie. We got things to do," her father said gently but firmly.

"But it's T, Daddy!" He gently worked her loose.

T stayed silent throughout the encounter. But as she walked away, he said, "Think you drop somethin' Tommie." She looked down and gasped at a beautiful wooden miniature of a sleeping bear. When she looked back up T was walking toward Jr. Wallace. On the ride home Kincaid had to explain why she needed to ignore him if she saw him again. He made it clear that it would

125

put her and T at risk if she didn't. In her mind, the only thing that came out of this lunatic conversation was that she needed to keep him safe. She reluctantly agreed that she wouldn't speak when she saw him, the decision made easier only by the miniature. He had not forgotten her.

Tommie looked up from her meal, "How much longer, Daddy? You said he would be comin' back, but it's been a long time."

"I know it Tommie. It won't be too much longer now. I promise."

This did not sit well with her. She stopped eating and crossed her arms in defiance, which alerted Rabbit, who looked from one to the other. "But he ain't safe, Daddy! I know it! Long as he's gone, he ain't safe!" she said, tearful and exasperated. "That's what I told him too," she finished. Rabbit started to whimper.

This was that raw moment in child rearing where the naked pain of your child can destroy you. And the truth of what she said could not be denied. Kincaid had to look down and compose himself. He then got up and walked over to her and opened his arms. She rose and fell into his embrace, crying out for comfort that was familiar and unquestionable. "Thing to remember, Tommie, is that they want T to work, so they're gonna make sure nothing happens to him. They'll make sure to keep him safe," he said as tenderly as he could. Not convinced of it for a minute. She did quiet down, though, as she considered the simple logic of the statement, and not the evil that men do. She didn't need to know the outcome of the trial or his visit to the bank. Instead he added, "I promise you we'll get him back. I'm not going to stop until we do."

CHAPTER 22

Even at 21, Rev. R was still the "boy preacher" and probably would be until his hair went from black to white or until he looked older than 15, with the former more likely than the latter. His father started preaching on the Sr. Wallace plantation after promising not to teach the niggers to read and to ensure they understood that God wanted them to obey their masters. This obsequious message grew increasingly untenable to Rev. R, as he witnessed the cruelty of the masters and the powerlessness of the enslaved.

One local white preacher went so far as to claim that he found a passage in the Bible that stated, "Niggers obey your master and mistress 'cause you just like the hogs and the other animals. When you die you ain't no more after you're thrown in the ground."

Black preachers, those who could read the bible, spoke much closer to the word. These were the sermons that would bring on shouts and testifying. The Sr. Rev. was legendary for his passionate sermons and kept a small supply of cooking pots on hand for folks to cover their mouths and shout into when they were overcome. This inspired bit of ingenuity was instituted after Sr. Wallace threatened to shut down the church if the niggers couldn't stop acting like wild animals. The unorthodox solution, though an interesting visual, did the job.

There was never a question that the son would follow in the footsteps of the father, though it was clear early on that Rev. R was not going to be the gifted orator he was succeeding. When his father died, a powerful and imposing presence was taken out of his life and out of the life of the plantation. A day did not go by without a memory shared with awe and respect for the "Sr. Rev." It was becoming clear to him that the old ones would never view him as anyone other than "The Reverend's Boy."

This did not diminish his deep sense of purpose whenever he observed the soul-comforting relief he was able to help God provide. And he thought of himself only as God's vessel, blessed to be able to share the word in a special way to people who lived on Satan's playground.

He was also a thoughtful young man and willing to entertain a more complex relationship to his calling. Though he didn't fully agree with Frederick Douglass' sentiment, "I can see no reason but the most deceitful one for calling the religion of the land Christianity," he continued to ask God to show him examples that Douglass was wrong.

His father dismissed these challenges as Satan playing on the minds of the unfaithful and positioned his calling as a simple battle between good and evil. Rev. R rejected this simple reading of his purpose and felt that he could bring more souls to Christ if he recognized the contradictions of the word and was willing to engage these non-believers with respect and a sincere desire to understand.

He was preparing his sermon for the following Sunday after T's return. It had been a couple of days and he was still shaken by the experience. He was aware of the sordid reputation of Jr. Wallace and had no desire to leave the senior's plantation, but also had no say in the matter. What took place that afternoon shocked his senses and his prayers for understanding were yet to be answered.

There was also that runaway. If Wallace had placed a bundle of dynamite on the bench it would have been no more explosive. When he got close to those bloodshot eyes he feared for his well-being, until they met his directly. Then they seemed to soften in recognition of his good deed, and in the process reveal an unmistakable intelligence that Rev. R couldn't miss. His heart rate did not slow until he had climbed down and was able to put some distance between himself and that angry, intelligent stallion.

His musings were interrupted by a knock. He opened the door to find Jerome, a middle-aged slave who walked with a limp from a birth defect that left one leg shorter than the other.

"Jus' coming to see if I help you out with yo' sermon." Jerome had been the preacher when Augustus owned the plantation and had taken Rev. R's promotion with begrudging acceptance. There had been the rare instance where they both spoke at the same service, but Rev. R viewed this as more of a transitional occurrence where Jerome wanted more of a partnership. To assuage him, Rev. R would occasionally ask for his assistance in preparing his sermons, but Jerome lacked Rev. R's courage and foresight, so it was more of a conciliatory gesture than of a true partnership.

Tonight was not a night for this gesture. "Much obliged, Jerome but I be fine."

"Well, I got some ideas that you jus' might want to hear. Like I tell you, I know these people and what can move 'em."

"I know you do. We talk next week. I be okay for now. You have yo'self a blessed night."

Back at his table he knew he had to address the death of the old man. His congregation would be preoccupied and less engaged until he did. Many would be satisfied not to question the wisdom of God but others, including himself, would need further explanation, and it was those he wanted to speak to.

There was nothing wrong with asking why, would be his introduction.

He would confess to having his own questions about what they had witnessed, and he would assure them that questioning God often led to a deeper love and understanding of His grace and power, as long as faith was not forgotten. It was this non-negotiable tenet of the true believer that welcomed in all that was God's promise.

Faith meant that God had a plan, even though it might not be obvious with the daily cruelties of their lives. It was faith that brought a sense of peace and joy and the promise of the beauty that awaited all of those that trusted in him. It would be this faith that would also bring understanding in the fullness of time. If he sensed that the atmosphere had settled, he would move off the topic and lift spirits with a new theme.

He had decided to revisit the importance of believing that God can work miracles. He had heard his father preach a version of this sermon countless times. It was guaranteed to bring a chorus of "amens" and "hallelujahs" as he recounted the parable of the loaves and fishes. He would start by asking if anyone was in need of a miracle today. This question alone could bring many to tears. He would encourage the crowd to shout out the miracles they needed.

He had witnessed congregations moved to a divine frenzy with this sermon. Some would start shaking and others would jump up as if the Holy Spirit held a cattle prod. A few could be convinced they were ready for the rapture at that moment and would plead, "Take me now, Jesus! I ready!" He vividly remembered one obese congregant who got her wish one heated afternoon when, after shouting, "Take me, Jesus," He did just that and she toppled over, taking several frightened and confused brethren with her.

This did not sit well with Jr. Wallace. He couldn't have his enslaved dropping dead in church and told Rev. R he would not be able to hold services if that continued to happen. Rev. R promised to be careful, which wasn't necessary as the congregation self-corrected when they saw that Jesus was actually listening and might want to amuse Himself again. The shouts were a little more subdued and "I'm ready, Lawd," or "Take me now, sweet Jesus," were never to be heard again. With God deciding He had no immediate needs, the sermon he preached that Sunday saw no one get their wings.

T was allowed back into the slave quarters after about a week. True to his word, he spoke to no one and kept his head down. On the second Sunday after his return, he was determined to take care of some unfinished business where Rev. R was conducting his service. He walked past the kitchen of the big house and through the window caught sight of a petite slave wearing an iron muzzle that her small neck cold barely support. "Joraye, come on over and help me with this pot," someone shouted, and she turned from T's view.

She got caught, he thought absentmindedly. This form of punishment was often used when a kitchen slave was caught tasting some of the fine food being prepared for the master. Something about her caught his eye. Maybe it was the contrast of that heavy muzzle she struggled valiantly to support or how she seemed isolated from the rest, or both. Then she turned toward the window, and he was startled by the greenest eyes he had ever seen.

He could not shake a sense of deja vu that was even stronger as he noticed her pecan skin. She caught him staring and turned away as quickly as the device would allow. T continued on in a slight state of wonder.

He got to the service just as the last of the congregants left. He approached and stood in the doorway. "You was good to me last week."

Rev. R was startled to see him filling the entrance but recovered quickly. "I jus' be doin' what God would call on any good Christian to do."

"But you the good Christian that did it and I be grateful."

"Why don't you come on in? Don't need to be standin' in that doorway."

"I say my piece. No need to come in," and he turned to leave.

"What you call yo'self?" Rev .R blurted out.

"T."

"What you mean "T"? What the rest of yo' name?"

"T." Rev. R cocked his head like a curious Spaniel.

"Mine Raymond, but folks took to callin' me Rev. R and I don't see need to change it. You don't come to the service today. You know you be welcome anytime."

"Got no need for this."

"How you know? You pray?"

"Only thing worth prayin' for is freedom, and it don't seem like He want to hear that one."

"I know people who was angry like you, 'til they start openin' they hearts to prayer and redemption."

"I hear you preach a bit," T said approvingly. "And don't take no wrong from me, boy preacher, but unless yo' God gon string massa up and turn his back bloody, you won't hear me thankin' Him for my good fortune. I believe in T. That be enough."

"Until it ain't. When I give you that water, I see the anger in yo' eyes, but I saw somethin' else too. You comin' here today tell me that some decency be in you and that's what God will grow in you if you let Him."

"I jus' do what be right for a man to do, if he do right by me. Yo' God can like it or not like it. I never give it no thought. Jus' look 'round you, boy preacher. All you see are miserable darkies, who can't understand why God deliver them back to the Devil one day after Sunday. Maybe God too busy helpin' white folks and jus' be too tired at the end of the day for us. No, T take care of T."

"Somebody say Massa Wallace don't rightly own you and that be why you run. We can pray you find yo' way back if that's where you want to be. God can help if you let Him."

"Like He help that old man? Don't want or need anything from anybody who able to stop that but don't."

"You talk like a man with no faith."

"Call me whatever you want but it seem like a fool take learning from somebody like that."

Rev. R took the insult in, but also T's willing to engage. "Until you walk with the Lord you won't understand."

"Maybe, but you a good man for what you did," and he left without waiting for a reply.

CHAPTER 23

"Come on here. I got something for you." T had been staring at the ground on his way back to his quarters after another exhausting day. It was near dusk and Miss Edna was standing on the road as if she had been waiting for him. "Follow me." They walked in silence.

When they got to her cabin, he spoke for the first time, marveling that she had such expensive accommodations. It was a single story, two room log house."I ain't never seen a slave with a house like this."

"Come with what I do. I keep everybody in the fields so massa gimme what I need." They walked inside and into another world. On one entire wall were shelves filled with pots and jars of dried plants, flowers and bark that made up her pharmacopeia. They were all labeled. *"She can read,"* he thought. There was a long worktable, four log stumps for chairs, a proper fireplace and a straw bed supported by an additional four stumps and several wood planks.

Along one wall was a box that was about six feet long and four feet wide that she used to transport her products for sale at the market. He could almost believe she was a witch as he took in the room. She had a stew going over the fire which made him nearly faint with the realization of his hunger. His stomach cried out for whatever was in that pot.

"Wait here." She disappeared into the other room and returned with a pair of pants and a shirt neatly folded in one hand and a pair of worn but intact boots in the other. "Take these."

"Why?"

"What you mean, why?" 'Cause you gonna need 'em, boy, that's why."

"Yeah, but why you give 'em to me?"

"Sit down." She indicated a chair at her table. "I know you ain't seen much kindness and I don't mean nothin' more than to show some good to you. I get all kinds of left behind things and I be thinkin' these may fit you. So, you go on and take 'em."

"Thank you, Miss Edna. You good to do this."

"Wait. Jus' sit a minute. In the other room is a tub with some fresh water and soap. You go on in there and clean yo'self up and see how those clothes fit. And I don't expect no back talk like I know you like to do," she added and held his stare. He did as he was told.

He had not touched a cake of soap in recent memory. The water was almost too hot and turned black immediately. He emerged from the tub feeling like he had been baptized. The clothes were a little too tight but at least the boots didn't hurt his feet. He walked into the front room and saw two places set for dinner. She appraised him. "So, this is what was under all that dirt. A fine man if ever there was one. The clothes ain't perfect but they clean."

"They real nice, Miss Edna."

She went over to the stew and spooned some out, blew on it, then tasted it. With her back to him she said, "Well, you can go on home now since you seemed to be in such a hurry. These ham hocks and turnips won't miss you."

He meekly sat at the table. "Uh, you be ok if I stay?"

"Figured you might want to," she said through a laugh. "Hand me that bowl." He did and she ladled in some stew. When they were both settled, she said, "When I first meet you and you tell me that strange name you give yo'self, I see you got some pride and feeling 'bout who you be. You got anger too and it make me happy and scared for you at the same time."

"I ain't scared of nobody. One day I leave this place and be free again."

"Free again? What you talkin' 'bout?'

"Mista Kincaid give all his slaves free papers once they work off what he pay for 'em, and he be fair 'bout it. I got my free papers. I ain't no slave."

"That be God working his miracles on earth. I ain't never know a man like him."

"Don't know and don't care it be God, I jus' know I got to get back."

"I know that. And I don't want that to bring you no harm. You ain't had a massa like Jr. Wallace in a long time. He 'bout as far from Mista Kincaid as the sun is from the moon. He and that wife of his be made from the dirt of the Devil. Mista Kincaid tells me 'bout how you be so good with that little girl of his and wherever that come from, that place in yo' heart that is still alive, I don't want you to let Wallace crush it out. And he will try mighty hard." T shrugged because he was afraid to speak. She had spoken what he could not, because he did not know how. He felt exposed, almost violated by her piercing insight. "I jus' want to let you know that I'm gonna be lookin' out for you. You good in a special way. I see that when I look past everything else, but you got to be careful, T, not to give this Devil a reason to hurt you. I can promise you, yo' time will come."

"He hurt folks if he want to. Don't need no reason," said T.

"Ain't nothin' you can do 'bout that. Their place in hell is set and ready. You jus' keep to yo'self and be careful. Hear?"

"Yes ma'am

The next morning T sprang up, disoriented and wide eyed. Slowly the straw, the snores of his roommates and the hard dirt floor, oriented him. Last night, after the bath and a meal from heaven itself, he fell into a coma-like sleep and was now in the groggy aftermath. His head was also pounding having rested the entire night on his new boots. There were thieves everywhere and using shoes as pillows was a common practice.

T didn't tell Miss Edna that his rib still hurt from being kicked by Samson, who promised to wake him up with a kick every morning if he wasn't outside and ready to work an hour before everyone else. "The smell of all you niggers in one room makes me want to throw up. Don't you make me come in here again." After that, he was never late again.

The hot August had moved into an even hotter September with no sign of Kincaid and doubt began to creep in. Maybe Kincaid didn't care about him. Maybe he was the fool that Miss Edna thought he wasn't. Kincaid promised him he was free, showed him a paper that was supposed to say that. So why was he still here? Was it a lie?

It wouldn't be the first time a white man lied to him. Maybe he would always be moved around like an ebony chess piece and any promise made to him could be wiped out by the highest bidder. From what he was able to understand, some evil Augustus did made him Jr. Wallace's' property now. It was all the typical white man lies at work.

But not this time. Kincaid made him foreman and he was paying him but T had never asked to see his money. Kincaid claimed to be "putting it away for him." But was he? These were questions T had not contemplated until now. The warm memories of his past were being rapidly usurped by the present, and if he didn't run soon, he might just lose all good memories of the Kincaid plantation. It was becoming harder to remember the longer he remained under Wallace's boot.

He had seen Miss Edna at the market and thought she was some kind of witch, at least that's what he had heard from others. He had no beliefs about that one way or another but had been cured by some of her medicine, as had most of the slaves he knew. Last night he was reminded of his first meeting with Ol' Pete. Here was another black elder that saw something in him and wanted to protect and advise him. It felt comforting in a way he had forgotten anything could.

When he got outside, on time, Samson shoved a hoe into his hands and marched him to the fields that needed to be tended. He was grateful that full light had not come up and that his new boots would be difficult to see. Samson would confiscate them, accuse him of being a thief and a beating would be in store for when he refused to reveal their true source.

Once at his destination Samson would move far enough away to watch him and the boots could be easily covered in dust and dirt, indistinguishable from the dozens of others that would soon join him. He attacked the soil with determination, while Samson lit a cigarette and didn't take his eyes off of him.

CHAPTER 24

He had heard his father called crazy for believing in Christ, but that was usually by a drunk who nobody paid no mind. It had never happened to Rev. R, until T leveled the accusation and probably would have had the same effect if T were a drunk, but he wasn't. Therefore, it stung.

Several days after their second encounter he was still in a quandary as to what to make of this impenetrable block of confidence and defiance by which a black man would fearlessly call his God a fool. If he had been like the others, full of hate and bitterness at the world without the capacity or interest to engage, that would have been the end of it. They would have gone their separate ways. But T wanted to engage, in fact, seemed excited by the challenge, as if he was just as interested in turning Rev. R into a non-believer.

This was frightening territory for Rev. R, but he was determined to fight the Devil for this man's soul and would consider it his crowning achievement to add T's name to his heavenly ledger. It would be a fight. He remembered thinking, *there be danger there,* after T left him standing at the altar.

Not so much in the physical way he sensed when he gave him the water, but in his fearless denial of God's presence. This would not be the last time his faith was challenged, but in the days that followed their conversation, he was shaken by the confidence of T's conviction. It seemed to match his own, opposite beliefs.

He remembered his father converting sinners with the carrot-and-stick method. He would extoll the glories to be had when one walked through the pearly gates adorned in the whitest of white robes against their

139

obsidian skin, a plumage of magnificent and unwieldy feathers protruding magically from intact backs. Their days would be spent floating in and out of each other's fully loaded mansions, while occurring as all things biblical.

If this didn't have the desired effect, then the stick: An equally graphic description of flesh eternally consumed by fire with every nerve ending registering the searing pain for all eternity. This usually had even the most ardent skeptic showing some concern, but Rev. R knew not to waste this technique on T. Even as he recalled it, it now seemed like a child's tale.

In the early months, it seemed that Jr. Wallace kept T working longer and harder than the others and fed him just enough to sustain him. This created an unforeseen opportunity for Rev. R to drop off a bit of extra food and continue in his purpose, when it was safe.

T was quick to establish guardrails the first time this happened. "This won't make me believe in nothin'," he told Rev. R.

"Then give it back." T looked up from his snack like a dog daring anyone to take his bone and Rev. R burst out laughing. "You go on and eat yo' food T, but if you want to give God thanks, I don'e t think He mind."

"You bring it. So I thank you." This was the first of several afternoon "prayer sessions" that they shared. Jr. Wallace gave Rev. R free rein to minister to whomever he wanted. He held the standard conviction that a Christian slave was more compliant and fearful than one who wasn't.

Some days Rev. R would offer a simple but sure-fire challenge that had most non-believers scratching their heads, "So how you explain the moon and the stars?"

"Don't need to," T would answer and would notice a crack in Rev. R pious confidence and smile slightly. This was how it went most afternoons. Rev. R would present a concept he hoped would stump T, and T would respond with his signature taciturn take on the subject.

One afternoon the conversation veered into the personal and, before T could stop himself, he started talking about Tommie. "She be the one thing I think I miss most 'bout that place."

"You say she be Mista' Kincaid little girl?"

"Yeah. She 'bout drown and I save her."

"Ain't no wonder why you miss her. You got any other people you know 'bout?"

"Maybe. Don't know. She be the closest. We talk. She teach me to read some. I make her these little animals sometime." For a minute T got lost in memory. "Don't matter. I never see those people again. Mista Kincaid say he gon' take me from Wallace but that never gon' happen and I won't go back anyway. He tell me I free but now I don't know. If I be free, why he don't come get me?"

"If he make you foreman and be payin' you, I believe him. That sound like a man of God to me." T shrugged.

"But I still here. If I really be free, don't know why I still under Massa Wallace."

"That don't mean Mista Kincaid ain't tryin' to get you back. You don't know what he tryin' to do."

"Maybe, but I can't wait to find out. Massa Wallace won't catch me next time. When I go it be to my freedom or my grave."

"I hope it ain't that."

"Me too."

"I don't know, T, I wouldn't be throwin' away that family, if you can get to them. Family like that don't happen every day with folks like us."

T shrugged and ate. "Don't matter none now. "

"Well, since prayer don't make it no worse, I be prayin' for you to get back to that family real soon."

"You got family, Rev.?" T queried.

"No, my mama die when I was a boy and my daddy die not too long before you come."

"Then you better get yo'self a wife," T said.

He turned to T. "You better get yo'self one too."

"Why I do that? Yo' God jus' let Wallace sell her and sell our babies and won't care nothin' 'bout it."

"That don't be God. That be the Devil."

"Same difference if he won't stop the Devil."

These challenges were not insulting to Rev. R, because he was under the misguided impression that any conversation that included God held the potential for salvation. They became friends that recognized the thinker, the searcher, the challenger in each other. They also enjoyed landing points, with Rev. R thinking their conversations were moving T closer to salvation. T enjoyed those moments of insecurity that would pass before Rev. R eyes, which he would desperately try to cover up with some biblical pabulum.

They were on the road to a true friendship, one that challenged that part of T's soul where a belief in "family" had been ripped out and replaced with a space that was impenetrable and dead. Rev. R was pushing through that space and T would find himself stopping in the middle of a task to glance around in the hopes that this was a day Rev. R paid him a visit and deflated when the day ended without the balm of their conversation. He would catch himself, though, from time to time, and move back into that comfortable space of trusting no one, even Rev. R, to be anything other than a potential instrument of deception and pain.

But this withholding was at the beginning. Through the months and hours of often-times soul-baring revelations, Rev. R started to occupy a place in T's heart that was as close to family as he had ever known. He felt safe with him in a way that was as exciting as it was confusing and the space that had been shut off started opening slightly to let in Rev. R and, maybe, form the seedlings of a new family tree.

What T didn't tell Rev. R was that his plan to run was as far along as it was. He heard about a church in Lexington where some woman was helping slaves get up north and this time he would not stop until he got himself there. If Kincaid came for him before then, he would know he was a good man. But he would not wait.

More and more he felt like he had been lulled into some abolitionist fantasy by Kincaid, betrayed, because just beyond those gates of Kincaid's fantasy lay a fresh hell whose deep scars he would forever carry in mind and body. This time, though, he would be no white man's fool. His freedom was a prize that he would die many times over to get.

Then he met Joraye.

CHAPTER 25

He was making his usual, exhausting slog from the fields to the slave shack, head down, brow furrowed and attitude grim. On this day he caught her in just enough of his vision to look up. She worked in the big house and their paths had never crossed. What first caught his eye was her isolation. Whereas other women were walking and gossiping in pairs or small groups, Joraye walked alone. As he got closer, he noticed that she was shaking her head and muttering to herself, but this did not put him off.

He had seen slaves fall victim to madness before, and he knew better than to think it was the Devil, or at least the Devil battling Jesus. If it was any Devil, it was the flesh and blood version that they faced every day. His reality, like his brethren's, included dark and unimaginable horrors that were always just breaths away. Those lost creatures, the ones whose unique horror was so unbearable that they were rewarded with madness or death, were a familiar presence in T's life. Like everyone else, he generally ignored these outcasts, not out of fear or hostility, but because he was T and he ignored everyone. Almost everyone.

When he passed her she looked up at him with startling green eyes and he recognized her as the girl he glimpsed through the kitchen window struggling with the muzzle and once again he was assaulted with the shock of deja vu. She must have recognized him too because she looked away with the jerky speed of a frightened animal, but not before he saw the terror and confusion spilling out of those eyes like an angry wound. Again, this did not put him off because he also saw, or imagined he saw, a pleading in those same eyes for someone, anyone, to show her simple human kindness.

He did not imagine the life he saw struggling to hold on, the spirit that was bowed but not broken, and his heart beat faster because he knew what would be. There was no predicting how long before she was swallowed up by darkness, the fight ripped from her, a descent from which she could not rise. T sensed that she was on a precipice, and that the clawing hands of insanity had not yet succeeded in tearing away her last vestiges of lucidity. And she was alone in this battle and it was that, as much as all else, that he recognized in his own soul. This all seared him with the shock and surprise of a lightning bolt, and in that instant he found a purpose.

The other women kept their distance from Joraye, afraid that madness was a contagion spread by close contact. Therefore, Joraye kept to the shadows, avoiding humanity as much as it wanted to avoid her. T had a disgusting premonition about the cause of her madness. She was the most beautiful woman he had ever seen, and therefore condemned to special horror reserved for those like her.

His first order of business was to let her know he existed. He tried a simple "Good afternoon," which had her flying away like a frightened sparrow, terror struck by the absolute threatening masculinity of this new addition to the plantation. But he was determined, and more importantly, patient. He didn't try to approach her again and avoided eye contact when they passed each other.

He could not explain how or why, but she exposed a level of empathy and sadness in him that spoke to his soul. He became desperate for her to understand that he could easily become a muttering half-man after one beating too many. As he watched her make her shunned way through the plantation, he most of all wanted to be her safe haven, her protector, and maybe, simply whisper, "You'll never be alone."

The only people she seemed to trust were Miss Edna and Rev. R. They took her under their wings and tried to bring some humanity to her tortured existence.

Her back story made her madness as natural as flowing water. T heard it a week later on a visit to Miss Edna when he was looking for a remedy for his cracked and bleeding hands. "What you know 'bout that woman with green eyes that be talkin' to herself?"

"That be Joraye. Why you want to know 'bout her?"

"Jus' do."

Miss Edna took a deep breath. "There be a lot there. She a troubled soul."

"What you mean?"

"You tellin' me, you don't be hearin' what folks say 'bout Joraye?"

"You know I don't be mixin' with folks. I do my work and eat and sleep."

"Like I said, you ain't no fool. You gon' live a long time, you live like that."

"So tell me."

"She show up some years ago and Massa Augustus take her straight to the big house. She look like a girl never touched by a man, and this put me to worryin' 'bout the child, 'cause I know what massa have in mind. Everyone did. But folks pay it no mind, 'cause she not the first nor she be the last. All you do is feel sorry, and that ain't helpin' the poor thing. I remember when it happened the first time. Someone be knockin' on my door and when I open it, there Joraye, lookin' beat up so bad almost didn't know it be her. Her lip be split open, and one of her eyes be shut. She say the missus sent her for me to tend to. When I ask what happened, she jus' cry and I hold her for a long time. After 'while, I ask if it be massa, and she jus' cry more then I know. Once she get her head 'bout her, she able to tell me. It no different from every other time massa do this. I tell her not to fight next time, or it be worse. She say she don't fight, jus' cried 'cause it hurt, and that's when he hit her."

Miss Edna noticed that T's jaw was clenching and unclenching, and he was barely breathing. "I know what you be thinkin', T. But no man here willin' to die to save her. It jus' be two dead instead of one. Massa leave for weeks sometime so Joraye heal a bit, then when he come back it start up again. 'Bout the time massa wife die, which be 'bout a year ago, she start with the head shaking and talking to herself. Some think the Devil got into her and be afraid to cross her path. Ain't no Devil! It jus' be too much pain and shame to live with so she start to lose herself. Now the Devil go and put her in the hands of Jr. Wallace. My faith be strong, but I don't know how God see fit to let that happen."

She could see T growing agitated.

"Think I need to stop now. This ain't doin' her or you no good. The world do what it do, and I think God don't even know what it be sometime. I love Joraye, but she be one of the unlucky ones. That jus' be life."

"She still come 'round here?"

"Yeah. She come 'round to pick up medicine for the big house sometime but I don't know what you see. Why her? You be thinkin' you can save her?"

"No man do that to a woman. No man!" He slammed his fist on the table overturning bowls and jars. Miss Edna silently picked up the pieces while T paced.

"I kill him! Miss Edna, I gon' kill 'him!" She went to him, took both his arms and forced him to look at her.

"No, baby, you not gon' kill nobody. It be up to God to give him his due. I see you got a strong feelin' for Joraye. You got to know who she be if you want to be with her. If you start up with her then get scared and leave, you as good as kill her yo'self. I tell you 'bout her so you know who she be and you can go yo' own way before you get started."

"What you say don't scare me." They grew silent. There was an unspoken acknowledgement that T was about to enter a fragile, potentially tragic experiment, whose success was hanging on a dangling branch.

Miss Edna took his hand and said, "Well, guess I can tell you now, I be thinkin' 'bout a way to get her out that house. Been thinkin' 'bout it for a while. Now I got to do it."

"I do whatever you say."

"Nothin' you need do. This only be me and Joraye, and you also be able to see her when you want."

"How? You say she live in the big house."

"Massa look to me to heal folks and keep 'em in the fields. I be thinkin' for a while now I can make him believe that Joraye act the way she do 'cause she be touched by the spirit of healin'. I tell him that she needs to stay with me, so I can help her become a healer and take over when I'm gone. He don't know nothin' 'bout spirits and healin', he jus' want to keep his cattle workin'. I say she ain't no good to him the way she be scarin' folks, with all that head shakin' and noise she make. I tell him, I take her in here, with me, and make her better."

"Then I come 'round to see her when she here."

"We see if this work first. Still don't know why a man like you have a heart for Joraye, but Lord knows she need kindness. You be a quiet, searching man, and that be good for her. Now, when she get here you got to give her time to learn you. She see men be the Devil, and she won't be fast to know you."

"That be good. It quiet here. She see who I am." Then he is struck by a realization, "He gon' ask for her back sometime. I can't let that happen, once she here."

"Oh, I know he will. He got to think he can have her back whenever he want. Been thinkin' 'bout that too. Lord bless us women folk with a monthly visitor that make you men folk look the other way. I figure that if he come after her that be what I tell him. I say she not clean and he need to find another. I know that be sending him off." T did not disagree.

"You men be so weak sometime, but it help us right now."

Joraye moved in the next week.

When she first saw T, she was terror struck to see the same man she ran away from now filling up Miss Edna's doorframe. She ran to a corner of the cabin and refused to move.

"Joraye, T don't mean you no harm. He jus' come to eat sometime. Massa don't feed us nearly enough and you see what a big, strong man he be. He got to eat. So you pay him no mind."

He inclined his head in a greeting to Joraye. "Like Miss Edna say, don't mean you no harm. I jus' come over sometime 'cause she gimme food."

"This here be, Joraye, T. She gon' be livin' here now."

"Then you be lucky, Miss Joraye, 'cause Miss Edna be real nice." He turned to Miss Edna, "I be outback, let me know when the food ready." He started to walk around to the back of the cabin.

149

"We got plenty room inside," she said, trying to hide her confusion.

"I know, but I be out back, jus' call me." And he left.

When the food was ready he went inside to collect his plate then took it back outside, to the utter frustration of Miss Edna. This was not like any courting she had ever seen. He did the same thing the next night. It was a full moon and she noticed Joraye stealing glances out the window. She looked herself and saw T sitting on a tree stump whittling on a piece of wood. Joraye quickly turned away. This dance continued for about a week until, just as incongruently, T decided to stay in the cabin and eat at one end while they ate at another.

The next night Miss Edna said to him, "T, come over here and move this pot off the fire." This would require he enter Joraye's space. She immediately tensed. He walked quietly over and moved the pot, deliberately ignoring her, then went back to the other side of the room. "T, come over here and put some wood on the fire." He looked at Miss Edna with an almost imperceptible smile. He took his time looking for just the right piece of wood. Joraye had to step around him while he tended to the fire.

Her mumbling did not completely stop when she moved in, though it wasn't as frantic and desperate as it was before. Her speech mostly consisted of "Yes Ma'am and "No Ma'am" when T was around. But in between those short phrases she still mumbled, until she stopped.

T almost didn't notice, it had been such a consistent part of the landscape since he started coming around to see her. He suddenly became aware of the silence and cautiously snuck a glance her way. She was chopping vegetables with her brow knitted in concentration, and she wasn't mumbling. He glanced over at Miss Edna who met his eyes with acknowledgement and a raised eyebrow. This was a small milestone but a milestone nonetheless, which is why she was completely shocked when T suggested that he not come around for a few days.

"But she actin' better round' you. Why you thinkin' to do this now?"

"She need to miss me," he said. Miss Edna shook her head and smiled in admiration.

"Boy, how you learn to make a woman want you like that?"

He shrugged. "She need time with her thoughts 'bout me, that's all. She see I don't mean her no harm."

"You got some knowin' 'bout women a lot of men don't have. Don't know where you come by that, but the way you be 'round her is different, and she startin' to be at peace a little. I do what you want. I tell her you ain't comin' 'cause massa put you to work on something new."

The next night, as they were preparing dinner, all went as usual, except every so often Joraye would glance at the door. Miss Edna waited until the third time. "Oh, I sorry baby, I forgot to say T not comin' by tonight," she offered up with sweet innocence. "Massa put him to work with the horses. Maybe he come tomorrow."

"No matter," Joraye said, more defensively than she wanted to reveal.

"He may come tomorrow. He don't come every day, you know."

She shrugged off Miss Edna's attempt at comfort and continued working.

The next day Miss Edna reported the evening to T. He listened, as she described the stolen glances toward the door and her failed attempt to hide her disappointment. "I jus' got to say, I be the one to make medicine, but you can put what you got in a bottle and men folk line up." She said, giddy with conspiratorial excitement. They agreed that T would make a surprise visit on the third night. Miss Edna did offer Joraye a little treat by way of telling her that she saw T and he asked after her.

On that third night, Joraye didn't steal glances at the door. She had resigned herself to the fact that she must have imagined the special way T acted around her. No matter that he asked after her. If he really wanted to see her he would have found a way. She felt like the imbecile that she was trying so hard not to be. How could anyone want what she had become? She had allowed herself to imagine the impossible and, once again, was reminded that she would always be the mumbling idiot, forever on the outside looking in. She became more aggressive with her tasks, infusing them with the anger and despair she was feeling.

There was a knock. "Well, I wonder who that could be." Miss Edna asked, almost chirping. "Who there!" she shouted out.

"It Simone, Miss Edna," a meek female voice answered. "Massa send me to collect Joraye." The air was sucked out of the room. They became still as mannequins.

Joraye burst into tears and started frantically pacing and shaking her head. "I can't, I can't," she repeated like a mantra.

Miss Edna was up in a flash and wrapped Joraye in her arms. "Tell massa she be in the blood and it be bad. She no good to him now. You go on, Simone, and you make him believe it!" she ordered.

"I will, Miss Edna. I promise I will. I say Joraye be in bed she be so bad with it."

152

"God bless you, child." She turned to Joraye. "You see baby? You ain't goin' nowhere," she said and stroked her hair. "We do jus' like we talk 'bout, and he leave us alone. I know you scared, but T and me gon' protect you."

Joraye was stilled by this and looked up. "Yes, baby, why you think he come 'round here every night? Ain't 'cause he courtin' me! When I told him I was gon' move you in with me, he say he come 'round every night 'til you see he a good man. He love you, girl, but he afraid he scare you away if he tell you."

"That be true Miss Edna, then why he stop comin?" Before Miss Edna can respond Joraye continued. "Oh. He find out." she said wearily.

"Joraye, he know all 'bout you and he don't care." She looked at Miss Edna, wide-eyed.

"How you know that, Miss Edna?"

"'Cause I tell him."

"You what? Why you do that?"

"'Cause best he find out from someone that love you, than from someone who don't. 'Cause he gon' find out one way or another, and you know somethin'? His heart open up even more for you. That man got a understandin' I ain't never seen. He real, Joraye. He stop comin' so you be thinkin' 'bout him, jus' like you doin' now. He got a way, that all I can say."

They both jump at the sound of someone else knocking. "Who there!" She yelled.

"It T." Joraye quickly stood up, wiped her eyes and moved to the fireplace.

"You good for me to let him in?" said Miss Edna. She nodded and Miss Edna opened the door. T looked more polished than either of them had ever seen. He was obviously in a courting mood. His shirt was cleaner than usual, and he had done something unexplainable with his hair. He was holding some wildflowers in one hand and a sack in the other. He set the sack on the floor.

"Don't you look yo' best and with flowers too! Look at this Joraye!" she exclaimed, a little over-enthusiastically. Joraye shyly looked up, then immediately looked away.

"These be for you, Joraye," he said and walked to the other side of the room and placed the bouquet on the table.

"Thank you." she said quietly to his back.

"You welcome. These all I could find. Don't look like much, but, you know, they still flowers." This is their first cordial exchange.

"Well, ain't that the most thoughtful thing?" Miss Edna said, as she searched for something to put them in. They fell silent as she tended to the flowers, and Joraye continued cooking.

He watched them and sensed the tension. "Somethin' wrong?"

"Oh, we jus' be a little tired tonight, that be all," was Miss Edna's' unconvincing response.

"I go then, so you can rest." He got up.

"Now, don't you go nowhere 'especially since we ain't seen you for some days. Massa been keeping you busy, and we been missin' you. You go and get all dressed up, and we makin' a nice meal, so don't you think 'bout goin' nowhere. Where you get these pretty flowers, anyway?"

"They was near where I stay."

"Well, I'm gon' see we do somethin' special for dinner tonight, you be so nice to bring 'em." She proceeded to help Joraye. There was a self-consciousness to their movements.

T's senses were on high alert. "I see Simone leave before I come," he probed, tying to tease out what he could.

"She jus' come to pick up some medicine, that's all," Miss Edna lied. He looked over at Joraye who was slowly shaking her head while quietly weeping.

"She come for you Joraye, didn't she?" T said. In response Joraye stopped cooking and rushed to a stool in the corner of the room. She rocked back and forth, holding herself tight through her weeping terror.

Miss Edna knelt beside her but addressed T. "And it work jus' like I said it would. I tell her she ain't never have to go back there again."

He wanted to rush to her and kiss her tears away and wrap her in his powerful arms. Instead, he slowly knelt on one knee in front of her.

Miss Edna tried to move discreetly out of their space, but Joraye grabbed her hand like a lifeline, as she shrank away from T and rocked more forcefully. "It's alright, baby," Miss Edna said and patted Joraye's hand. "You remember we talk 'bout T. He here for you and I be right here too. I jus' need to tend to the pots real quick, but I'm right here." She gently slid her hand out of Joraye's and moved to the fire.

Joraye refused to look in T's direction as he began quietly. "He never touch you again. Long as I be breathin'. I swear, Joraye, he never touch you again." He paused, but she still refused to face him. "I. . . know you, Joraye." At this her eyes shifted in panic toward him. "Ain't nothin' happen to you that scare me away. Nothin'. These Devils try and destroy me too, so we both seen pain and maybe we help each other with that pain. When I first see you, all I want to do is take it all away." She stopped rocking. "All you got to do is let me. I come 'round here and sit like I do jus' so you see me, you see I good." He paused, considering whether to share this next revelation. "I was gonna run. I ain't even tell the Rev. that, and he be the only other one I talk to. Then I see you and my whole world change.

That be true, Joraye. Can't say I be knowin' why, exactly, but it somethin' in my heart that come up on me all a sudden when I see you." She had been as still as a statue, almost not breathing, as she took in T's confession. "Please jus' listen to what I say. It been in my heart for a while now and I glad you know it. You don't want me, I leave you alone. I promise, but Wallace never touch you again, I also promise you that."

Miss Edna had been quietly completing the meal, now done, she moved toward the door with a bag and a digging tool. "I'm gon' gather some plants. They be some that only come out at night." Joraye looked up, brow knitted. Miss Edna said to her, "Don't you see what this man tryin' to tell you, Joraye? You bein' here with him 'bout the safest place you be. I won't be gone long, baby. You be fine." She kissed her on the forehead and headed into the night.

They didn't talk for several minutes. T moved to a chair across the room. He contemplated his hands in search of what to say.

"Miss Edna, say she told you 'bout me," began Joraye.

"It like I say, we all been done wrong by these Devils, Joraye. Ain't yo' fault. I supposed to be free but I ain't."

"Then why you here?"

"'Cause the white man be the Devil. At least a lot of 'em do. The world do what it want with us, Joraye. I be a man, so I fight back. They beat me for it, but I fight back anyway. You can't fight these Devils, but I fight for you, you let me."

"Why you say that? Why you say you fight for me? You ain't even know me."

"I know all I need to know. What happen to you, ain't nothin' worse than that, and it don't stop me."

They fell back into another awkward silence then, before he resumed. "I see a girl a long time ago that have eyes like you. I ain't never see another one. I could only see her with my one good eye. The other one was all big 'cause someone tried to steal my food and we fight."

Joraye looked at him sharply. "Was you jus' sold?"

"Yeah, I was. I was walking to the wagon with Mista Kincaid. I knew it," he smiled, slightly. "The first time I see you in that kitchen, something make me think I see you before. You was with a big woman."

"That was Tessie. I see you too." She said, more breathless than she meant to show. "I remember thinkin' yo' eye was bad as I ever see. How it be now?"

"Not right like the other one but I can see some."

The had mood shifted. There was a heightened sense of anticipation. Neither one could say what it was. Another even more awkward silence descended.

"Miss Edna say she tell you 'bout me," T said. Joraye shrugged. "What she say?" She shrugged again. "Was it good?" Another shrug. "Was it real good?" This time a hint of a smile. "Then whatever she say be true," he said in playful triumph.

"You not really 'bout to run is you?"

"Yeah. Would be gone a while ago ain't for the Rev. We friends now and it been a long time since I talk to anybody like I talk to him. I don't believe in all that God mess but he still listen like he care 'bout what I say. There be this little girl on Mista Kincaid Plantation, it be his little girl, and she real nice to me. She the only other one close like family."

"You not a Christian man?"

"No, and that ain't gon' change, Joraye. God got too much to answer for, is the way I see it. Like there be bad Christians, there be good people that ain't." She pondered this.

"Who Mista Kincaid?"

"He my massa before the Devil that steal me from him and sell me to this new Devil."

"Sound like he good to you."

It was T's turn to shrug. "You still be scared?" he asked gently. She shook her head. "Oh," he said. Remembering something, he walked over to the bag he brought with him and took it to his stool. As he took out its contents he said, "I like to do stuff with wood, this be for you." He presented her with a crude but nevertheless beautifully realized carving of her face. What it lacked in refinement was replaced with startling emotion and strikingly obvious love of the subject.

Joraye gasped. She took it as delicately as fine China and traced the lines and grooves, gently brushing over each feature, almost as if bringing it comfort, before she quietly started weeping. "This…" she barely whispered, "nobody ever. . .," then through tears, "Thank you."

T walked over and again knelt before her. "Now, I think you see. This say it maybe better than my dumb talk."

"Yo' talk ain't dumb," she said, trying to regain some dignity as she wiped her eyes with her sleeve. They remained together like this until it became awkward. "You maybe be hungry?" She said, needing to put some distance between them. She was no longer fearful of him but fearful now of how she was responding to his physical presence.

"That sound real good, Joraye." He rose. She went to the pot that Miss Edna left for them. T watched her for a few minutes then began to touch the pedals of the flowers he had brought. While focused on the table, his back to her, he reached out a hand behind himself as if trying to find something to grasp and stood stone still saying nothing. The silence had the desired effect and Joraye turned to see his extended hand and tentatively placed her small one in his.

He turned to face her and could not hide his urgency. "This all I want, Joraye, jus' touch yo' hand, please."

She looked at him, quickly looked away, but did not remove her hand. He took it with both of his and brought it to his lips. Her throat caught, as he kissed her palm with a tenderness she had never before felt. She flushed, sensing warmth in places that embarrassed and surprised her. He slowly brought her hand down, and true to his word, turned to go. She grabbed his arm, and as he turned around, rushed into his chest. He gently enfolded her. Slowly, they met each other where they could, and for the time it lasted, transcended the horror.

His night with Joraye forced a clarity. He was reminded of the soul-annihilating behaviors of his daily existence. The whippings, the rapes, the burnings, the beatings, the mutilations, the shackling and imprisonments that lay in wait for the disobedient nigger must never touch Joraye again. There would be nothing or no one who could stop him from exploding into that house and revisiting the dark fantasies of his fever dream if any of this were to happen to her now. The security inherent in his detached participation in life on the plantation was gone. Now he was more like a raw nerve, keenly sensitive to the myriad landmines laid out for them both.

They settled into a routine as lovers as best they could. Miss Edna was happy to offer her cabin as their rendezvous point. It was away from the other slave quarters and so was able to offer them some privacy. The routine usually consisted of some kind of meal for the three of them or sometimes four. Rev. R might show up with sweet potatoes or some other nourishing contribution. T might go back to his shack and other times he would indicate he wanted to be alone to "talk" with Joraye, whereas Miss Edna would excuse herself to gather nighttime roots. If, in fact, she gathered roots as often as T wanted to talk with Joraye, every bush and tree in the south would be uprooted.

They were in a blaze for each other, and Miss Edna could only move aside and let them get their fill. After a while, she made no pretense of gathering roots. She'd leave without being prompted and return at a time she hoped was tactful.

The relationship also created a potent new weapon of abuse for Jr. Wallace, a harsh fact Miss Edna made clear to them. "Don't be knowin' one another outside this cabin. Massa get it in his head to work some devilment if he find out. You only safe when you close that door, and I mean it."

"Joraye always be safe with me," was T's quick answer.

"We know that, but still don't mean you got to give 'em cause to go crazy, and they still lookin' at you real close. Jus' go on 'bout yo' business-like you strangers and save yo 'selves for this cabin. That be the only way to keep you safe." They understood the wisdom of her warning and behaved as instructed.

It was nothing short of a miracle, Rev. R thought, as he watched Joraye interact with T and Miss Edna. He was witnessing her astonishing transformation firsthand, as he sat at the roughhewn piece of oak that served as Miss Edna's dining table. The muttering, the darting eyes and defeated affect were simply gone. She wasn't a chatterbox, but she was engaged and hung on every word that T uttered. One evening, T made a proclamation, "Me and Joraye jump the broom, Rev. She be my woman. What you think?"

This phenomenon should have had Rev. R exalting God's hand in their lives, but nothing like that occurred. Even he didn't understand his muted response. He could only offer a perfunctory, "Well, praise Jesus. You both look real happy." He did not have the emotional vocabulary, nor the courage, to admit that in every way this commitment felt like a betrayal, and he became uncharacteristically self-conscious. He had come to expect that that his intimacy with T was unique.

Now that someone else occupied the space he thought was only theirs, he felt abandoned, like a puppy dropped in a dark forest. He was losing a cherished friend, his only friend.

The rest of the evening proceeded in a fog of conflicting emotions that were brought to a head when T said, "I was jus' 'bout to run again, then Joraye come into my life." Rev. R rubbed his forehead.

"Guess I was more tired than I realized," he said. "Thank you for a meal that make God proud, Miss Edna, but I got to go now. God bless you two." And he made a hasty exit.

***

"The Rev. not hisself tonight," Joraye commented as they lay together while Miss Edna performed her nighttime foraging. T was surprised she noticed what he had also sensed. But his mind was elsewhere. He continued to marvel at the depth behind those beautiful green eyes.

"He think 'cause you my woman he not be my friend." A silence stretched between them.

161

"Those be the feelings of someone who feel real strong 'bout you, T," said Joraye.

"I feel real strong 'bout him too. He the first one show me kindness and we talk like I ain't never talk to no one. Maybe he think we not do that now I be with you."

"Maybe. You know, it be him and Miss Edna only ones good to me before you come."

"I see him like family. Like I see you, Joraye. I mean, I feel close to him, like I feel close to you." He struggled to get this out, trying to make her understand while he didn't fully understand himself. He only knew that he must tell her. He would always show his heart to her, even if it was a struggle. "But different, you know?"

"Why this be so hard for you to say? We not talkin' 'bout somebody bad."

"I know we ain't. It jus' that I don't feel this way before."

"You need to keep him close, T. The way I see it Rev. and me both be lucky."

"What I say don't scare you?"

"You save me when most people run away. They all say the Devil be in my head and treat me like I with a sickness. You be the only one ain't scared to come to me. You love in a strong way, T, and you love ME in a strong way. If you love the Rev. in a strong way too, ain't nothin' 'bout it scare me."

***

While the lovers talked, Rev. R was setting a brisk pace back to his cabin. He shook his head in confusion and disbelief at T's confession. They had talked about him running, but not right away. Now it sounded like he was going to stay because of Joraye.

162

He had thought he was going to wake up one morning to find T gone without a word.

That it mattered this much whether T left or stayed was disconcerting to him. There had been times when he blessed a slave on Sunday and that same slave was gone on Monday without a word. He would say a prayer for him then go about his business believing God for the best. Why should T be any different? In addition, T was only doing what he had told him he needed to do. He found a woman.

In all of it, T had done nothing wrong. Yet why wasn't he pleased? Rev. R felt abandoned, rudderless, like he was watching a beacon of light being pulled from his life. Watching their intimacy made him feel rejected, as if Joraye were inserting herself into T's life in a way that was meant only for him. Time away from T just increased his hunger for the friendship. T was someone who excited him intellectually and wasn't cowed by the suffocating fear of a punitive God.

He often revealed to Rev R uncomfortable cracks in his own belief and forced him to better define ideas he had long taken for granted. T's reaction to Joraye was pulling back the veil on his own crushing loneliness.

Rev. R kept himself busy to stay away from his friends. He distracted himself with other ministries and hoped for some divine understanding and forgiveness for his unholy feelings. Prayer brought him some comfort but could not completely excise them. The routine he set for himself helped him regain some confidence. After a week or so, he felt ready to talk. He found T during a rest break, shading himself under an oak and approached him warily.

"Ain't seen you for a bit," T offered, wary himself.

Rev. R sat and after a silence answered, "You gon' tell me before you run off?"

"That what got you beside yo'self? I been thinkin' bout running since the day Jr. Wallace bring me back."

"But you tell me before you go? You do that?"

"You my friend, Rev., and I don't be running without coming to you. Don't you have no worry 'bout that." Rev.R's relief was immediate and overwhelming. T continued, "You know, you was right 'bout getting me a woman. Never had no feeling like I have for Joraye. Can't really tell you what it be. It like she jus' come over me when I first see her. You and Miss Edna pro'bly gon' go to yo' heaven jus' 'cause you been the only ones that treat her right."

"That girl has suffered, T. She in need of God's grace more than most."

"I know all 'bout her sufferin'. She think it make me scared, but I tell her we all suffer under a massa. I tell you this, Rev., won't nobody hurt her no more."

"You the only one that come along for her. God must have bring you here for Joraye."

"Guess He do somethin' right, sometime." They smiled. "What 'bout you, Rev.? Seem like God owe you a lot more than He owe me. You need to let Him know He owe you a wife. You tell me 'bout these women that bring you all that food. You tellin' me ain't none be right for you?"

"Come close a few times. Jus' ain't happen yet."

"Well maybe you jus' need to look a little harder."

***

Emerging from the ravages of mental illness, Joraye moved through her days as if airborne. She floated around Miss Edna's tiny cabin as if she had burst from a dark forest, into the healing warmth of the sun. T shattered the dark future she and everyone else assumed was hers, and everyday brought greater confidence as the fog continued to lift.

T was swept up as well. His second skin of steely detachment visibly thawed when he stepped through Miss Edna's door, and he relaxed into the sanctuary they created behind those four walls where he was free to open his heart and soul. If asked what brought them together, Miss Edna and Joraye would say it was God's grace, and T would say he went after what he wanted and got it. He was not about to give credit where it wasn't due, especially to a God he felt was always looking to take credit for the sunshine and the light.

Though Joraye was making progress, there was still work to do. She didn't come by her troubled state in an instant and neither would there be an instant resolution. Her illness had served as a shield, preventing her from looking out and others from looking in. Now, with a thirst for all she had missed, a new set of challenges presented themselves. The outside world was all of a sudden recognizable and overwhelming. The first time the new Joraye ventured out, the one that wasn't mumbling and shaking her head, she was still ostracized and because of her revived self-awareness, it cut deep. She would forever be the stuttering idiot to passerby, the one who made you cross yourself when you passed, no matter the miracle that was happening behind the doors of Miss Edna's cabin.

As for Miss Edna, she wouldn't stand for any of it. She was not one to use foul language indiscriminately. But when she got wind of Joraye's continued harassment, Joraye listened in shocked silence to her expletive-laced response to those, mostly women, that threatened her charge's fragile progress. Joraye said a special prayer to remain on Miss Edna's good side. After the tirade, Miss Edna explained to Joraye that people would respond to her based on how she responded to them. She needed to carry herself like the proud woman she had become.

To help Joraye along, she proposed a simple way for her to demonstrate her improved health. They would go back out together and, after Miss Edna's greeting, Joraye would ask one simple question. It could be about health/family/weather, anything to show she that was in command of her faculties. It wasn't long before folks took notice. Greetings were more common and there was genuine change in the air. There was still the occasional slap to her psyche, but it landed less painful as her confidence blossomed.

Miss Edna had been working up to what she considered the most essential rite of passage for Joraye, attending a worship service. Joraye had never returned after one disastrous meeting where her muttering and headshaking had her sitting alone with Miss Edna. Everyone had walked quickly past them, as if trying to outrun a contagion. After that dreaded experience, whispers began of demon possession and lunacy culminating in her almost complete exile within the community. Since this is where it began, this is where it would end, determined Miss Edna.

Joraye was not enthusiastic. She had been deeply scarred by her worship experience, and even though she was gaining confidence, she wasn't ready to subject herself to a potential repeat of that horror. It was T who finally convinced her to go when he said he would be there too. Not beside her, but at the service so she could see that he was there giving her his strength. With this, Joraye cautiously agreed, and she and Miss Edna went to work planning on how she could look her best for the day.

Miss Edna's desire to make Joraye shine was not altogether holy. It was inevitable that some of the women got wind of the relationship between Joraye and T. Miss Edna had heard several befuddled and resentful sisters marvel at how T, the model of a man, could choose someone so Devil-possessed. Those vipers couldn't be kind, even in the best of circumstances, and this ensured that Miss Edna would delight in making Joraye shine like a diamond.

On Sunday, they made their way to the service with Joraye holding tight to Miss Edna's arm. She held her head high, as Miss Edna had instructed, and heads turned. In fact, the chatter started even before they reached the gathering. Gone were the headshaking and muttering. The green eyes were clear. She was very much a different woman from the one they were used to seeing.

"Good morning, Miss Edna. Good Morning Joraye. Don't you look nice today." This greeting was said on more than several occasions. Joraye was all but beaming by the time they got to the benches.

Her mood abruptly changed when she didn't see T."He ain't here, Miss Edna," she whispered in a panic. "He promised he would be here."

"And he will. He ever not keep a promise to you?"

This calmed her and, true to his word, just as Rev. R was about to start, T made his entrance. He caused just as many heads to turn. Joraye felt like a queen. Also true to his word, he stayed in the back of the room. After the service he made a hasty exit. Miss Edna and Joraye stayed behind and held court to make

The Old Ones

clear that Joraye was now an unashamed and confident young woman who, additionally, had won the prized stallion. The experiment was an unequivocal success.

"That was a brave and wonderful thing you did, Miss Edna," Rev. R offered as he, Joraye and T sat at Miss Edna's table for Sunday dinner following Joraye's debut.

"Thank you Rev. Joraye deserve a blessing jus' like everybody else. Ain't nobody got a right to deny her that, but I ain't the one be brave. Joraye held her head up high."

"You right 'bout that," said Rev. R. "What you think of the service Joraye?"

"It be good, Rev. God talk through you in a strong way."

"I think you be the voice of God to those folks," answered Rev. R. "You be the miracle I tell them God can grant. And I must say, you turn some heads with that head wrap and dress that Miss Edna put together for you."

"Oh, that was nothin'," said Miss Edna, though she took the compliment. "In the Lord's house we got to be lookin' our best. Joraye only go to show her thanks to God. We ain't studin' 'bout turnin' no heads," she finished.

"Oh, come on now, Miss Edna. I see how you be smilin' and grinnin' when Miss Carlyle tell you how good Joraye look, and what a good Christian woman you are for takin' her in," Rev. R playfully challenged.

"Well, she do be nice to say those things," Miss Edna responded, glowing with false humility.

"Now, you be 'bout the best woman in the whole wide world, Miss Edna. Everybody know it and if they don't you sure to tell 'em," T needled.

"I ain't studin' you neither, you ungrateful thing," she answered with a broad smile.

168

The rest of the meal continued along the same lines. When the evening was over and Rev. R announced he was leaving, T offered to walk with him. Joraye mentioned before the evening started that she was feeling tired, so they wouldn't be talking tonight.

CHAPTER 26

As they walked, the opening salvo of spring was their backdrop, with the sun not fully set. Just a few weeks before, they would have been walking in darkness. Now dusk was just descending.

"You know, you had true second sight when it come to that girl. I was barely able to keep my mind on my sermon from watchin' how people be chattin' 'bout her change. God right to bring you two together."

"Whole lotta things bring me to Joraye. My ol' massa had to let me go, Jr. Wallace had to buy me and before all that, my back get bloody by the whip. God let a lot of bad happen to make this good happen."

"Like I tell you, no one know why He do what He do. We not supposed to. Even those that believe don't know."

They walked most of the remaining distance in silence. As they approached his cabin, Rev. R said, "Why don't you come on in? I got some sweet potatoes one of the sisters gimme. I give you some to take with you. Got to get rid of 'em before they turn."

Soon as they entered the cabin, T noticed two tree stumps. One with a bible on it. There were also two large burlap sacks filled with straw on opposite sides of the room with threadbare blankets covering both. T was awestruck.

"How you able to have all this?"

"Big Wallace tell Jr. to take care of me when he bring me here. So he gimme this." He indicated the room. "It ain't much but I thank the Lord for it."

"If you ain't happy with it, you welcome to my shack and I take this one."

Rev. R smiled. "I 'ppreciate yo' kindness, but this suits me just fine." He moved the Bible off one of the stumps so T could sit. He took a lid off a small bowl, took out a sweet potato, sliced a small section off for himself and gave the bulk to T. They ate in silence for a minute or more.

T broke through first, "It jus' like you say. It be quiet in here without yo' daddy."

"Don't mind it quiet. It give God room to come to me."

"You and Miss Edna be close. It like you family. You lucky."

"We all be family. Miss Edna take on Joraye and treat her like she her own. Then God make sure you here to take care of her. You family too."

"What if I never show up? What happen to Joraye then?"

"God's will is what happen. It not always what we like, but it be in His plan, and we trust in Him." Rev. R answered, more confidently than he felt.

"He let the Devil have his way with her, that be what happen. Joraye lay with me, not God, and I think she like it that way."

"You be one somebody that got life all straight in yo' mind, T. Most people be needin' some help to figure things out."

"I don't got it all figured out, but good and bad don't be hard to know."

"That what God do. He help people know that evil happen, but it don't win, if you walk with Him. The faithful know they got beautiful crowns comin' when they meet they God."

"Why He make us wait? Why don't He give us those crowns right now, when we need 'em, instead of waitin' 'till we ol' and dead? It not right to watch all this bad happen, and not do nothin' except ask us to wait 'till we dead to be happy. That not never gon' sit right with me."

"There is things you can't see 'cause you don't walk in grace, T, but I be prayin' for yo' soul. We talk 'bout that. It yo' eternal soul that heaven be waitin' to bring home."

"My soul gon' do whatever it do. I jus' tryin' to keep it with me long as I can."

"Well, you be lucky 'cause you be in my prayers. But He gon' need to hear from you real soon."

"Like I be needin' my freedom back. We wait and see when He make that happen and how much I suffer before then. But you keep up yo' prayin', Rev., 'cause it can't hurt, least I hope not," T said as he got up, stiffly.

"You hurtin?"

"My back scars be tight sometimes. Joraye put oil on 'em to make it better," he said as he headed toward the door. He was about to open it, then hesitated, "You do it for me? I sleep better when they don't be so tight."

"Uh, I ain't got no oil," he managed to get out. T reached into his pocket and pulled out a bottle.

"Miss Edna gimme this for my hands. Should be good for my back too." Without waiting for an answer, he took off his shirt, and lay face down on one of the sacks of hay. Rev. R walked over and sat on the floor beside him. He put some oil in his hand and tentatively started to rub the thick, ropy scars on T's back. T's eyes were closed as he murmured his relief. As Rev. R's hands traced the tragic history written on T's back, every line, every ridge, assaulted him with its painful origin. He fought to keep his emotions in check. His friend had suffered unspeakable pain.

"You got good hands. Not like the hands of a field nigga." This brought Rev. R back to the present.

"When you get whipped the first time?" T turned his head from facing the wall, to face Rev. R.

172

"That be a long time ago, before Mista' Kincaid. He never raise a whip to me. Be 'bout the only one that didn't. I think I be on the Jackson Plantation, the first time it happened. He crazy hateful, like Massa Wallace. I remember watchin' him teach the overseer how he wanted his niggas whipped and watchin' that nigga die. You know I speak my mind. Always have. Never hang my head for nobody. So I knew I be on that tree one day, and I say, no massa ever see me shed a tear. The day it happen, I finish with my work and as I walkin' to my shack somethin' hit me on my back. I don't know I be shot, or what. I turn 'round fast and see massas boy laughin' and callin' me names. He got a bucket of tomatoes, and before he could let another one go, I pick up a rock and showed that little peckerwood what a good aim look like and hit him square upside his crooked head. He run screamin' like he really be shot, and I got me a good laugh and the tree for my troubles. That whip feel like fire throw'd' on my back at first, and then the pain go even deeper. People die sometime, like the ol' man. But I took that whip and no tear fall from my eye, and not one fall since."

Rev. R had stopped breathing. His had resting on T's back. "No boy should ever be whipped like that," he said quietly.

"No man neither. You done?"

"What?"

"With my back. Yo' hand ain't movin'."

Rev. R started rubbing again. "No, you good to stay."

"You ain't been whipped, have you?"

Rev. R shook his head.

"I guess you got a deal with yo' God that most slave men don't. You lucky too. I see some of these crazy Devils take a whip to a preacher soon as anybody else, and Wallace be jus' the one to do it."

"I take the whip, God ask me."

"Don't know why you do that, 'cause He ask you to take the whip for Him one day, and He let a baby die the next. I think 'bout that, if you ever get that fool thought again," then added, "Yo' hands right for my back. It feel better than it do for a time. I can turn now." He rolled over on his back, and a startling presence entered the room, in the form of his erection. He placed his hands behind his head, quite comfortable and unselfconscious. Rev. R immediately responded with one of his own. He was clammy with tension, not sure what to say or do, except drag his eyes away.

"You scared?"

"What? What you talkin' 'bout?"

"I get like this 'cause yo' hands. You got a touch."

"Oh," Rev. R stammered.

"You scared?" T asked again.

"Why I be scared?"

"I mean, you scared to be my friend."

"I am yo' friend and yo' preacher," the Reverend sputtered.

"Ain't never ask you to be my preacher, jus' my friend. You the first one be good to me here. You easy to talk to, and that different for me, Rev. It feel warm, like home. When we talk, it like you see me and I see you." He paused, waiting for Rev. R to look up. He had been staring at the floor the whole time. When he looked up, T continued. "This been on yo' mind too. I know it and you be scared, but I ain't."

"I been tryin' to bring you to God. Like, like I do for everybody," he said. "How you can talk like this, when you got Joraye?"

"Joraye be my woman. Don't want no other woman. I always be with Joraye. She know what I feel for you. She love you too. You be so good to her. I tell

174

her I feel strong for you like I ain't never feel for a friend before and she understand 'cause she know you a good man. I show her every day how I feel 'bout her, too. I say maybe we be a family one day."

"But this? She know this?"

"I ain't never lie to you or Joraye. She know she never lose me and she say this won't scare her away. Jus' like I ain't scared by what the Devil brought her, and this be only from good. She smart and I prove my love to her. I want to be with you, if you want, and it don't scare me to say, Rev. Yo' God don't want me to share pleasure with you, but happy enough to watch me get whipped and to keep me in chains. He don't care 'bout me, which be fine, since I ain't got no use for Him either. I make myself T, so I always know I can make my own life too and I say I want Joraye, and I say I want you in my life. You ain't feel pain like I have, Rev. I be in my head and quiet, 'cause I don't know where the pain be comin' from next. That be my whole life, but there be no pain when I with you and Joraye, jus' good. That be what I want to share."

He reached out to touch Rev. R, who jumped back as if attacked by a snake. T sat up and dressed to leave. "I sorry, Rev. You a good man and be my friend. We never talk 'bout this again. I promise."

"Wait," Rev. R halted him. "I jus' be outta' sorts by what you say. You always speak yo' mind, and I still be gettin' use to it. This be strange to me, but I leave it in God's hands. We don't need to be speakin' 'bout this ever again, like you say, but you stay. It be late and you already comfortable in bed."

"That'd be good," he agreed and lay back down. "You put me in a real easy spirit, like always." He yawned expansively. "I glad we good Rev. That real special to me. We still talk like we do?" he asked, almost beseechingly.

"Yeah, T. You always be my friend."

"But never 'bout this thing, I promise. See you in the morning."

"Night, T," Rev. R said and proceeded to clean up. When he was done he blew out the candles then lay wide awake on his side of the room.

His pants are too short and the boots too tight. His teenage body will not stop its climb toward the heavens. T carries a hoe to dig up some beets, which were buried by his friends when the overseer wasn't looking. He is looking forward to having beets again. It has been a long time since he had beets, and beets are one of his favorites when they boiled up and soft. His feet make a sucking sound as they slog through the soil, still muddy after recent rains. He is moving by moonlight and is fortunate to have a sky without a cloud, only the brilliant moon. Earlier in the week, he and his friends hatched their plan. They decided that of the three conspirators, T would be the one to collect the beets after the other two buried them in the designated spot. The overseer studied them like a bloodhound to make sure that none of 'em don't walk off the field with food.

"Well, if ain't a little lost darkie!" The unmistakable voice of the overseer cut the nighttime silence. With the speed of a cougar, T explodes away, except he's not moving. Every step he takes drives him deeper into the mud. The only way the overseer could have known where he would be was if his friends told on him. He had let down his guard and trusted and now he is running for his life, only he isn't. His feet seem to weigh a ton as he tries to lift them out of the mud. The more he struggles the deeper he sinks.

"What's wrong, boy? I thought you was gon' try to run away, before I blow your head off. But look like the mud tryin' to claim back one of its own."

"Please help me, massa!" T pleads, as the mud climbs past his waist, and he continues to sink. His heart is pounding in his ears, and then he becomes the boy he is and starts to cry.

"Help me, massa! Please don't let me die, massa. Please...please!"

"Looks like it be a little too late for that, you stupid nigger. But why you scared? You gon' be with your other mud people. That be after the mud fill up your nose, then your mouth, then your eyes."

"No!" but his scream is cut off as his head goes under and mud rushes into his mouth. His hands try to fly up but can't because his arms are glued to his sides, as the mud squeezes like a vice. He tries shaking his head but the mud has hands that hold his head in a vise. He is dying, suffocating, mud pouring into every orifice. He chokes and gasps in his last breath of thick, airless mud .

"No!" T woke with a start, wild-eyed and breathless, to find Rev. R kneeling next to him, hands on his shoulders.

"Hey, you was dreamin'," Rev R said, trying to comfort him.

T grabbed Rev. R's arm. "The mud. I couldn't breathe," he said through gulps of air. "It be so real!"

"I know, I know." whispered Rev. R. "You alright now. You in my house, and ain't no mud come in here." T looked around, still not sure, still panting. "What kinda dream you have?"

"I was young, going to dig up some beets and an overseer catch me. I try to run, but I start sinkin' in mud."

"Never did like beets. Now I know why," Rev. R said, attempting to lighten the mood. "It jus' a bad dream, T. You go on back to sleep now and I see you in the morning."

He attempted to get up but T grabbed his hand. "Tommie say she have a bad dream 'bout me too. She so scared by it, she don't even tell me, and I don't ask 'cause it upset her too much to talk 'bout it."

"She Mista Kincaid little girl, that right?"

"Uh, huh. I ain't think 'bout that overseer for a long time. He look jus' like I remember him. I hope he dead now, and I hope it was bad." He is quieting down. "I know you say don't talk like that, but a bad death is what he deserve."

"I say nothin' 'bout that. God also a just God."

"Guess our talkin' make it all come back. I say things with you, I don't tell people. You truly got the gift."

"Givin' folks bad dreams ain't no gift. You good to sleep now?"

"Think so. I ain't have a dream like that for a long time, glad you be here Rev."

Rev. R slipped his hand out of T's and stood but didn't move toward his bed. His breathing was loud and rapid in the silence. T gently pats the bed, and Rev. R slowly sat. Still not speaking, he places his hand on T's chest. T took it and gently moved it down and pressed firmly, where it remained

"You 'wake?" Rev. R turned his back to T. "You don't have to say nothin'. I got to go and I know you gon' talk to yo' God 'bout what we do, but I want you to think 'bout this. Every day I be in the fields or the stables burnin' up in the summer and freezin' come winter. The overseer lookin' to beat me for lookin' at him the wrong way. Ain't never enough to eat and at the end of the day I go to a shack ain't fit for a dog. Last night, with you, I get peace from all that and I hope you able to get peace too. I never be sorry for it. I see you, Joraye and me like a family. That be what I want. You and me, Rev.? Somethin' powerful be here. We got to grab it 'cause ain't nobody gon' hand us what life we want, and just maybe God say you work hard for Him, so now He gon' show you His love. If you don't feel what I say, we ain't never' do this again and I hope we still be friends Rev. I do whatever you want." He gently touched Rev. R's back and left.

Rev. R did not turn from the wall as T walked out. He wanted to crawl inside it, have the wall cover him from his life. He was empty. Numbed by this shift in his universe, unable to process a single thought. This would not be the life prayed for by his father nor the one sanctified by his God. But what left him hollowed out was that he knew this would be his life. There would be no wife for appearances.

This was not a drunken night to be lost in guilty stares then eventually forgotten. Like all those who had tread a similar path, last night was not a discovery, but an awakening of desire that survival dictated remain dormant, but not excised. Some, the lucky ones, maybe, had acceptable desires as well and navigated lives of rewarded deceit. He had one desire. With every fiber of his being he wanted T.

And what T proposed was unbelievable, ungodly and a slap in the face to Joraye. It was a the same time fantastically intoxicating. The proposal shattered any reality he thought he knew. But T made it somehow sound like a forgone conclusion, one that he would make happen through sheer force of will and shamelessness. If what he said was true, that Joraye knew his feelings, then just maybe there could be the miracle that T imagined. Ultimately, it was one truth that gave him to T: *How could a loving God prescribe them both to the hell that was their every breath, then condemn a rare chance at true salvation?* Then he thought, *but did He condemn?* His indecision took a back seat to everything that was T, and he crossed over.

He took T's unshakable confidence in the beauty of their union and wrapped it around himself, a shield from a shame that threatened to go so deep as to destroy him. He pulled strength from T's strength and gave himself over to joy. There would still be times of hand wringing and doubt. God was his blood and there would never be a life without Him. But now his prayers would be more challenging and less supplicating.

Yes, the flesh won out, as it usually does in these passion plays. The need was too great, and not just for the sex, but for the intimacy, the closeness, those quiet, deeply fulfilling moments of shared fears longings and thrills that bond lovers. With Jesus sitting on one shoulder, and Lucifer on the other, Rev. R threw his lot in with T, even as he continued praying for guidance, for forgiveness, for some sign that he was not abandoned by the only good force that had ever brought order to his universe.

Once again T simply took what he wanted from life, but not from anyone that was unwilling to give. He didn't steal, cheat or lie his life into the one he wanted, nor did he ask for permission or validation. He simply showed himself to the people he chose, and they responded or not. Joraye and Rev. R made their own choices, T's powers of persuasion notwithstanding. Fortunately for T, he was living a dream he very specifically engineered and without an ounce of guilt.

He had been on a long path toward the same crippling future that awaited most of his peers, until Rev. R and Joraye grabbed his large hands and held on tight, and he held them right back. He saw his night with Rev. R as a culmination of a bond that was forged from the moment the young man climbed up that wagon and gave him water. Now he felt intertwined, bonded together with an ache for him, even as he continued the healing and joy that was his relationship with Joraye.

He kept nothing from her. He told her that he considered the three of them family. He said that Rev. R was the best man he ever met, and that he loved him like he loved her, as family. Rev. R had been such a comforting presence in her darkest hours and T remained so passionate, if not more so, for her, that she was thrilled that T had grown to love him as she did. She looked on their trio as God continuing to work miracles in her life. For her, there was no other explanation.

Miss Edna suspected something but said nothing, There seemed to be a new, almost tentative energy in the air, as if there were a shared secret bursting at the seams to reveal itself. The sheen of guilt was most evident on Rev. R's face, and her heart sank when she recognized it for what she thought it was. In her years, she had known men and women to fall under this satanic spell.

The signs were all the same in him. If her suspicions were correct, she knew the fault lay with T. He paid no mind to anything or anyone when it came to getting what he wanted. She just never thought that would include Rev. R. She had rarely seen such threatening virility as emanated from T. And she also knew that anyone who didn't walk with God was ripe for any sinful and ungodly act that Satan could sweetly offer.

But this sin was different. If he drank too much or cursed too much or even went with other women, Miss Edna could point to several other men who made up that fraternity and commiserate with Joraye about their weaknesses. Murderers, rapists and thieves would comfort one another by claiming, "at least I'm not like that,". This sin seemed to occupy a space several places below all others.

What gave her pause in this tragic assessment was his treatment of Joraye. Most men that she had known who had this affliction broke away from the beds containing their wives and concubines, if they had them. She had given comfort to several women who wanted her to help them get these men back. But T seemed to be even more loving and attentive toward Joraye. So maybe she was wrong. Maybe T was different in this respect as well, and there was hope. She prayed. She had grown to love all three of them and could not, would not imagine Rev. R and T condemned to that tortuous, hell-bound existence.

CHAPTER 27

Overseers were often seasonal help, hired around the time of harvest to maximize crop yields. This could be the overseer's most important result, determining if they were asked to stay on as the permanent deputy of misery. Jr. Wallace had landed on a particularly effective one a few years back, and Samson was given a large amount of latitude. He was exceptionally skilled at the delicate art of pushing the enslaved to their limits, but not exhausting them to the point of uselessness. Few of the approximately seventy slaves that were quartered on the Jr. Wallace Plantation were left unmarked by his vigilance.

He was also able to convince Jr. Wallace that the stocks offered an effective addition to their menu of savageries. He appreciated that they allowed a sustained visual of the suffering of their guests and Jr. Wallace enthusiastically embraced their use. Criminals locked in the stocks would often soil themselves, as there was no other alternative and when this happened the overseer would throw a bucket of water on them to calm the stench. Because of this, in the summer, they prayed for full bowels if they were so condemned. This was not a wintertime device. Property was too expensive to continually replace due to icy deaths.

Contact was strictly forbidden and after the first few Samaritans had been whipped for their efforts, most walked past these prisoners with heads down, pretending to ignore the incoherent mumbling or the occasional lifeless body waiting to be thrown unceremoniously, into a hole. Like everyone else, Rev. R knew to stay away. He'd been caught offering water and wiping the brow of one of these unfortunates and his collar saved him from the whip, with a warning that the next time there would be no reprieve. His calling would not permit him, though, to ignore these tragic souls and he endeavored to be wiser and more watchful of the lurking Samson, timing his walks past the stocks when he knew Samson was otherwise occupied.

An older cook with arthritic hands had dropped a roast twice in a week and an incensed Lady Wallace sent her to the stocks for a few hours of reflection. Rev. R had eyed her when he was out earlier that day but Samson was within view so he could do nothing. If he followed his usual schedule, Rev. R knew Samson would be far away from the stocks midday as he patrolled the fields. He would make his move then. He packed some bread and a cup for water and set out. When he got to her, her head was dropping, almost to the point of falling off.

He filled the cup from a nearby well. "I bring you some water," he said gently as he tilted the cup toward her lips, most of it spilling, as she had barely enough strength to sip.

"You jus' don't listen, do you?" Rev. R whirled around to see Samson coming from around the back of a shack, tightening his belt. "Get the hell away from that bitch and come on over here." Rev. R was too stunned to move. "I said get over here, nigger." He came out of his daze and walked slowly over. The overseer walked to a barrel, took out some shackles and put them on Rev. R's wrists. "I don't think I ever whipped a nigger preacher before, but God did tell us we got to keep all you in line, preacher or no. Ain't that right?" Rev. R was hyperventilating.

A small crowd started to gather. "Y'all 'bout to see what happens when you don't do what the master tell you. Now, this here nigger think he help that there nigger in the stocks, even though I told him he be punished if he do. Well, we'll see if he ever do it again after I'm done with him. Come on see the show y'all'!"

The overseer dragged Rev. R to the whipping tree, as the crowd followed. There was always a crowd. Jr. Wallace insisted his slaves witness these events. The stunned crowd was silent, as a contagion of fear made its way through. Most had never seen a preacher get whipped. Several stared at one another as if waiting for God to intervene. But there was no celestial reprieve, and Rev. R started his own prayers as others joined in. "Y'all go on and say your prayers. See if the hand of God stop this whip from tearing up his back. Don't think so." Rev. R was not reacting with bravery, as he described to T that he would. He was not going to that tree with reverent acceptance of God's will. He was in stark, blinding terror.

"No!" All heads turned to see T tearing through the crowd. Panting, he came upon the overseer, who struck a defensive pose with the whip. "Take me," he said between breaths, hands on his knees. "Let him go and take me."

"T! No!" shouted a stunned Rev. R.

"Well, what be goin' on here?" said an intrigued Samson. "This ain't somethin' I see every day. You tellin' me you want to trade places with this nigger and take the whip instead?"

"Don't be right to be whippin' a man a God," T said. Many in the crowd stared open mouthed.

"You wrong there. Like I told this one, God say we got to keep you animals under control. I'm performing His work here," he laughed, then paused for a moment and considered T. "Just so I know what you're sayin', 'cause I'm 'bout ready to oblige you: You want me to let this boy preacher go and you take the whip for him?" T looked at Rev. R then back at Samson and slowly moved his head up and down.

"Well, it be your lucky day, boy preacher, get over here." When Rev. R was standing in front of him, Samson grabbed the shackles and yanked them off. To T he said, "Been waitin' to do this since you come. Hope you don't think 'cause you doin' some kinda good deed that I care. You will know that you ain't never been whipped until you whipped by Samson. Now walk your crazy ass over to that tree." He turned back to Rev. R, "You better thank God tonight, 'because he saved you from meetin' up with him."

The whip tore through T's flesh like a dull knife through tough meat. The snap of the cowhide flung blood and bits of tissue into the air. The spectators stood at a distance, letting the blood and skin turn the black earth blacker.

Rev. R watched from a distance, where no one could see him vomit. He would surely give T and himself away if he were near the group. They would wonder at his particular anguish. He typically gave silent prayers while stoically witnessing these beatings. That control would have been impossible today, and T would not want the spectacle. This physical sacrifice to be his alone. So alone, he watched the shattering oblation, which surely saved his life for he would not have survived the savagery he was witnessing. Samson was whipping his lover with such grunting, maniacal glee as to appear unhinged.

Something brushed against Rev. R. He jumped back, almost knocking Joraye over in the process. He didn't hear her approach, focused as he was on the unfolding horror. She rushed into his arms, and he held her through her wracking sobs.

"12. . . 13. . . 14. . ." rest. "15. . . 16. . . 17. . ." rest. There was no crying out, no pleading for mercy. T's face was a twisted mask of silent rage. "20. . . 21. . . 22. . ." rest. Thirty-nine lashes were the number that was standard on most plantations. Since that was the number of lashes Jesus was given before his crucifixion, slave holders were exhorted from pulpits throughout the south that good Christians give their slaves no less. Of course, more was also acceptable. Samson continued and T's entire backside became an unrecognizable, oozing stew of tissue and blood.

Jr. Wallace had been watching the proceedings with his wife and their visiting ten-year-old nephew, William, who sat queasily in a corner of the porch.

"Hold it, Samson," Jr. Wallace called out. He turned to his nephew, "Get on down there boy and show us what you got." William stared petrified at Wallace and didn't move.

Lady Wallace had been fanning herself and watching the proceedings with the detached curiosity of a day at the races. "Now don't dally, William," she chimed in. "This is not easy for any Christian, but you need to understand, dear, that they're not like us. These niggers are like the other animals on the plantation that do our bidding, and God demands we keep them in line like we do our goats and pigs. It's His will. Don't we feed them like we feed our goats and pigs and give them a place to live?"

He was too shocked to respond and stared at her as if in a daze.

"Well, don't we?" she coaxed. He nodded slowly. "That's right. They would be wild animals running loose, if not for our decency, but when they do wrong, we have to punish them. Sometimes the right thing to do is not the easy thing, isn't that right, my dear?" William numbly moved his head up and down.

"Then get on down there," Jr. Wallace cut in, startling William into movement. He slowly put one foot in front of the other until he was standing next to

Samson, who placed the whip in William's small hand. He then covered it with his own, massive fist.

"Now, I'm gonna help you out, young Master William, until you get the feel for the whip." He drew William's thin arm back and landed a light blow. The only comfort this new horror brought was that these lighter blows might also count toward the thirty-nine. Before Samson could bring William's arm back for another blow, the boy broke free and fled into the woods.

"Well, there goes our little tree fairy," remarked Jr. Wallace.

"Now, be kind," his wife responded. "This was only his first time. My sister won't let him whip her niggers." The contempt in her voice betraying any sympathy for the adolescent.

"He's soft. He'll never have what it takes to keep these savages in line. When I was his age, I pleaded to whip the niggers. Maybe one day soon you'll give me a son before you go dry."

"Well now, that's not only up to me, is it? Lady Wallace snapped. "Try coming to bed sober one night a month and we can pray for a miracle." She took two steps forward and called out "William!" Hearing no response, she went looking for him.

"Get the salt this time. I want to see if we can get a rise out of this mute monkey!" Jr. Wallace yelled out. Samson grabbed a handful of salt from a bucket not far from the tree and pressed it against T's back. A sharp intake of breath was the only sound T made to acknowledge the searing burn.

"You one strong nigger," admitted Jr. Wallace. "The next time you get whipped, I might just tie those limbs to my horses and give him a swift crack. Samson! Add ten extra then come see me."

188

When it was over, the overseer dropped the whip in total exhaustion and headed to the big house. Moving tentatively, the crowd tentatively swelled towards T. Rev. R told Joraye to wait and rushed through the crowd to be the first to reach him.

"Hold on. We got you." He worked silently, avoiding eye contact, as if shamed by his existential helplessness in the face of the horror. Others joined in, just as silent, and reverently removed him from the tree.

"Bring him," was all Miss Edna said, and she disappeared to prepare a bed.

"Can you walk, T? Do you want to wait?" asked Rev. R. He and the others negotiated the best way to move him.

"Walk," he whispered. Rev. R took one arm and placed it around his neck, and someone took the other and did the same. They gingerly grabbed hold of the rope that held up his trousers to give them added leverage. Experience with this ritual taught them that this was the least painful way to move someone who'd been whipped. They proceeded to half walk; half drag him to Miss Edna's cabin.

Rev. R was keenly aware of the heat and sweat on his neck and hoped T took some comfort from this closeness. "Almost there. You want to rest now?"

T shook his head. They continued.

Miss Edna was standing in her doorway. "Lay him on his stomach," she instructed, and they carefully placed him on one of the straw beds against the wall.

Joraye crept in behind them and went to a stool in the corner of the room, where she took to moaning and rocking. "Oh, Miss Edna," she cried hysterically, "He look like he die. He can't, he can't! You got to make him right!"

Miss Edna walked over and took Joraye's hands, "Look at me, baby." Joraye focused on her.

"Now, I see this before and T gon' be all right, I promise. But right now he need you to be strong for him. You do that, baby?" she asked gently. Joraye nodded. Miss Edna turned to Rev. R and his helper, Shadrach. "Now, one of you needs to go. Massa won't want two out of the field. I can say I needed one of you to hold him down while I work."

"You go on," Rev. R told Shadrach. Miss Edna proceeded to take thick mustard paste from a shelf, and a piece of leather, then dragged a stool next to the bed. T was passed out. She gently woke him and made him drink half a cup of a tonic she had also prepared. He saw the piece of leather and opened his mouth. As she cleaned the wounds and applied the paste, beads of sweat broke out on T's forehead, and he grunted through clenched teeth, testifying to the never-ending horror of this plantation ritual.

Rev. R sat on the floor in front of him, and could only offer helpless encouragement, "You be ok T. Not too much longer."

Miss Edna occasionally glanced over at him with an unreadable face and continued working. When she was done, she removed the leather from T's mouth. "Now you lie still and let my medicine work. You be here least 'til tomorrow." To Rev. R she said, "He gon' go back to sleep now. Nothin' more for you to do here. But you stay, you want to."

"Need water, Rev...," T said weakly.

"I be right back," and he was up in a flash.

"He a good Christian boy and very devoted to you. Good to have a friend like that," Miss Edna said.

"Where Joraye?" T whispered.

"I right here," she answered meekly.

"Don't you worry, Joraye? Miss Edna take real good care o' me. Ain't that right, Miss Edna?"

"Oh, yes. I have you healed up in no time. That why I tell Joraye not to be worryin'."

"That good, Miss Edna," he said.

Rev. R entered with water. Miss Edna said, "Let me have that." He handed the cup to her. She took a potion off the shelf and added a few drops to the water. "This help you sleep," she said held the cup to his lips. He drank, thirstily. "Not too much," she said.

"I can stay," offered Rev. R.

"No need. Joraye and me be fine. You had a day too. Go on home and get you some rest, son."

"I come check on him later." He went over and embraced Joraye. "He be alright, Joraye. Miss Edna and God gon' work some magic, you watch."

T woke before light the next day. Samson was waiting for him in front of Miss Edna's cabin. She had instructed him to leave his shirt off so the sun could dry out his wounds, and scabs could form. She was also able to convince Jr. Wallace that T needed to stay with her for the next week so his scars wouldn't get infected.

During those first few nights Joraye tucked in with Miss Edna. She did not want to be in his bed, fearing that the slightest movement might 'cause him pain. His wounds scared her. They were in various stages of healing and the scabs and welts brought back fresh memories of her dark past. She would stare at them then involuntarily shake her head to dislodge horrific flashbacks that threatened to undo her hard-fought victory over darkness.

Miss Edna shifted the narrative of T's wounds. She explained that they were hurting the man she loved, the man who saved her, and now, when it was hardest for her, she needed to put aside her fear and do the same for him. Miss Edna delivered this admonition with kindness but made it clear that T deserved the best of her right now. On the third night, as Miss Edna was cleaning his back and gently patting it dry, Joraye quietly knelt beside her. Miss Edna handed her the cloth.

T put no pressure on her. He knew that those demons and shadows that swirled and skittered about her might seize this opportunity to claim her back. He expressed more concern for her well-being than his own. She took to heart what Miss Edna said, and the intimacy of caring for him brought her close to him in a way she had not imagined. Putting her hands on his wounds and learning what was painful and what wasn't made her feel intimate and involved with him for the first time since the beating. Soon they were able to lay together and discover fresh and unique ways to bring each other comfort.

Rev. R was a changed man. The unquestioning devotion to Christ that marked his life previously was now the source of confusion, anger and betrayal. His father was no longer able to be that unshakable voice of blind faith whenever the real world splattered blood and cruelty onto his angel's wings and pearly gates.

Like Joraye, he had seen beatings before, but witnessing T being savaged was as if someone had reached into his gut and grabbed onto whatever could be held and ripped it out. T was a flesh and blood example of someone willing to die for him.

He had not abandoned his faith, not yet, but was asking questions of his God and waiting for answers that did not come, would not come. He could never be like T, but neither would he relinquish to God a faith that was blind to the point of being nonsensical. There simply was no excusing what He had allowed to happen to his friend and lover while the Devil remained alive and well in so many others.

About a week after the beating, Rev. R opened his door to find T, silent and brooding, on his doorstep.

Anthony Henderson

They didn't speak, Rev. R simply moved aside and let him in. T didn't sit, just stood in the center of the room with his head down, overwhelmed by what he wanted to say but didn't quite know how.

Rev. R moved toward him, and T wrapped his huge arms around him. "I never, never, see you hurt," he whispered.

"I know, T, I know." Rev. R's rested his hands on T's arms, his back still too raw to touch.

"You know, I die first Rev." He could not get the rest out. Rev. R silently led him to bed. There was a poignancy and depth to their coming together that could only come in the aftermath of the savagery visited on them both.

"You never do that again, T, never. Do you hear me?" Rev. R said, in the languid space that followed. "It was a fool thing."

"Long as I be livin' a whip won't touch yo' back. Don't care what yo' God say."

"It hard for me to pray now, after what I see."

"What'd you think gon' happen, Rev.? A big hand come out the sky and grab that whip? I ain't never seen that miracle. I think He watch you get beat to death and do nothin'. That's what I think yo' God do."

"Wallace be the Devil if ever I see it."

"Devil or no, yo' God supposed to be able to protect folks. Especially folks like you. I ain't never see that happen yet."

"He send me you."

"What? To get beat almost to death? And I'm supposed to say "Thank you, Jesus?" How that make any sense? No. I take that whip 'cause I feel for you. Yo' God jus' as soon see me die."

Rev. R separated from T and hugged his knees, unable to meet T's eyes. "Maybe it be God tellin' us we wrong," he confessed.

193

"Wrong for what?" What we wrong for? You kill somebody? You cheat a man out his money? How many white men get whipped for the wrong they do? You go on believe in yo' God Rev. I not take that away from you, but don't let Him take away this. I remember you say God want His children happy. Maybe that what He be sayin' to you and me."

Rev. R shook his head. He was totally unsettled. "How you do this T? Nobody talk like you do 'bout God. I don't know it be right, all you say."

"Nothin' I do 'bout that. But we good people, that be livin' in hell. So maybe yo' God give us each other. Why can't that be true? 'Specially seein' how hard you work for Him."

"I got to tend the fire," Rev. R said.

As he worked on the fire, T got up and quietly took a broom that was leaning against the opposite wall and placed it on the floor.

When Rev. R turned from the fire, T was standing in front of the broom. "I want you like this Rev. This how I want us to be."

Rev. R stared at T, his face a portrait of confusion and fear. "This be too much, T. I don't know God forgive us, we do this."

"You already with me Rev. This jus' be one more way. I jump the broom with Joraye 'cause I always be with her. I always be with you too, Rev. Always. He stepped over the broom. Rev. R did not. After a minute T asked, "Who be yo' life?" Rev. R stepped over.

194

As our old ones sugared their coffees, staring down into the swirling liquid, lives were replayed. Sad smiles, mostly, marking their responses. Then back to their rockers, their chairs, their beds, where they waited. Some might have placed themselves by windows, counting stars and glimpsing angels, marveling at how soon they would be able to touch them both. But for now they tucked in, with their kaleidoscopes of lives lived, and this one tale....

PART 3

CHAPTER 28

"*W*here is that goddamn broach?!*"* he cursed, as his stubby fingers felt around the watch pocket of his vest for the third time. He had just completed as many trips through every pocket of his formally elegant suit, now moth eaten in corners he hoped no one noticed. Jr. Wallace was confident he put the damn thing in his coat but now was not so sure, preoccupied as he was for it to have the desired effect. Which was to take The Lady's mind off their current disaster.

This was not very likely: she went through the ledgers, bills of sale and every other financial document with the detail of a dyspeptic banker. She realized early on that if they were to survive, she would be the one managing their unpredictable finances.

If there was a way to be swindled, lied to or cheated, Jr. Wallace was your man and could give as good as he got. He never met a bad deal or unlucky card game he didn't lovingly embrace, which is how he found himself in this freshly minted disaster. He was certain, at least fairly certain, that he had settled all his outstanding gambling debts and had been able to outrun the rest.

The bad news came in the form of a gun toting "sucker" that Jr. Wallace had cheated and written off. Unfortunately, this same sucker managed to find him and go unnoticed as he followed him to his bank. As Jr. Wallace exited the bank he was greeted by the barrel of a Colt pocket revolver and relieved of Richards' next loan payment. This constituted much of what was left of their savings. When The Lady inquired about the money, and he sheepishly related the story, any ceasefire between them vanished. The payment was due in two months, and they didn't have it.

In his infinite wisdom, he decided that an exaggerated show of their respectable social status would remind Richards that he was dealing with a Wallace, and that it was imperative they remain in the southern land and slave-owning hierarchy. To that end he had conjured up a scenario that he hoped would remind Richards of the weight and influence of the Wallace name.

Keeping up appearances was The Lady's life purpose, so he thought she would warm to the idea of a grand evening of entertainment, demonstrating a social status that existed only in his imagination. So he bought a fancy broach as a peace offering, hoping to establish a semblance of détente as he continued to push for his magical evening. She, the other hand, thought he and his proposal had reached a new level of idiocy. That was the first conversation. It was to be continued tonight.

He continued his search, looking on chairs, in closets, under the bed, but still no broach. As he swept the room, his eyes landed on a daguerreotype of his fleshly face and head with three or four wisps of hair staring back at him in mocking disapproval. Whatever possessed him to part with fifty cents for this insult, he would never know, except that it seemed like a good idea to a drunken idiot, easily taken in by a desperate photographer. The only redeeming feature was that it was not much bigger than a calling card, so you had to have decent eyes to make out detail. He knew the details well enough, and they did not sit well with him, then or now.

Even more insulting, was the Lady's reaction. To say she was horrified was only a slight exaggeration. She was unequivocal, "This monstrous thing will not be seen in my house!" and that's why it sat on his bedside table, a constant reminder of one more bad decision. Well, no more! he thought and flung it out the window, where it lodged in a tree just off the property and was found on the ground a few nights later by Miss Edna on one of her foraging expeditions. She, too, was initially horrified but decided to keep it. It was so unusual and lifelike; she could imagine some future use.

"Are you ever coming down!" came screeching up from below. The Lady was hungry and irritable.

"In a minute. You go ahead and start without me," he yelled back, wiping sweat off his brow at the thought of impending disaster. In his frustration, he grabbed his bed pillows and threw them across the room and there, lying innocently on the bed covers, was the mischievous little broach. He grabbed it, but it slipped through his sweaty fingers and onto the floor. When he moved to retrieve it, he instead kicked it under the bed. "Sweet Jesus," he muttered and grunted onto his hands and knees.

His bad luck continued, as the broach was far under the bed, and completely out of reach. His only recourse was to lay flat on his corpulent gut and scoot as far as possible under the bed. He snorted and wheezed as far as he dared while willing his short arms to stretch just one more millimeter. "Blessed Lord," he muttered when his hand finally closed around the cursed thing, and he was miraculously able to emerge from under the bed like some freshly birthed baby elephant. Dust and sweat stained his shirt and waistcoat.

He put the broach in a pocket and tried in vain to clean himself up. Composing himself, he headed downstairs with the enthusiasm of a man walking to the gallows and failed to notice that he had put the broach in the same threadbare pocket that caused this farce. Once again it slipped through that same hole and now gleamed triumphantly up at him from the floor.

He entered the dining room and attempted to plant a kiss on the top of The Lady's head, but she flinched away. He chose to ignore the spurn; there were bigger fish to fry. "Sorry to keep you waitin'."

"My God! What was going on up there? Do you need a doctor? Which we would have to pay for with loaves and fishes, by the way." She made no stab at pleasantries.

"Don't you worry 'bout me. Here I am. All in one piece." He smoothed down his hairs and his hand came back dirty. He sat a safe distance away. "How's the soup?"

"How's the soup? Is that what you'd like to talk about? Really? The soup?!"

"Just initiatin' some pleasant conversation, that's all."

"Well, let's pleasantly converse about this little beggars' banquet you seem so driven to force on me. To think this is where we've arrived, and you being a Wallace. I can promise you this, if Richards does not agree to change his terms, I'm going to pick up what's left of my sad life and go to my father's house. You can rot alone in this trash heap for all I care." She finished in a full flush.

"Aren't you spirited this evening?"

"Go to hell!"

"Darlin', I know you don't think this will work, but I want you to know, I got it all figured out. Richards is an honest man, and he'll be drinking our finest whiskey, smoking our finest cigars, and seeing how hard we've been working to meet our debt. And I know you'll be just as charming and lovely as you always are.

He's not an unreasonable man; and if we sell a few things, we can get close to what he needs."

"He doesn't care about close, you idiot! Close! That orange-haired baboon has put families out their homes for pittances! How do you think he got so rich? And just what do you propose we sell? Another nigger? We don't have enough niggers as it is. Next, you'll be asking me to get on my hands and knees to help with the harvest. He's going to look at the money we're throwing at this ridiculous party and wonder why it's not being put toward what we owe. I would! I have a very bad feeling about this, Wallace. It's a desperate, stupid move and turns us into beggars. He's probably gossiped about our circumstances to those other buffoons that are coming. They won't be fooled, not for one minute."

"We men don't talk like that, and this ain't just about the payment coming up. I intend on askin' him to change the whole thing so we don't go through this again. He's got to see we are important. Besides it's only nine or ten people coming over."

"And he owns the lot! Anytime Richards shows his face, at least half of the people staring back are in his debt and they act like it. I've never seen so much shamelessness from otherwise respectable people."

"But you could never do that. That's why I got you a little something that will make you the most respectable Lady in the room." He reached into his pocket and felt the empty space where the broach was supposed to be. "That's mighty strange. I could have sworn I put it in this pocket," he said as he gave himself a nervous pat down.

"Please, dear God, don't tell me that you wasted more money on some stupid trinket, when we are absolutely drowning."

"Oh, but you don't understand, my sweet. This is real special." He continued to search in vain. "Where is the goddamn thing?" he finally hissed in frustration.

"Are you saying that not only did you waste what sounds like a precious amount of money on something needless, but that now you've lost it? My God, there is just no end!"

"It's here. It has to be. I put it right in this..," he broke off, as his finger found the hole. "Oh, my lord, not again." He stood in exasperation. "I'll be right back."

"Don't bother, really. Don't." She signaled a slave to help her with her chair. She stood. She was quiet, resolved. "I'm done for the evening. But make no mistake; I meant what I said about leaving."

"We won't come to that. This'll work like a charm. You'll see," he delivered to her back.

The next morning, he woke up feeling like an abused street hound. After The Lady stormed off the prior evening, he proceeded to finish her glass of wine, as well as several of his own. The drapes weren't closed last night, and his arm could barely block out the sun as it jabbing his eyes. His mouth felt full of sawdust and his head throbbed.

Once he crawled out of bed, he plodded around his bedroom preparing for his monthly excursion to Owenton for supplies. He was hoping to secure much of it on credit, the more honest description of which was by begging. He had the magical thinking of a gambler. Each day was going to be "the day," the one where his fortunes turned just because he believed they would.

And today his fortunes were better than last night. He found the broach and, once he returned it, he would have enough money to show those fools at the

202

saloon who was boss. He might even use some of the proceeds as a good-faith advance to Richards.

He had no intention of telling The Lady. She didn't believe in him and never would, he thought. Well, she would not see a dime from the sale. After last night, to hell with her. Every cent was going into his pocket, all drinks on him. If anyone had doubts about his finances, this would settle it. He deserved at least one round of drinks with people who respected him.

The wagon made its lazy way to town. Did she really mean to leave him? *Well, good riddance*, he thought. He would be free to be his own man again. He had tried everything he knew to please this woman. "Ain't no real man that don't drink a little and enjoy an occasional card game, even if he's a holy man," he had told her. If that's what she wanted, she should have married herself one.

And she had Richards all wrong. She didn't understand the bond there was between them. If only she could've been there to hear Richards tell him how men with similar good breeding and reputation had also come to him, but he trusted none more than Jr. Wallace. That's how he knew that once Richards saw what a respectable home he ran and shared some excellent cigars and enjoyed his best spirits, all would be right. *What could a woman possibly know about such things?* he thought. Especially one like his wife, who refused to let a man be a man.

His confidence rose with each passing mile and by the time he arrived, the scars of the previous night were tucked away and he was ready for business. The first order being to sell the broach.

Once the wagon was tied up, he sought out the only pawnshop in Owenton. He thrust the broach forward with such eagerness that the counterman knew he had a sucker and offered him half of what he paid, take it or leave it.

"Did you look close? I paid almost double that," protested Wallace.

"That's real interesting and it's a very nice piece, but that's all you'll get from me," the counterman answered.

Having taken the offer Jr. Wallace fast-walked to the bar. His intent was to buy as much instant gratification as could be found amongst the thirsty patrons. This restorative charade always worked wonders for the few hours that it lasted, and he was thirsting for it like a bitch in heat. He refused to let the needs of the plantation or the debt owed to Richards prevent him from reestablishing the good Wallace name to those captains of industry swigging their drinks mid-day in the filthy saloon.

Five of the nine patrons paid him no mind as he entered the bar. He heard the other four whispered about that "Black Wallace" as he made his way to the bar top.

"Who in here got a thirst?" he yelled out. This changed the dynamic instantly and enthusiastic shouts of confirmation roared back. "Well, you 'bout to have a drink compliments of the Wallace family. Fill every man's glass that wants one," he instructed the bartender.

It was Christmastime and Santa was surrounded by nine drunken elves that praised the generosity of their clueless host. They quickly drained then held up their empty mugs with the speed of mortal thirst. The false camaraderie was energetic and had the desired effect on Wallace's feather weight ego. He grinned and preened like some conquering hero returning intact from battle.

Kincaid watched Wallace enter the bar as he tied his horse to a post a few storefronts down. He eyed him with a mix of anger and anxiety. What was to come would be difficult at best if Wallace were sober. Hearing him praised and celebrated like some drunken Caesar was unbearable. Kincaid had seen him that once since the ruling and things had gone about as south as they could go. He needed to get him alone to present his proposition. Today would be the day. The thought of negotiating with a sadistic murderer made the whole affair rancid.

If I have ever prayed for anything, let me be a tool of justice for that poor girl and for T, he thought. But in the intervening months, a path to justice had not revealed itself. But it would. It had to. The murderer was there, doors down, several steps away.

He had considered riding back out to the plantation to make an offer, but reconsidered his plan. He knew that Jr. Wallace needed to be away from the influence of The Lady. She was an Iron Woman, as unmovable as a wall and as shrewd as she was hard. He figured if he stood any chance it would be to play to Wallace's ego, man to man. No woman should be allowed to challenge what two men decided. Still, Jr. Wallace would be faced with a dragon when he communicated the proposal to The Lady and she could derail any possibility of a positive outcome. He faced a formidable task.

At least Tommie was no longer having nightmares. Thankfully, those ended after the first month, but what replaced them was almost worse. A listlessness had enveloped her. The endless curiosity that would exasperate him and that insatiable thirst for each new day, had disappeared since T was taken. That it happened on the heels of her mother's death was a blow too great for her to overcome, he feared. He had to get T back. If he failed, he might lose her altogether.

He entered the saloon with his head down and managed to place himself against a wall opposite Wallace, without being noticed. As he surveyed the room it became clear that this might not be the place to have a conversation like the one he needed to have. Word had circulated quickly that some sucker was throwing his money around, and people seemed to materialize out of thin air with mugs thrust at the bartender. The overwhelmed server wiped the counter then his forehead with a stained rag, wondering how much liquor was left in his barrels and fearing for his well-being when it began running out.

Kincaid was struck, once more, by the change in Jr. Wallace. He would have walked right past him without a hint of recognition had he not been told his identity. *Maybe a form of justice is working on the man,* thought Kincaid, as he observed his jowly, desperate behavior. He also wondered if he were back in the good graces of his family, as he watched a parade of grateful riffraff toast their generous host. If this were the case, then he stood no chance. He had placed Wallace in the same category as other gamblers, cheats and liars. The type of men who were always in need of money because someone was surely waiting just around the corner, looking to settle a debt. If he was now flush with a steady flow of cash he would have no reason to bargain. It would become some drunken game for him as he tossed out outrageous numbers. All the same, Kincaid had to see it through.

Jr. Wallace was finally sitting alone. It seemed that once they had their drinks and said one or two disingenuous remarks, his new friends moved back to their true comrades. There was something pathetic about him, thought Kincaid. His attempts to find a companion had almost turned to begging. They would raise their glasses with a loud, "You're a fine gentleman Mr. Wallace," and move on. This might be his best or only opportunity, he thought. The mood had noticeably shifted. It was still noisy, but people were grouped into their own tight pods while Wallace looked on, like a fat little schoolboy staring longingly out at a game of Annie Over, nobody had chosen him for. Kincaid made his move.

"Good day to you, Mr. Wallace," he said in a voice overreaching for warmth.

"Mr. Kincaid! Well, I have to say this is quite a surprise. You ain't struck me as the type to frequent such a fine establishment as this!" Wallace shouted with consonants slurred.

"Every man can get a thirst," Kincaid replied gamely, straining for a show of camaraderie. "Mind if I join you?"

"Not if this is the day you plan on making good on your threat," he cackled. Kincaid answered with a slight smile. "Look, Kincaid, I know we didn't leave on the best of terms, and I didn't mean to be so harsh that afternoon, but when you tryin' to break in a hardheaded nigger you do what you gotta do. We are both respectable businessmen, ain't we? And how was I supposed to know I wasn't being presented with a legitimate offer? Or so you say." He leaned in closer, "And I just got to tell you, that nigger is prime. May not happened like it 'sposed to, but I still got you to thank." Kincaid gritted his teeth. "So here's to the man who helped me get a mighty fine nigger."

He held up his glass to toast and Kincaid, disbelieving even as he did it, met it with his own. He simply could not afford a confrontation if he hoped to be successful.

"Had to give him his first taste of Wallace leather. And I gotta tell you, I ain't never seen a nigger take what that one took. Even when we added some salt for good measure, he didn't holler once! And, you know, he didn't even do nothin'! He took the whip for some soft little preacher boy, 'cause he don't think it right, to go whippin' a nigger who talks the Bible. To hell with that! If a nigger do me wrong, he gets the whip! He can hold the Bible while I whip him, he want to, but he still get it."

Kincaid stared ahead in stony silence, Jr. Wallace took obvious pleasure in his discomfort.

"Never seen nothin' like it. Well, he got what he wanted. Only reason he ain't dead is 'cause he's a Goddamn bull." He paused to emphasize the next statement. "I can see you still ain't too happy 'bout what you saw. But that one come with a whole bucket of attitude and, like I said, he won't have nothin' but gratitude for scars when I'm done with him."

"Can I ask you a question, Mr. Wallace?" Kincaid said with a calm he didn't feel.

"'Course. I'm enjoying our little neighborly chat."

"Would you consider selling him?"

"'Scuse me?"

"I'm interested in buying him from you."

Wallace stared at Kincaid for a silent minute. "You a strange one, Kincaid. I ain't never known a white man so attached to a nigger. He a good one, no doubt, but he ain't the only good one. Does he got gold teeth? He sure ain't shittin' rubies."

"My reasons are my own, Mr. Wallace, and, by your own admission, you can buy another slave just as young and strong as this one, if not better. He's nothing particularly special to you."

"How much?"

Kincaid was caught off guard by the question. He was not expecting to get there so fast. Maybe because Wallace was too drunk to put on a poker face, or more likely was never able. The stench of desperation oozed out with the question.

"I'm not blessed to be a Wallace, like yourself, and able to be so generous to all my friends." He cocked his head toward the room. "Money is obviously not an issue for you. But I am not so lucky, Mr. Wallace. I would ask that you take that into account. I can barely afford to offer you the $150 dollars that I have in my hand." They both knew that T was worth three times as much. Kincaid was ready to bargain up to $250.

"Know what I think? I think you tryin' to insult me, Mr. Kincaid. You and I both know I could walk out on the street and in less than ten minutes get at least twice that much."

"No doubt. I respect that you had nothing to do with my dealings with Augustus. But the fact remains that he did me wrong. I was hoping with you being a Wallace that you could bring some grace to this situation."

"I appreciate that you're in a tough position, Kincaid, but it ain't my doin'." *This man obviously knows who I am and knows his place*, thought Wallace. He felt more inflated than he had all afternoon.

Kincaid feigned rubbing his chin to keep from smiling. He leaned back and watched Wallace bask in the cheap adulation.

"You are a gentleman to understand. Why don't you take this cash and we can settle this here and now and you can move closer to your place with the Lord."

Jr. Wallace eyed the wad of cash. "One thing I can tell you, Kincaid, if you do get him back he won't be the same ornery nigger that left you.

CHAPTER 29

About the same time that Kincaid walked into the salon in Owentown, Sr. Wallace pulled up to his son's plantation a few miles away. He had business that took him in the vicinity and he figured it was time to check in on what was his investment as well. Julius Wallace was still in a quandary about his sanity regarding this arrangement. When Jr. showed up on his doorstep, like some vermin sniffing around a food source, his first instinct was to have him thrown off the property. But his mother saved him, like she always did, and he always allowed. But no more. The Wallace reputation had suffered enough damage because of their misfit son.

Their other children had found their way, especially his artist son, Ira. Vincenzo, an Italian youth the same age as Ira, had come to Transylvania University in Lexington to study medicine. He also happened to have a love of art. Mutual friends thought Ira could be a proper host because of his growing renown as a painter. They became fast friends, spending almost every waking hour together. Sr. Wallace and his wife treated Vincenzo as their own and watched the two young men become inseparable. They had hoped that Vincenzo might spur Ira into finally finding that illusive wife. So far that hadn't happened.

The main house was far from what he expected. It was a good size but most of the exposed wood was in need of paint and there were a few porch boards that were warped and needed to be replaced. Overall it left the impression of a home with potential but past its prime. Much like the owner.

The screen door opened, and out stepped The Lady.

"Mr. Wallace! Well, this certainly is a surprise! I wish I had known you were coming," she said, making a futile attempt to hide her annoyance.

"My apologies for intruding on you like this, Lady. I like to look in on my properties from time to time and I just happened to be in the area."

Lady Wallace reddened at the reminder that the property was as much his as it was theirs.

"But I will try my best to give you ample notice in the future. I'd like to speak to my son, if you'd be so kind."

"I'm afraid that won't be possible. My husband went into town for supplies. I'm so sorry you wasted your valuable time, but I'll be sure to tell him you called on him."

She made the conscious choice not to afford him the common courtesy of a refreshment, reaching a new height of insult, even for her.

"Since, as you say, my time is so valuable, I think I'll wait a bit so as not to have to come back." He stepped down from the wagon. "If you could be so kind as to have some refreshments prepared. I'd like to hear how you all are getting along." He said this last part as if he were addressing a servant and she was outraged. But there was nothing she could do. He was the Patriarch and she had much to lose if she were to engage in battle with him. "And while you're in the kitchen, I think I'll have a stroll around the property. I should be back in half an hour or so." He left her fuming on the porch.

He walked past the house toward the stables. He noticed a few empty stocks and was reminded of how far the fruit had fallen from the tree. He, for one, was not tentative about disciplining his own enslaved, but he considered discipline and torture far apart. This was closer to torture in his mind.

"I see you admirin' our friends over there," Samson said, referring to the stocks.

"And who might you be?"

"I'm Samson, the overseer here."

"Mr. Wallace." He did not extend his hand in response to Samson's. "Looks like my son has landed on a rather nasty device to control his niggers."

"That was my idea. I seen it used at another place. Master Wallace liked it."

"No doubt. I was hoping to catch my son, but it looks like I've missed him. I'd be much obliged, Mr. Samson, if you could spare a few minutes to show me around."

"Yes sir, Mr. Wallace." They walked together as Samson explained the plantings, showed him property lines and described the slave distribution. One of his agents had done the initial inspection, so Wallace was only familiar with the written details. It was an overall solid piece of property that needed proper tending, he concluded. As they made their way back to the main house, they walked past the tobacco fields. Wallace paused.

"Who's that tall nigger with his shirt off?"

"That's a troublesome nigger that we had to beat last week."

"Looks like a strong worker. What did he do?"

"Didn't do nothin', sir. He took a beatin' for this boy preacher we got."

"That would be Raymond. His father was a preacher for my niggers. What do you mean, "Took a beating for him?"

"Well, that preacher know he ain't supposed to give nothin' to the niggers we put in them stocks and I catch him tryin' to give one of them water."

"And you're sayin that tall nigger in the fields took a beating for him?"

"Yes sir. Claimed it don't be right to be beatin' no preacher and said take him instead."

"Remarkable. Mr. Samson, isn't it?"

"Yes, sir."

"Mr. Samson, I want you to do me a favor. I want you to tell that useless piece of humanity that I'm ashamed to call my son, that if I get wind of him or anyone else laying a hand on that preacher, I will personally bring my whip and my gun to address the outrage. Do we have an understanding?"

Samson swallowed. "Sure do sir. I'll see to it nobody harm that preacher."

"You do that. His father was a good man and his son seems to be following in his footsteps. Now go bring that nigger to me."

"Scuse me, sir?"

"You heard me correctly, go bring him to me." Samson hurried off to get T. When he got back with him, Wallace said, "It's my understanding that you took a beating for the preacher."

"Yes, sir."

"And just why did you do a fool thing like that?"

"Ain't right to go beatin' on a man of God."

He examined T a moment longer then told Samson, "Put this nigger on my wagon, Mr. Samson. I got use for him."

"Uh, what should I say to your son, sir?"

"Whatever the hell you like."

CHAPTER 30

L ady Wallace soaked in her reflection with the eyes of a hawk scanning for its next meal. She was looking for that new crease, that new stress crack that might bespeak their desperation. She sat at her vanity gently caressing the tiny lines around her eyes and mouth with quivering hands that were usually as steady as a surgeon. She was incensed, and her outrage was reflected in the trembling journey over these unmistakable hints at her rapidly fading youth. This self-regarding exercise usually had a calming effect, even as it invariably confirmed the march of time.

She took the opportunity to remind herself that, although age spared none, the upturned nose, high cheekbones and general sense of superiority would always separate her from others. This time, however, the pep talk wasn't working. Those tiny lines that she had been able to repurpose now leapt out as gorges and valleys. She slammed her hands down on the vanity, sending three bottles of expensive French perfume tumbling onto the carpet. *How dare he!* She thought. That he showed up unannounced and then treated her like a servant was insulting enough. But then to steal one of their best niggers? This was beyond the pale.

He made some weak pretense of asking her permission, as if she could refuse him. He would take the nigger anyway, leaving her humiliated and shamefaced in front of any fieldhand witnessing the debacle. So she pretended to be enthusiastic and nobly asked him to consider it a show of gratitude for all he had done for them. Which would have been his words to her had she refused. But it was as sure a theft as if he had stolen the nigger from them in the cloak of darkness.

She heard a wagon approaching and thought it must be her husband back from Owenton. As she stood to go to the window, she noticed the perfume bottles scattered on the rug. When she reached down to pick them up, several small moth holes in the sleeve of her dress caught her attention. *My world is crumbling before my very eyes,* she thought. Moments later, she heard a knock.

"You decent?" a breathless voice asked.

"Not now, Wallace, please."

"This 'bout that nigger that was just beat. Got some news that's gonna solve our problems. Just wanna talk to you." She was not expecting this and opened the door. He stood before her, sweaty and reeking.

"Good lord, don't you set foot in here. You stink like a gin barrel."

"Just had a little something for the ride back." He stood straighter and brushed at his clothes, but made no attempt to enter the room.

"How did you hear about that nigger so fast," she asked.

"What are you talkin' 'bout?"

"Didn't you just tell me you heard about what happened?"

"I ain't heard nothin'. I was gonna tell you his old master wants to buy him back."

"Well, he's gone."

"What? When I catch him this time he'll hang after he's beat. Stupid nigger."

"Your father came by when you were gone and stole him."

This news backed him up a few steps. "Stole him? What the hell you talkin' 'bout?

"You heard me right. Your great father came by this morning to rub his generosity in our faces and after treating me like a servant informed me he was taking the nigger."

"He can't do that! Ain't got no right!"

"Rights be dammed for Sr. Wallace! He did it. Now, what's your news?"

"You remember that Kincaid fella that claimed he was cheated out of that nigger by Augustus?"

"Go on."

"Well, he wants to buy him back."

"So what. We can't sell these niggers."

"Don't worry 'bout my daddy. He came by today, but it was the first time in almost a year. We sell the nigger, buy another one and use the left-over money to pay Richards." Despite herself, she was intrigued.

"He had each one marked, he'll know if he ever wants to check."

"Then we say he ran off and we had to buy another one."

"You've got to get him back first."

"I'm gonna talk to my daddy. Let him know he got no right."

"Well, that just added a nice bit of comedy to this tragic day," and she slammed the door.

CHAPTER 31

Miss Edna started in The Lady's bedroom. Her bag of lavender and mugwort sachets was draped around her shoulders. She opened drawers, chests and closets and placed a bundle inside each one to ward off moths. This single example of her skills seemed to be the most important to The Lady as she had seen some of her best dresses destroyed. She begrudgingly admitted that whatever Miss Edna put in those little bags worked. Miss Edna knew she was thought of as a "witch doctor" by The Lady but paid it no mind. White people could think of her as they liked, long as they left her alone. She also enjoyed the access he was given to the private spaces of her master's home and wasn't beyond doing a bit of snooping.

T's abduction weighed heavily as she went about her tasks. He could be thrown from master to master on a whim and was helpless to stop it. Her worry now was that the oven door of his anger and rage would be harder to keep shut. If that door were to explode open, it would be his death. She had tried to stop Sr. Wallace by claiming that his scars might still go bad.

"Is there something you put on them?" he asked her.

"Yes, Massa Wallace."

"Well, go get me some. I'll have another nigger put it on his back." She did what she was told, and they were off.

Joraye was inconsolable. She told Miss Edna that she really must be cursed, and that's why T always seemed to find so much trouble. Miss Edna did what she could to reassure her of his quick and safe return, but found it hard to focus on. It was Rev. R's reaction she found most absorbing and telling.

He was also distraught, but his heartache seemed deeper then that of just a "friend." This only fueled her suspicions about the devilment flowing between the two. The time was fast approaching when she would have to call him out to save both their souls. She knew that if they had truly fallen under Satan's spell it would be up to the Rev. to put a stop to it. T answered to no God and she feared now he might be answering to God's nemesis and drawing in Rev. R in the process.

She had moved onto Jr. Wallace's bedroom and the marked difference never ceased to amaze her. The Lady's bedroom was outfitted with matching drapes and bedding, fresh flowers and clothing, folded or hanging where it should be. Even though an attempt had been made at housekeeping, Jr. Wallace's bedroom reeked of myriad stale odors and all the linen were dirty and threadbare. It looked like a vagrant had settled in for an extended stay in a hostel. As much as she held no affection for The Lady, she could always manage some vestiges of sympathy when she walked into his room. *There was nothing that would make a woman want to be a wife to this man,* she thought.

After she placed a bundle in the last drawer of his dresser, which was leaning to one side, she moved onto the closet. She held her breath as she opened the door, anticipating the rank odor that would be rushing out. She liked to give the smell a few seconds to dissipate before she began breathing again. Bad chicken was how many of the enslaved described the odor of white people, but Jr. Wallace's closet exuded an odor that was something else entirely. Miss Edna had to actually back away from the stench lest The Lady find her on the floor. She normally dropped a few sachets on the closet floor and quickly closed the door but today something caught her eye in one of his shoes.

It was a shoe that didn't seem to have a match. There was the chain of a delicate gold necklace just peeking out of the opening. She took it out and found it supported three small pearls set in a gold disc. She turned over the disc and saw an engraving "to our Jesse." She was not sure why this should be familiar to her, but it was. The more she tried to place the object, the more her mind filled with a jumble of images and thoughts all disconnected. *Why is it in a shoe?* she thought. *Why is he hiding it from The Lady?* She put it back thinking it had to do with his gambling, finished up and then headed downstairs.

"All done, ma'am."

"Good. Next time come sooner. This house seems to attract vermin."

"Yes, ma'am." She continued out. As she walked down the stairs, she froze mid-step. She remembered where she saw the necklace. *But no, that was impossible.*

CHAPTER 32

He had his answer. At least that's what Rev. R concluded as he sat in his oppressively silent room. He looked down at his half-eaten meal and stared. He abruptly got up, opened the door, and threw the food out for the first grateful creatures that came along. His appetite and much of his will had disappeared. God's will pulled them apart. Had to be. There was no other answer. The beating and now this. It was clear that misfortune would follow them so long as they, or he, or either of them, decided to live against the will of God. T once said that maybe God gave them each other as a gift for the Rev's faithfulness. It was an idea that could only come from someone that did not know that God was as vengeful as he was loving. But He had also promised to not let someone be tempted beyond their ability, and Rev. R remained helpless to his desire.

It was as burning right now as it was when T first rode onto the plantation. If it was God's will that they be apart, then He was right to take T away. There would be no other way to keep them from each other. But Joraye was being sacrificed too. *The wages of my sin*, he thought. If their desires drove her back into madness, he would ask God to condemn him to hell. There would be no plea for redemption, no shouting for forgiveness. "If we destroyed that innocent and loving soul, then deliver us both to the lake of fire," he spoke out loud.

He felt like a charlatan as he continued to offer prayers and blessings to his congregation. Maybe it was right they not be together because the conviction and unyielding belief that the faithful depended on had left him when they came together. Since finding himself through T, he had seen too much, felt too much that challenged the very marrow of his beliefs. But his pain was irrelevant to those who only wanted relief from the pain and despair of their day-to-day existence. So he prayed for and with them hoping that God could see past his troubled soul. He found purpose in giving comfort to those more deserving than him.

He could not know that this discovery between men was hardly ever a revelation, that it might be buried under layers of denial, until someone touches that part of the soul that says it's safe and then a floodgate would burst. For anyone who wished him happiness, they could never know he had already found what is soul was searching for, even if the discovery incurred God's wrath. There would not be a celebration, no warm hugs from the elder women, no camaraderie from the men. His would always be a shadow life, one that had him looking over his shoulder for a knowing snicker or worse. Any hint of his true desire would have many calling for their heads, while the more pitying would exclaim how one should "love the sinner, but not the sin," secure in their condescending piety as they walked around in their own soiled linens.

What possible future did T imagine for the three of them? he thought? But that was just it, wasn't it? He had come to realize that T lived with no expectation for the future, or even of a future. There was a stark, clean and fiercely selfish logic to how he lived. He truly answered to no one and had unyielding confidence in his instincts to guide not only his own existence, but theirs as well. When he talked about their family of three, Rev. R could almost believe it.

CHAPTER 33

"**M**assa's daddy took him," Miss Edna said to Mr. Kincaid from the back of a wagon where she had set up her temporary apothecary. She and Samson were in Owenton on one of their twice monthly trips where she sold her goods. The proceeds were a dependable source of income for the plantation and Samson served as the banker as well as the driver. Before she proceeded to bring Mr. Kincaid up to date, she noted that Samson was well out of earshot and engaged in conversation with one of his peer overseers. She still kept her voice to just above a whisper.

"You mean he bought him?"

"No. I mean he took him. He jus' come by one day and took him. Said he needed another strong nigger for a bit. Said he would give him back soon, but I ain't seen him since."

"Probably wasn't anything Jr. could do about that, but sure puts me in a spot."

"How you mean?"

"I offered to buy him back. He can't stay there. Jr. Wallace will kill him. He's beat him once already." She took a deep breath.

"It was bad, Mista Kincaid, 'bout the worst I ever see. He a lot better before he go but not all healed up like I want him to be. I hope you get him back. I know that precious little angel of yours must miss him somethin' awful."

"She's better now but, yes, she has suffered greatly."

"Well I know for a fact he ain't buy him so he got to bring him back sometime. You keep on prayin' on it, Mista Kincaid, 'cause it be right for you to get him back."

He was a regular client and Miss Edna had been filling a small sack with his typical order as they spoke. She handed it to him.

"Thank you, Miss Edna." He took the sack and walked over to Samson to make the payment. As he headed back to his wagon, Miss Edna call out.

"Mista Kincaid!" He and Samson both looked her way. "Oh, it jus' somethin' I forgot to tell Mista Kincaid 'bout what I give him," she called out. Samson didn't turn away until someone walked over to him and started up another conversation. When Kincaid was back at the wagon and safe from Samson's curiosity Miss Edna said, "I jus' remember somethin' strange I mean to tell you 'bout. I was puttin' out some sacks to keep away moths in massa's bedroom and see this necklace in one of his shoes. When I pull it out, it a necklace with this picture in wood on it. There was also pearls hangin' from the piece of wood. Somethin' 'bout it was known to me, but I don't remember what it was right then. After a bit, I remember who that necklace belong to, and it don't it make no sense for massa to have it. And he hide it too like he don't want nobody to find it."

"Who did it belong to?"

"You remember that poor girl that throwd' herself into the falls? The one they say was Judge Whiteside's daughter?" Kincaid was speechless. He stared at Miss Edna as if she were a ghost. He was barely breathing. "You all right Mista Kincaid. You look upset."

"I'm fine."

"Thing I don't figure to know is how he get that necklace 'cause I remember everybody talk 'bout how she never take it off. People say she treat it like the most special thing her daddy ever give her."

223

He drew closer to her. "I need to ask you to do something very important for me, Miss Edna."

She creased her brow at his seriousness and became a little wary. "This really seems to have you in a state, Mista Kincaid."

"I don't mean to scare you. But if you do what I ask, you will be performing Gods work."

"What is it?"

"I need you to bring me that necklace." Her back turned straight as a pole.

"That not be possible, Mista Kincaid. I take it, he know it be me 'cause I the only one that go in his closet. Even The Lady don't go in there."

"When are you supposed to be in there again?"

"In 'bout two weeks."

"Okay. If it looks like it has not been touched since the last time you were in there, he doesn't take it out much. Don't put a sack in his closet when you go in this time, just take the necklace. That way you can say you ran out of sacks and didn't go in his closet if he accuses you of stealing the necklace. But I don't think he will, Miss Edna. He won't even know it's gone. I will only need it for a few days then you can put it back."

"This jus' don't sound right, Mista Kincaid. Why you want that necklace?"

"Can't tell you right now. But you know me to be an honest man, don't you?"

"God as my witness, I know that be true."

"Then I need you to trust me with what I'm asking you to do. You will be making a very bad wrong right by doing this. Will you help me, Miss Edna?"

She didn't answer immediately, then said, "Long as you don't keep it too long, I guess I can do it. And if you say it be in the service of our Lord, then I guess it can't be wrong."

"God bless you, Miss Edna.

Anthony Henderson

CHAPTER 34

The building that housed the Sheriff's office was at the end of Main Street. It extended further toward the back of the lot than most properties to accommodate five jail cells. Kincaid had had a couple of occasions to pay a visit, so he and the sheriff were familiar by the time he entered the small office.

He approached a desk whose occupant was almost completely obscured by a cloud of cigar smoke. The smoke cleared to reveal the bald head and thick mustache of Sheriff Brooks Davidson. He had been sheriff for the ten years it took to watch his hair disappear, as if it were pulled from his head, through his nostrils ending in the gaudy and magnificent mustache he spent fifteen minutes shaping each and every morning. He was fleshy and offered no threat to criminals on the run, seeming to prefer his cigars over the earnest pursuit of justice.

"Good day to you, Sheriff Davidson," Kincaid extended his hand. "Still see you're enjoying your Figurados."

"Indeed," the Sheriff said as he stood and took the proffered hand. "God gives a man limited pleasures from which I was never one to walk away. Have a seat." Kincaid took a seat opposite him. "What is it I can do for you, Mr. Kincaid?"

"I need your help to see that justice is served."

"I always do my best. What seems to be the trouble?"

"It has to do with what happened to the Widow Whiteside's daughter."

"You mean the girl that killed herself all those years back? I ain't thought about that nasty piece of business since it happened. They say that's what really killed the Judge, why his heart gave out. Can't think what you got to say on that."

"I was there."

"Beg your pardon?"

"I was there. I heard everything. Didn't see it exactly, but I heard it happen. That girl was murdered, Sheriff. She didn't kill herself and Jr. Wallace did it."

The Sheriff was tapping the ash off his boxcar sized cigar and missed the ashtray as he looked up in astonishment.

"I know what you're thinking. But you have to understand, Sheriff, I was young and too scared to say anything when I realized what happened," Kincaid got out in a rush.

"Go on," prompted the Sheriff, his brow wrinkled.

"I had an argument with my daddy the night it happened. It was a pretty bad one and I ran away. I ended up falling asleep against a tree that was close to the falls. Don't know how long I was asleep, when some voices woke me up. Then I heard a splash. I was far enough away so whoever was up there couldn't see me. Then they started heading my way. Something told me there might be trouble if they saw me so I hid far enough away where I could still hear them. It was three boys and one of 'em was Jr. Wallace. One of them started talking about what would happen if they got caught. That's when I heard that they had just thrown the widow Whiteside's daughter, Jesse, I think her name was, into the falls." Sheriff Davidson had been sitting back listening intently. At this last bit, he took a massive deep breath. Kincaid continued. "That's when Jr. Wallace threatened them and their families if anyone said a word. He said that his family was so powerful no one would take their word against his anyway. Even though I didn't see anything, it was like he was taking to me too, and I believed him."

"Hold on," Davidson interjected. "Are you telling me that you overheard Jr. Wallace, of THE Wallaces, admit to murdering the widow's daughter?"

"That's right. But don't you see? There was nothing I could do. Who would believe me over somebody with that much money and power?"

"I get that you were scared. But that still don't explain why you walked into my jailhouse. You would have the same problem today, especially with no proof. And just so you know, I would love to show that good for nothing piece of horseshit the inside of one my cells. He has cheated and lied with nary a consequence for way too long."

"Well, I got something now," Kincaid said quietly. He reached into his pocket and took out the necklace. "One of Wallace's slaves found this in his bedroom. She was cleaning up and saw it in one of his shoes, like he was hiding it."

"Whose is it?"

"She told me it belonged to the widow's daughter and that she used to brag that her daddy gave it to her 'cause he loved her so much. There is only one way Wallace could have gotten this necklace. He took it the night they threw her into the falls."

Neither man spoke for several minutes. The Sheriff slowly nodded as he put it all together then said, "The word of some nigger that that's the same necklace won't fly with no judge. It would be her word against everything the Wallace's can throw at her. We need to pay the widow a visit, which could be problem."

"How so?"

"She ain't been out of that house for some time and it's my understanding that she don't take visitors. I also don't know what this would do to her if it is Jesse's

228

necklace. Might be enough to put her to rest." He paused, thoughtfully. "You know, people said that girl killed herself but Judge Whiteside nor his wife believed that for one minute. Neither did I. I remember Jesse. She always seemed to be happy to see you. Then they claimed to have found out who did it. I´always wondered how that little nigger boy could have done all they said he did. Didn't make no sense, but they wanted blood and that's what they got. Could barely find his teeth when they was done, but that's just how we do things around here, Mr. Kincaid."

Kincaid lowered his head as he was reminded of the blood on his own hands. The Sheriff seemed to read his thoughts.

"Nothing you could have done about that, Kincaid. No way they was gonna bring a Wallace to justice over this."

"Appreciate that, Sheriff. That's just one more reason why we got to make this right."

"Look, let me try to talk to widow Whiteside. Our families were friendly when I was growing up. Would be God's will that she don't go to her grave not knowing the truth. I'm also hoping it would be His will to give Wallace a good kick straight to hell."

"But not before I get what I want. I've got more to say," added Kincaid

CHAPTER 35

K incaid sat next to Sheriff Davidson waiting for the widow to descend the stairs. Miss Edna had been true to her word and had managed to secure the necklace which was now in the Sheriff's possession. Her servant had seated them in a foyer that was bigger than the entire first floor of most other homes in Owenton. It had been darn near impossible to get this appointment. The widow had become a recluse over the past several years. She was close to ninety and rumor had it that she was unable to get out of bed and that her nose was pressed firmly against deaths door. She agreed to the interview only after the Sheriff said it had to do with a legal matter of the utmost importance and he would be unable to complete the investigation without her assistance.

"I don't know how that one small nigress can get her out of bed and down those stairs. I hear she has to be carried," Sheriff Davidson said.

"I have always found my legs to be a suitable method to move me from here to there." They looked toward the staircase and saw an elegantly dressed woman with a snow-white braid cascading over one shoulder, held together at the end with a tasteful pearl clasp. Her nigress held one of her arms more for insurance than out of necessity. She was clearly in possession of her faculties and far from the bedridden recluse of rumor. The men leapt to their feet.

"We meant no disrespect Mrs. Whiteside," the red faced Sheriff blurted out.

"So sorry for our insensitive comments, Mrs. Whiteside," Kincaid added.

"Oh now, don't you both look like a set of twins with their hands in the cookie jar. Sheriff you should know better than to participate in such gossip. I might have to spank you like I did when you were a little boy, or have you forgotten?" she added with an amused grin.

"No ma'am. I do remember," he replied.

"Oh, and it looks like your good-looking friend with those magnificent blue eyes finds the thought rather amusing."

"Very much so, Mrs. Whiteside," Kincaid shot a glance at the Sheriff who was now grinning.

"And we're off to a pleasant start, Mr?"

"Kincaid."

"A pleasure sir."

The Widow and her servant descended slowly, but at all times she was on her own two feet. Although no one would mistake her for fifty or sixty, her ninety years remained a mystery. With alert eyes, unbowed bearing and a fully intact wit, she was not what most would imagine. This was not the bedridden, mentally challenged relic they were expecting. They sat up straighter as she was helped into a chair across from them.

"Now tell me what pressing legal issue needs the attention of an old widow?"

"Mr. Kincaid brought a matter to my attention and I agreed with him that it was vital that we speak with you. Let me say from the outset that this will be a sensitive matter and we come to you only with a desire for justice, and a prayer for your comfort," Sheriff Davidson began. He was hoping to preempt any shock.

"A curious start, to be sure. Go on," she said, her clear eyes clouding over with suspicion.

"He has something that we'd like you to take a look at, if you would be so kind." She nodded her consent. Kincaid took the necklace out his pocket and handed it to her. She reared back as if it were some cursed talisman.

"How could you have this?" She said in a shocked whisper. "She never took it off, never." She reached for the jewelry, her translucent, unsteady hand revealing the ancient woman she was. "Jesse, my Jesse." A single tear fell onto the necklace. The servant handed her a handkerchief. She wiped her eyes and regained her composure.

"That's what we needed to know, Mrs. Whiteside." Sheriff Davidson said.

"Where did you find it?"

Kincaid and the Sheriff exchanged a look. "You are certain that she never took it off?" the Sheriff asked.

"Yes. Now, please, tell me what is going on here," she said impatiently.

"We are reasonably certain that Jesse did not take her own life."

"Of course she didn't! I never believed that for one minute. My poor husband was nearly driven to madness with the not knowing. Am I to understand that you now have someone in custody?"

"Not just yet. Another reason for our visit is we'd like to ask for your help in bringing our suspect to justice if, in fact, he is the one that did it."

"Gentlemen, I am at your service."

CHAPTER 36

Rev. R was spreading the healing word of Jesus to shouts and exclamations on this Sunday morning. It was a few days after Mr. Kincaid and the Sheriff had had their conversation with the widow. Miss Edna paused in her assent to listen to the Rev. and say a silent prayer for her own safety. She was heading up to Jr. Wallace's bedroom to reinstall the necklace in its hiding place. In was in an apron pocket, tucked securely out of view. Even though Mr. Kincaid had told her that her bravery was key to his plan, there would be no peace for her until it was safely put back.

She had several sleepless nights while it was in Kincaid's possession. She also figured that since he had hidden it from The Lady, he wouldn't be too vocal with his suspicions if he discovered it missing. But he would be desperate to find it, and a desperate Jr. Wallace was enough to keep her eyes open.

Even though she couldn't imagine it, Jr. Wallace and Jesse must have had a powerful relationship, thought Miss Edna. That necklace was too important to her to give to just anyone. How else could it have ended up in Jr. Wallace's possession? Just when Miss Edna thought she had lived long enough to have seen everything, this was proof she had not. There could not be two more unlikely people to find love. Then there was Mr. Kincaid's excitement about the thing. She couldn't understand why he found it so strange that a girl in love would give a boy a gift.

Her plan was simple: she would claim that she needed to put a few more moth sacks in Jr. Wallace's bedroom. This was not unusual, and The Lady consented.

She fingered the menacing item with hands that were moist as she snuck a glance behind her to ensure that The Lady, for reasons only known to God, had not decided to follow after her on this day. Fortunately, The Lady was continuing her vain attempt at needlepoint. She was turning it this way and that, trying to figure out how everything had gone so horribly wrong.

The staircase was wide with threadbare carpeted stairs. This partially muffled the squeaking of the old wood boards as Miss Edna continued her assent. In the past she paid no attention to these groans and protests, but today each one became a little shard of indictment that she imagined would soon have Jr. Wallace raging toward her in murderous accusation.

Now at the top, she had to hold onto the banister and wipe her brow. Beads of sweat revealed the toll the short journey had taken. Jr. Wallace's bedroom was a few doors down and after another minute she walked toward it on more steady legs.

She turned the doorknob, but it didn't turn. Or at least not enough to open the door. She tired turning the handle in both directions, but it only spun on the shank that joined it to its partner on the other side. Her eyes shifted nervously, fearful that someone might accuse her of trying to force her way into Jr. Wallace's bedroom. She abruptly turned away and made her way back downstairs.

Her mind was ablaze as to what her next move might be. Then she realized that since she had been given permission to enter Jr. Wallace's bedroom, she was within her rights to ask the The Lady about the door. Even though Miss Edna could not imagine that

she would know how to open it. That was one room
the entire plantation knew The Lady did not enter.
Just as she was about to enter the drawing room, she
heard a wagon pull up. Jr. Wallace ambled down and
walked quickly into the house.

"Mornin', Massa Wallace," she said, hoping
her surprise and anxiety didn't show. He ignored her
and headed toward the stairs.

"I forgot some papers," he hollered out as he
continued up the stairs.

"'Scuse me, Massa Wallace," Miss Edna
spoke up nervously. He turned around, clearly
annoyed. "I tell The Lady that I got to put more moth
sacks in your room but the door don't open."

"That damn lock just broke a few days ago,"
he answered out of frustration. "Come on, then." She
followed him up the stairs. When they got to his
bedroom door, he took out a folding knife that she had
never seen before and stuck in the keyhole. After
moving it around and cursing his lack of skills he was
able to get the door open. They both walked into the
room. Miss Edna started placing sacks in various
corners, not wanting to go straight to the closet with
Jr. Wallace in the room.

"Wallace!" They both turned at the sound of
The Lady's voice from downstairs.

"Dammit. What now?" Jr. Wallace said to
himself and left the room. As the conversation
continued, Miss Edna darted to the closet and opened
the door. With necklace in hand she scanned the floor
and saw the shoe was where it was supposed to be.
She took a step in and reached out to drop the
necklace in.

"What the hell are you doing in my closet?" Jr.
Wallace shouted. She snatched her hand back and

whirled around to see him glaring at her. She grabbed one of the small sacks and held it up.

"Like I told you, Massa Wallace, I was jus' puttin' out these moth sacks," she blurted out, hoping he didn't notice her hand trembling. She had slipped the other hand into her apron.

"Not in there you don't. You stay out of that closet. Do you hear me?"

"Yes, massa," she said as she closed the door, but not before she reached back and let the necklace drop into the shoe.

CHAPTER 37

The Lady took in the activity downstairs with the enthusiasm of a condemned prisoner listening for the footsteps of a priest about to administer her last rites. She was up at first light to prepare for the evening's festivities. At the moment, she was resting before returning to strike fear into the lazy and unsuspecting. She could not stop her errant spouse from moving ahead with his beggar's banquet but she was resolute not to go down with what she was convinced was a sinking ship.

She had contacted her father and said everything she needed to say to prepare him for her imminent return. He had been against the marriage from the start. But his ambitious daughter held his heart in her hands, and, in the end, he acquiesced to the union against his better judgment. Even so, the only blessing he would bestow was the promise to be there when the union fell apart. He responded to her distraught letters with no smear of reprimand or blame. His home and his heart would always be open to her, was the gist of his replies.

If they lost the plantation, the humiliation would be crushing, no question. Even as practiced as they were at failure, it was a coat that never went on well. *And it would be lost,* she thought, as she rose from her fainting divan and started rummaging through her closet for what she might wear this evening. Fortunately, she was well practiced at holding her head up through walks of shame. The surprising gesture from the Sr. to help with the purchase of the plantation, gave her hope that father and son might be on their way to reconciliation. When the father showed up unannounced and stole their prime nigger right from under them, she was freed from any misconceptions she'd long clung to regarding his true feelings toward them.

Tonight, Richards would take in this act of desperation and find special pleasure in being one of the few men in the history of Owenton, to chip away at the Wallace dynasty. *And it would happen the same way it happened with every peasant,* she thought. Richard was flush with cash and had discovered an unoriginal way to grow his wealth. For those poor souls that banks turned down, Richards was their man. He would lend money at impossible terms. And much more often than not, within a year of setting his devilish terms, payments would fall behind and he would promptly repossess the property. She admitted some sour admiration for his ruthlessness. They were cut from the same cloth. But it seemed certain he would beat the Wallace's at their own game. Still, to also snatch this place from the Sr., and the contract she looked over all but ensured Richards would, gave her a flicker of warmth.

As she rifled through dozens of pairs of shoes, a fresh wave of anger rose up. *All of this should have been a celebration!* She fumed. *One that showed off their high standing to the curious vultures that would be attending.* Instead, she would be forced to endure their condescension. Most would see through the pretense of the last-minute invitation; Richards was just as deeply in their pockets. Nevertheless, they would happily accept the food and drink at the well-appointed wake.

She took a deep breath and steeled herself. If this was to be their requiem, at least her guests would remember and recount her skills as a consummate host, head held high. She put on day clothes and made her way downstairs to oversee the preparations. Her eyes

238

immediately set on a bare end table. "Why aren't there flowers on this table?"

"They bein' picked, ma'am," answered the closest servant.

"Well get them in without delay. They will need time to open."

"Yes'm."

"And make sure the table is set for ten, not eight."

She stomped to the kitchen. When she smelled the meat roasting and the pies baking, she admitted to the kitchen staff, "at least the food won't be a disaster," then added "Where's that nigger that was sick?" she asked no one in particular.

"You mean, Shawna, ma'am?" someone answered.

"How on earth should I know who I mean? Someone told me we might need extra help because someone was sick. Is she sick or not? And if she's not, where is she?"

"She over at the end of the table, ma'am. She be fine." Lady Wallace walked over to an adolescent servant, who was carefully laying a lard crust into a pie tin. She kept hAnytime her down during the scrutiny.

"Lift your head up so I can get a good look at you." She did as she was told. "Your eyes look a little feverish to me. Just make sure that you don't go sneezing into the food." She didn't notice that Shawna was holding onto to the edge of the table for support.

"Yes, ma'am."

Lady Wallace moved on thinking that the last thing she wanted to do was to ask that babbling idiot that lived with that witch woman to come back. But, she was very good in the kitchen, always coming up with special dishes. *It's not surprising that she and that witch are partners,* she thought. They were both

239

maladjusted. Though she had to admit, the witch did seem to keep the darkies healthy. Whatever magic she pretended to know, served the plantation well. Plus the idiot girl was learning the trade. *Well, that would truly take some magic,* she thought. A pot start to boil over. "Who this watching this pot?!" she demanded. A flurry ensued. Two black women rushed in, almost knocking her over in the process. "Will you watch where you're going!" she shouted. The women moved the pot off the fire, averting a disaster. "Pay attention!," she shouted. "We are not spending a small fortune on food only to have it ruined!"

She could only hope that the liquor and cigars, and whatever else is supposed to impress men, had been tended to by her husband. This thought did not bring her comfort, but there was nothing she could do but trust him. She started out of the kitchen just as Shawna went crashing to the floor.

***

Upstairs in his room, Jr. Wallace gazed at himself with the same preening intensity as The Lady had minutes earlier. That's where the similarity ended. As his puffy and pocked visage stared back, he was not bemoaning the tragedy of their current state; he laid that responsibility squarely at the feet of his emasculating wife. Instead, as he examined his profile in clothes that wouldn't stand close scrutiny, he imagined himself thinner than he was. He also saw a face that featured the strong jawline of a Wallace. When in truth the jaw was buried under layers of chunky chin. He held his head high, convinced that staring back was a man deserving of the respect associated with his legacy, even as his name was being stricken from its history books.

Tonight will be damn good, he mused. He waved a used handkerchief in a grandiose bow to himself, then tossed it on the floor like a giggling fop. They were throwing the kind of event that was expected of a family of his stature. It was well past due. He might have capered around the room with the grace of a rhinoceros, if his corns had not flared up making each step excruciating. He had promised The Lady that he would take special care with the wines and cigars, even though it took the remainder of what he got for the broach. After tonight it wouldn't matter. Richards would be enchanted by the show of pomp and pretension and gladly refrain from quibbling over a few pennies. He was as certain of this as he was of the sunrise.

He would sell that unruly nigger, too, soon as he got him back. He went to his father in petulant outrage at the insults leveled at his wife and made a whining demand that he return T immediately. This show of rights was met with stony silence.

When the Sr. finally did speak he offered a compromise. "I will keep that nigger as long as I want. However, you can expect to have him back in the next couple of weeks and not a second sooner. Please send my regards to your lovely wife. You may go now."

Jr. started to speak but thought better. He had a promise of T's return, which could just as easily be retracted if he were to irritate his father any further. He left without another word.

Ain't no way Kincaid will get that nigger, he thought. He and The Lady decided to accept not a penny less than $600 and unless Kincaid stumbled head first into a pot a gold, there was no way he would find that kind of money. All that talk about a Christian duty was for another man, one that said his prayers every night. Wallace only raised his hands to God for a blessing when there was dice in one and money in the other. He had been thinking, though, that there might be trouble if his father came looking for that same nigger and he was gone. Well, he was going to replace him with a far less expensive stallion and if his father came around to steal another one there'd be something here for him. He would give the rest of the money to Richards and they could breathe a little easier.

The used handkerchief had fallen behind a chair and Wallace retrieved it, thinking it would make a nice pocket square. He proceeded to shake and fluff it as he imagined those refined French people did and with each flick of his wrist, he became more confident that tonight he would show his emasculating harpy who was boss.

"Wallace! Get down here!" Lady Wallace yelled from the kitchen. And like a dog hearing his master's call, he rushed down and stopped cold as he to saw one of the cooks passed out on the kitchen floor.

CHAPTER 38

"This here be called Devil's Dung on account of how it smell," instructed Miss Edna, as she held up a thin, dried stalk. Joraye looked on feigning interest. She had been listless, hopelessly depressed since T was taken away. But Miss Edna told her since nothing could be done about it, she needed to focus on other things. So she was trying mightily to immerse herself in learning Miss Edna's secrets. She had mixed results.

"How you make people take somethin' that smell like that?" she asked.

"They don't have to take it. Gimmie that bag over there." Joraye handed her a small cotton sack. Miss Edna cut up the root, put it in the bag, then attached a string to the bag and put it over her head.

"This what you do with Devil's Dung. You wear it 'round yo' neck if it hard to breath. So every time you breathe, it get deep inside you and help you be able to get more breath when you sick."

"And that work?" Joraye asked skeptically.

"If you believe it do. You see, it matter that you make people believe it work. I see miracles happen jus' 'cause someone believe somethin' work. That be a lot of what people like us do, Joraye. You know, I think Mista' Kincaid gon' be with you on the smell of this Devil's Dung, though. Don't think he picked this up from me before. I'm gon' have to convince him it work real good," she said with a laugh. Joraye smiled slightly and walked slowly to the corner of the room and sat on a stool. "I see that baby startin' to make itself known. You lookin' more like you with child every day. I hope you told T, like you promised me you would." Joraye was silent. "Oh no, baby! We talk 'bout it and you give me yo' word you tell him. He ain't no stupid man. He gon' know in a minute, the way you be lookin'. But it be so much better you tell him."

"No!" she declared, forcing Miss Edna to stop what she was doing and look her in the eye. "Massa gon' take it anyway. T ain't got to go through that. You got to do somethin' Miss Edna!" This was where Miss Edna could only rely on her faith because Joraye was painfully right. Her chances of keeping her child were slim to none. But Miss Edna had not allowed that reality to set in. She had hoped God would intervene, but so far He had sent no intervention or guidance. Regardless, she was not going to let Joraye destroy the child.

"I hear you say that but maybe God got plans for yo' baby," she said gently. "Maybe God make massa leave it with you."

"If massa take my child, I die Miss Edna. I can't live, that happen."

"You got faith, Joraye?" she asked soothingly. Joraye nodded, knowing where this was going. "Then you got to trust that our Lord Jesus will protect you, your baby and your T. I be prayin' on it every day. When that man first see you, he come to me and talk like you the only woman ever lived in the whole world. I know he be 'bout the happiest man on God's earth he know you with child. Ain't no way I take that joy away from him, or from you. You carryin' a gift from God, that will lift him like nothin' else. You say he be good to you. Well, havin' this baby be the best way to show him how much he mean to you." She paused to let all this sink in. "And I be almost happy as T, to have a baby 'round this house." Joraye started to calm. "'Course, we can only hope it don't have yo' big head or his big lips." Joraye smiled slightly. "We all family here, honey, and all you gon' do with that child is bring joy. Do you understand that?"

"Yes Miss Edna." She did not mention the sleepless nights beside T, wondering if she was carrying a child that would be touched like she was. *No man would stay with a woman who couldn't give him a right child,* she had thought. Even if that man be T. She had convinced herself that there was only one option left to her. So she had listened closely when Miss Edna described the various herbs and roots for any mention of a remedy that was not safe for someone with child. She knew that some medicines could hurt a baby and she planned on taking just such a medicine as soon as she learned of it. She reasoned with T gone it would be easier to go through whatever pain the medicine caused, and she would be better by the time he returned.

But now, as she sat on her stool listening to Miss Edna, who seemed to be speaking directly to her heart, she wanted to curse herself out loud for letting the Devil fill her with such evil thoughts. Every gentle and loving word of support that Miss Edna offered, peeled away the layers of fear that she had built. What had been something she thought would destroy them was becoming something beautiful that she never imagined. She would pray hard for massa to leave her baby alone.

Miss Edna concentrated on pounding spices with a pestle while Joraye sat with her thoughts. Tentatively, with the nervous anticipation of opening a wonderfully wrapped gift, she put her hands on her stomach and now marveled at what she and T had created. "How soon I feel it, Miss Edna?"

"Anytime now, and believe me, you know when it happen. It one gift God give us, which no man will ever know and can never take away. When you feel that baby for the first time, that when the love really start, and it only grow from there. You be blessed, child, that you bringin' this baby into a family that want it, so yo' mind need to be only on the love."

"You have any babies?" This question caught Miss Edna off-guard, and she answered without looking up.

"I be blessed with three. A girl and two boys." She was not kept pregnant because of her other uses. "I pray every night they be safe and in a good place."

"You never see them again?"

"No, child, I never see them after they sold. But that be so long ago and I help so many people, I know God bring us together in His kingdom."

"T won't let nobody take our baby," Joraye said with quiet conviction.

"I know you be right, Joraye, and times be changing all the while. I pray the world be different for you and yo' baby than it be for me and mine." They fall into contemplative silence.

Noticing the activity at the big house Miss Edna said, "Guess they be workin' hard to save this place."

"What you mean?" Joraye asked.

"I hear that massa in trouble with money and this party be 'bout doin' somethin' to save it. Look like they be workin' real hard to make somebody think they special."

Joraye was immediately put on edge and much of the joyful energy seeped out of the room. Miss Edna walked over and draped her arm over Joraye's shoulders.

"Don't you even think he can make you go over there. He ain't asked after you for a while now. What we tell him been workin'. So don't you worry. You jus' focus on yo' baby and how happy T gon' be when he hear the news."

A scream came from the big house. They went to the window.

"Somethin' wrong," Joraye said, grabbing onto Miss Edna's sleeve.

"With all that goin' on over there somethin' bound to happen. It sound like it come out the kitchen," Miss Edna added, "Pro'bly spilled a pot of somethin'."

Joraye moved away from the window, tense and silent. Miss Edna followed and said with more conviction then she felt, "They got plenty folks over there to do all the work needs to get done. Now, hold yo' nose. and come on over here and help me make more of these necklaces. Mista' Kincaid want five. Gon' be some smelly darkies walkin' 'round his place." Joraye smiled, despite her apprehension. Miss Edna paused and looked up at her. "By the way, you know what you gon' name the baby?"

"This caught Joraye by surprise, and fully refocused her. "Ain't never thought 'bout it, really. How you name yo' babies, Miss Edna?"

"I give 'em my own special names. That way I keep 'em close to my heart. I call 'em Matthew, Mark and Sara, from the Bible. You want to give it a name it be proud of. Not somethin' like, Ham Hock or Mustard Green."

"But maybe T like "Mustard green," Joraye answered through her laughter.

"I guess yo' next be Cornbread. Heck, people get hungry jus' repeatin' the names of yo' children," said Miss Edna through her own laughter. This exchange helped them get back to a place of warm anticipation for the new baby and they refocused on their tasks.

"Miss Edna! Miss Edna!"

They both froze, as the front door vibrated from incessant pounding.

"Miss Edna open the door, please!" came the insistent cry of a female voice.

"I comin', Simone, jus' a minute," Miss Edna said. She opened the door and Simone darted in.

"Oh please, Miss Edna! She say she gon' have me beat, if Joraye don't come this time. I ain't never been whipped! Please! Please! She got to come with me this time!" Simone blurted out in stark terror.

Joraye's eyes darted from Miss Edna to Simone and she started to shake her head and back up against the wall. "No, no..." came out in a disbelieving whisper. "Miss Edna, my baby, he kill my baby I go there. He kill my baby!"

"Nobody do nothin' to yo' baby, Joraye. You got to settle yo'self." She turned back to Simone, "Tell him she be in bed sick and can't come unless he want everyone else to be sick tomorrow."

"That ain't gon' work this time. The missus say she see Joraye outside and tell me not to let you make up no lie. I sorry Miss Edna. It be her that sent me, and she promise to get me beat if Joraye ain't come back with me. That why she got to." While Simone spoke, Joraye listened. The moment Simone finished, she darted past them and out the door.

"Joraye!" shouted Miss Edna. "Go after her," she instructed Simone, who sprinted as fast as her legs would move.

Outside, Miss Edna heard, "Over here, Miss Edna!" Her eyes went to a large, leafy, oak tree. Joraye was sitting against the tree weeping. Simone had her arm around her shoulders.

"I tell her I take care of her, Miss Edna," Simone said. "I tell the missus we need help with something easy and far away from massa. We all look after you, Joraye, 'especially now we know you got T's baby."

"Who know?" Joraye blurted out in shock.

"Jus' us, Joraye, Jus' us. Folks say you look like you with child for a while now," she said and quickly added, "No white folks know. They don't be payin' no mind 'bout that 'til the baby 'bout to come. I swear before God, ain't nothin' gon' happen to you, Joraye. But you got to come, else I get the whip!" She pleaded for understanding.

Joraye looked at the ground and shook her head in shock and confusion. "Miss Edna, you promise me. You say never again," She spoke these words with quiet, angry accusation.

"I know what I say, and I mean it. Now we got to make sure you safe and Simone don't get the whip."

"But how you do that' less I go?!" Joraye responded helplessly.

Miss Edna kneeled in front of Joraye and took her hands. "You got to listen to me and be strong."

Joraye turned away, knowing what was coming.

"I rather go to my grave, than to see you in that house again. You know that don't you?" Joraye reluctantly, nodded her head. "But I know you with me and don't want no harm to come to Simone, like she don't want harm to come to you. Ain't that right?" Again, slow acknowledgement. "Now this be a terrible thing the missus leave us to do, no doubt. But we plan on it and I know no harm come to you or Simone. What I see is that there be a lot goin' on in that house right now, and Simone can slip you in any place she want. Jus' stay close, and no harm come to you, jus' like she say."

As tears dripped onto her dress Joraye started to tremble. Miss Edna held her tight. "Oh baby, I know how scared you be, I know, but you not by yo'self. Simone told you they all be lookin' out for you, and I know that be true. Before you go, we gon' ask God to protect you and that baby, then you do what Simone say, and I know you come right back to me, and to T."

"She right, Joraye. I put you somewhere far off in the kitchen, then tell the missus I make you come. She too busy to care, so long she know I make you come. Massa ain't no worry neither, he got a new one he fancy, and he take no notice of you. You be safe, you will, but we got to go now, Joraye. I can't be gone too long."

Miss Edna held out her hands, and they started a prayer circle. When they finished, she said, "You protected now, Joraye. No harm come to you or yo' baby. God got His arms 'round you."

Joraye turned mute and stone cold. Simone led her off. Miss Edna stared after them and continued her silent prayers, which brought little comfort.

CHAPTER 39

The buzzing pulled him from Rev. R's touch and the warmth of his skin. T opened his eyes at the end of a dream and on the tip of consciousness. The blackness that surrounded him was disorienting. Then in almost the same instant he was in the present. It had been several weeks since his arrival to the Sr. Wallace plantation and there had been other nights like this. Minutes before he had been lying with Rev. R in all the sensory reality of a dream and was now faced with a pesky fly insistent on enjoying the sweat and dirt that was as much a part of his face as the mahogany color he'd been cursed with. He swatted at the pest and lay motionless. The other slaves snored and moaned. This sleeping arrangement was not the sadistic equivalent of his introduction to the Jr. Wallace plantation, but with ten to a space that uncomfortably slept half that many, it was better only by a margin.

Sleep had not been a risk those first nights. He was consumed with worry for Joraye and Rev. R. Sr. Wallace had promised that no one would ever raise a whip to Rev. R again, then road away with the very one who had saved his life. But it was Joraye who grabbed him from the depths and set his heart pounding in a sweaty panic. Rev. R would have his own unique pain but also the peace of a mind free of demons.

Before they rode off, he had seen Joraye pacing back and forth in Miss Edna's cabin. She was muttering and wringing her hands, inviting the specters that had been pushed aside the last several months to come back and claim her. She kept her back to the wagon as it pulled away, not wanting to witness another example of the inevitable betrayal she felt was her destiny. He knew that if the whirling tentacles of madness

251

reclaimed her, she would never come back. He felt this result with a chilling certainty.

Thinking about Miss Edna helped calm him. She would not let any harm come to Joraye. He had witnessed her lioness-like protection and received some solace from it. But if Jr. Wallace wanted Joraye, he knew Miss Edna would be powerless to stop him. These thoughts were the way to his own madness, so he willed himself to believe the absurdity that she was well protected in Miss Edna's warm cabin.

As he lay foot-to-head with his enslaved brethren, it became clear what he must do. They could never be a true family under the boot of a master. With each sunrise, he or Joraye or Rev. R could be ripped from each other's lives at any moment. He would find a way to get his fragile family to safety. He was a free man and he would claim it back. Mista Kincaid would give it to him what was rightfully his. He would take his family north and build a free life. Miss Edna would help. As he imagined a new life with Joraye and Rev. R, one where they could live without fear, he was able to fall into a sleep that was near unconsciousness.

CHAPTER 40

Back at the big house the Lady surveyed her table. Despite her misgivings she had to admit that at least this part of the charade was impressive. The ham and geese were gleaming and fragrant. The barley soup was thick and savory with healthy chunks of bacon resting on the surface. Completing the cornucopia were fresh baked bread, potatoes au gratin, butter beans, fresh peaches and Kentucky burbon pecan pie. Even her guests seemed to have found various skirts and trousers that made an attempt at style. She was grateful for these small surprises. They would help with the alternate reality she was intent on crafting.

She smiled and cooed warmly accepting copious compliments on the table, her dress and various decorative fine points. Her false modesty, expected of the occasion, was also on pitch. This critical part of the affair, which set the tone for the evening fell completely on her shoulders. She could not depend on her husband. Indeed, she would have to work against his instinct to call attention to himself with some embarrassment that would leave no doubt as to why his own family had chosen to disown him. Still, her best efforts could not erase an unmistakable chill to the proceedings. Conversation was halting and forced. The men chitchatted about the impact the weather was having on yields and the women mostly said nothing. This stiff artificiality was generally the case whenever Richards was sitting center table.

As The Lady took all this in, small cracks started to appear in her veneer. She realized the herculean task ahead of her, if she and her bungling husband were to end this evening with a shred of respect. Richards was basking in his ability to hold court. He practically dared anyone present to compete for the floor. He droned on about the superiority of French-cut suits versus those made in America, as if his audience were blue bloods, instead of second tier landowners who had never left nor would ever leave the state, much less travel to France.

"I just don't know how they make this material. It's soft as a baby's bottom. Feel this!" he demanded of the man on his left, whose soup spoon was halfway to his mouth. At Richards abrupt command, he dropped the spoon and it splattered in his bowl, splashing hot liquid soup onto Richards' jacket. Richards reared back. "My God, man, this is a dignified affair please be more careful."

"So sorry, sir."

Richard turned to the man on his right. "What do you think, sir? Have a rub. Ignore the stain."

"Feels nice," he responded demurely.

"Feels nice! Indeed! I picked up this fine article of French culture on my last trip to Paris. I know most of you won't ever get to Paris, but let me tell you, they know how to live over there, those French do!"

How odd, thought Lady Wallace, that someone who engendered so much fear and loathing, could so resemble an orangutan. His hair was not so much blond, as it was a shade of orange most had never seen. Frankly, like some horrible accident, it was hard to look away and yet this clownish man had everyone at the table acting as if they were in the presence of royalty. *Well, not for long,* she thought. With or without the buffoon at the other end of the table, she was determined never to suffer another humiliation in life.

"Had you ever thought of staying put when you were over there?" she asked, in a tone as sweet as honey. Lips pursed. Dinner plates clanked. She went on. "I ask only because it sounds like Paris was just a dream, the way you are describing it. Especially to us ladies who so love the latest fashion and to cultured gentlemen like yourself. Wouldn't you agree Mrs. Silvestri?" Mrs. Silvestri was the only one at the table not beholden to Richards and therefore not the least intimidated by him.

"Lady Wallace, it's nothing short of uncanny, how the exact same thought just now crossed my mind. Maybe I could find a lovely outfit like yours, Mr. Richards, for my Galen. And I would look just like a peacock when we returned with all them colorful hats, gowns and feathers I would just have to buy," she said through a flurry of giggles.

"Oh my," said Richards in mock surprise, "If I were a sensitive man, I would conclude that you two ladies are conspiring to get rid of me, which would be tragic, since I would miss this lovely, and dare I say, uniquely important occasion. However, I must agree, you would find Paris delightful, Mrs. Silvestri. I do hope you have the opportunity to visit, though I know how challenging it must be even to contemplate such an extravagance in these most unpredictable times."

Lady Wallace winced. She did not miss this slight and would not be outdone. "Aren't we the lucky ones, then, to have won out over gay Paris. I'm sure I speak for us all, when I say how much you brighten up any room fortunate enough to have you in it."

Richards reddened. The other guests shifted in their seats.

"What lovely peaches!" Exclaimed Mrs. Silvestri. "Ours are bigger and peachier looking, but there is just no taste."

Before The Lady could get another word out she was cut off by Jr. Wallace. "You probably ain't growin' em' in the right place, Mrs. Silvestri. Peaches are a funny fruit. They need lots of sun. They got to be cared for just like little babies."

"We know how to grow our peaches, Mr. Wallace," Mr. Silvestri responded coolly. "I can assure you."

"Then it must be the amount of sun we get, or the quality of the water, or who knows what," Lady Wallace interjected with some levity. "But thank you, Mrs. Silvestri. Please, have another."

"Thank you, my dear. And I must tell you I was so pleased to receive this invitation, even though there was hardly ANY notice. But I do understand that sometimes one cannot anticipate when the desire to bring together old friends completely overwhelms."

"I could not agree more," chimed in Richards, feeling the need to remind everyone that this whole affair was for his benefit. "I always look forward to seeing my friends and neighbors. There is always so much to catch up on. I want to say, again, how grateful I am to be included, and what a magnificent table you've set, Lady Wallace."

"Well, that's mighty fine of you to say, Mr. Richards," Jr. Wallace shouted out. "And you ain't even seen the brandy and cigars! Now there's a treat you'll be glad you didn't miss!"

"Let's not get ahead of ourselves, my dear," Lady Wallace said through a clinched jaw. "We have so much more of this lovely meal to make our through."

"To the Lady of the house!" Richards raised his glass. Everyone followed suit. "You continue to be a shining example of southern charm and gentility and I look forward to a most interesting evening."

Looking him directly in the eye with a slight smile and eyes that could slay a dragon she said,

"As do I. Mr. Richards. As do I."

He knew he would have her. Not tonight but soon. The thought had been with him from his first meeting with her. This evening the circumstances aligned. Other men's wives were no stranger to him. Lady Wallace would be the top prize. She was arrogant, critical, and proud, just like him. To break her would be his most delicious victory. When you held the purse strings, in the most fundamental ways, you held life. He had determined some time ago that another man's wife was so much more delectable than one's own, who could be so demanding and always... there. *"Lady Wallace was right"* he concurred. There was, indeed, so much more of this lovely evening to get through.

***

The commotion coming from the big house stood in sharp contrast to the stillness in Rev. R's airless cabin. The contemplative silence that he so proudly boasted of to T had become unbearable. He was now so easily distracted that a few minutes with his tattered bible was all he could muster. Inevitably T's presence would rush forward and thrush him into an emotional cauldron that made concentration impossible.

He thought, hoped, that Joraye and Miss Edna might still be up given the noise and decided to pay a visit. Joraye's presence had been a particular comfort with T gone, and he sensed she felt the same. His relationship with Miss Edna, in contrast, had become more complicated. Initially, he felt a gnawing anxiety every time he contemplated the reason for the change in behavior. But T's unyielding and infectious confidence soon made him hold his own head up when

257

he was around her. If she didn't feel the need to talk about it, then neither would he.

As he headed to Miss Edna's cabin, he could see lights blazing in the big house. There was talk of some kind of trouble that massa was in and this party was supposed to help. *Massa always seemed to be more in trouble than out,* he thought. As he approached Miss Edna's cabin, he couldn't see lights nor could he hear anything. Even without the activity at the big house this would have been a little early for them to turn in.

He considered waking them, dreading the possibility of, once again, being alone with his own miserable thoughts. He dismissed this idea and was about to turn around when he remembered that on some nights Miss Edna would go into the woods behind her cabin to forage, especially during a full moon, which there was tonight. Preferring a moonlit night to his own four dreary walls, he headed into the woods. As he walked, he realized why she liked to go out on a full moon; he had no trouble finding his way through the luminous darkness. The moon carved a path through the red maple and oak hickory that composed the land beyond the cleared acreage of the plantation.

"Miss Edna," he called out when he was deep into the thicket. When he got no reply, he decided that he might risk his safety to continue deeper into this uncharted territory and he started to retrace his steps.

"That you Rev.?" His heart skipped a beat.

His head swiveled anxiously around. "How you able to come up on me like that?! I didn't hear nothin'!" he said. Miss Edna stepped out from behind a tree.

"These woods my home. I know when somebody in my house. I don't say nothin' 'til I know it ain't somebody bad. Why you all the way out here lookin' for me?"

"I stop by yo' cabin to look in on you and Joraye, and when I see no lights and don't hear nothin' I remember you come out here sometime when the moon be full."

"You sure make a mighty effort to be neighborly, Rev.," she said with a raised eyebrow. "But I appreciate you thinkin' 'bout us." She started to walk and Rev. R followed.

"I be thinkin' Joraye might be with you, but I guess she go to bed early tonight."

Miss Edna stopped and took a breath before she answered. "Joraye at the big house tonight." She may as well have slapped him across the face.

"But you? I…"

"I know what I said! I know! But she safe, Rev., I promise you, she safe this time. She left with Simone who swear to look after her."

"But what 'bout yo' plan? Why don't it work this time?"

"It be The Lady that sent for Joraye, and she promise to see Simone get beat if she don't bring Joraye to the big house." Rev. R fell silent. "Simone say she keep Joraye close, far away from massa and I know she will. I can't let Simone get the whip and Joraye was with me on that. So she go. We pray before she go, Rev., so God got her in His bosom. I know she be safe."

Rev. R still did not respond. He closed his eyes and softly prayed. "Sweet Jesus, please wrap yo' daughter, Joraye, in yo' loving arms tonight and keep her from danger. In Jesus name we pray. Amen."

They moved on with Miss Edna leading the way. "I also be prayin' for T," she began after a few minutes of silence. "He be gone a while now and I hope God be keeping him safe. Joraye worry 'bout that too. You pro'bly worry 'bout the same thing," she added, not turning to look at him.

"He in my prayers too, Miss Edna, like you and Joraye."

"Oh, I know he be in yo' prayers." She began digging at a root and started to stab and thrust at the ground with the force of her pent up frustration from the last several months. "I know that for a while now. I know jus' how much in yo' prayers and in yo' life he be. One thing be clear, he got you in his mind in a strong way and I got to tell you Rev., it ain't the way of God." So, here it is, thought Rev. R. She continued, "He tell me 'bout you two and I be thinkin' he sent by the Devil, if not for Joraye. I see the way he truly love that girl and it real. Then he tell me he feel that way 'bout you too! Like he not afraid of God! I tell him maybe it be you that put those thoughts in his head. You supposed to keep folks away from Satan! How you gon' let this happen, Rev.?"

She had succeeded in voicing his darkest fears. "I pray every day and night for a cleansing, and it don't come. It don't come, Miss Edna. It like he got power over me that even stronger than God. The way he talk confuse me, Miss Edna, 'cause it sound right. But it not from God. I know it not. But it sound so RIGHT when he say it." He wiped away tears.

"He mix me all up too," Miss Edna said sympathetically. "He such a good man. Don't be drinkin', don't be gettin' into trouble. Be like magic what he do for Joraye. But God be clear 'bout men laying with men, Rev. Don't matter what T say. He even make Joraye think it right! You can't let him put her soul in danger too. You can't do that! You got to be the strong one. I know it be hard. He got power like I never see, and I know how strong you are for him. But you know in yo' heart it wrong. That what I see when I look in your heart. And that what God see too. He know the flesh be weak. But He also give you strength, you jus' need to ask Him for forgiveness and he make things right."

"Maybe God desert me, Miss Edna. 'Cause in my heart it don't feel wrong when me and T together. He say things 'bout God that I can't answer. Like maybe God put him on this earth for Joraye and me. T not scared to believe like that. He say, I give my life to God and maybe God give me somethin' back for all the good I do. Maybe that be true."

She grabbed his hands. "He give you the gift to deliver the gospel! That gift was with yo' daddy and now it with you. Ain't but a few folks be blessed like that! You able to bring peace and happiness where there be pain. That's what God give you. But this other thing? This other thing ain't nothin' but the Devil, no matter what T or anybody else say." Rev. R. bowed his head. Another thought occurred to her. "What yo' church think if they find out? You answer that question. That make you do what's right."

"I think 'bout that too."

"Then do what God want you to do and stop it!"

He shook his head. Utterly defeated. "I can't, Miss Edna, I can't. I feel like I got no control over this."

"God help us. You sound like you demon possessed," she whispered with real fear.

He continued shaking his head. His mind was a cauldron of competing truths. Finally he shouted, "No! No! No!" Miss Edna stepped back, stunned. "How you condemn me like you know what God be thinkin'? You don't! We all got our own relation to God. You don't know nothin' 'bout mine! Jus' 'cause you say God don't want me and T to be happy don't make it true! You don't speak for Him! I pray like you do! Jus' maybe He listen to me, like He listen to you! You go on and pray for yo' own soul. I be prayin' for it too. I also pray for mine. 'Cause T be right when he say maybe God bring us together, all three of us, and so I give thanks for what He bring me. I be grateful to God He bring me T."

"Miss Edna! Miss Edna!" The cry filled the night.

"That be Simone," Miss Edna said in a panic and pushed past Rev. R.

When Simone reached them, she blurted out, "Come quick! It Joraye!"

CHAPTER 41

Simone had been true to her word and stationed Joraye in an obscure part of the kitchen. The other women were cordial and protective, knowing that she was with child and being assured that she was not carrying a contagion of the mind and spirit. Joraye's anxiety stepped down a notch as she focused on a specific task. She spoke to no one and kept her head down.

While Lady Wallace soldiered on, the men followed Richards into the parlor for cigars and cognac. The ladies gathered for mints and sour candies in the front room. Perched on a divan, Lady Wallace waxed poetic about a hat she had recently purchased, "Oh, and the feathers are like watercolors. I only regret that there was not room for more."

"Why are you hiding it? We would certainly love to see it!" urged one of her guests.

"Perhaps I'll wear it to the next party or some such other special occasion."

"I don't know about these other ladies, but I can't wait until then! Oh, why not bring it down now, Lady Wallace? It would be such fun!" prompted Mrs. Silvestri to a chorus of agreements.

"Well, I suppose it could use a trip outside that dusty old closet. It's been such a long time," she demurred. She beckoned the closest female slave. "Go up to my room and look in my closet, toward the back for a yellow box with a, oh, you've never been up there have you?"

"No ma'am."

"But that idiot that lives with the witch is downstairs, isn't she? And she knows my room."

"What charming names!" interjected Mrs. Silvestri. "The idiot and the witch!"

"Poor thing was born with less than half a brain. At least the half she's got knows how to make divine desserts," said Lady Wallace.

"An idiot made the pecan pie? How delightful! You say she lives with a witch? This is turning out to be an evening I might never forget!"

"Lady Wallace turned to Simone. "Go fetch her from downstairs."

"Ma'am, I think she be working on somethin' else special downstairs, so I go find the hat right now. I listen to you real good and know right where it be."

"Are you disobeying me? I asked you to fetch the idiot woman and I will not ask again."

"Yes ma'am, I go right now," said Simone, and ran out.

As she passed the study, she overheard Jr. Wallace say, "He's weak. These abolitionists lead Fillmore by the nose. Any self-respecting southerner would never let a black baboon like Frederick Douglass give a 4th of July address, but he jus' goes and caves in." Simone prayed that he stay put until Joraye completed her task and was back in the kitchen. She dashed down the stairs and up to Joraye.

"You got to go upstairs, the missus want you." The knife Joraye had been using fell to the floor. Heads turned. "It only to get a hat out a closet then you come right back. It be easy, Joraye, you do it real quick."

"No, Simone, I don't go upstairs. That what we say!"

"I know what we say, and I tell her I find the hat, but she want you. You don't go up there, missus come down here, and there be some trouble. Just go and be quick about it. I ask the missus if you can leave right after 'cause we don't need you anymore. Please,

264

Joraye." She became a statue. "Please." They are at a standstill. The servants in the kitchen have all stopped moving. Some not breathing, as they waited for her response. She tenderly placed her hands on her belly and slowly moved towards the steps.

As she retraced Simone's steps, she passed the study and heard Richards say, "So, I can assume by your comments, Mr. Wallace, that you are not among those fortunate enough to actually hear the nigger speak?"

"Well, no," Jr. Wallace answered, a little unsteady, surprised that it was Richards who challenged him.

"Please don't get me wrong, sir," Richards offered in mock apology. "I agree, he is one of ugliest excuses for a human being I've ever seen. And I, too, am extremely disappointed that our President doesn't demonstrate more resolve when confronted by these heretics who call themselves abolitionists. But I also believe it's important to know what the enemy is up to. And I must say Mr. Douglass is smarter than your typical nigger and therefore extremely dangerous."

"Oh, here's the idiot now," said Lady Wallace, spotting Joraye.

"Can it speak?" asked a guest.

"Can you speak?" asked Lady Wallace

"Yes, ma'am."

"Well, there you have it, and that's about all you'll get," remarked Lady Wallace. "I need you to bring me that hat with the peacock feathers that's tucked away in my closet. Do you know the one I'm talking about?"

"Yes ma'am."

"It's in the same place it was when you last put it away. Do you remember where you put it?"

"Yes ma'am."

"She's just like a parrot!" laughed one of the guests.

"As I said, that's all you'll get." To Joraye she said, "Go on now and make sure the feathers are fluffed out before you bring it down."

"Yes ma'am."

As she headed up the familiar staircase, a firm grip on the railing was the only thing keeping her from collapsing. Memories of the savagery she experienced threaten to overwhelm her. She mumbled prayers and kept her head down, fearful she might see a demon leap out of the mildewed air. At the top of the stairs, she moved with purpose, desperate for the sanctuary behind the closed door of The Lady's bedroom. She went straight to the closet. She looked to where the hatbox should have been but wasn't. Her eyes darted from box to box until she saw it toward the back of the closet. She picked it up, took the hat out, and started to work with the feathers. Focusing on the task calmed her a bit and after a few seconds she was fully engaged.

She was running her hands across one of the feathers, when she heard voices in the hallway, directly in front of the bedroom door. One of the voices belonged to Jr. Wallace, and the closet door was wide open. She crept toward it, praying she could reach it without a sound. *Maybe they jus' stopped to talk,* she thought, as there could be little reason for two men to enter The Lady's bedroom. Just as she reached the closet door, the bedroom door opened. Jr. Wallace and Richards entered. At that moment, God put his hand on hers and silently closed the closet door.

Richards entered first and took in the space. "Yes, this will do just fine," he said and moved further in.

A confused and uncomfortable Jr. Wallace followed. "I want to respect your wishes, Mr. Richards,

266

but I'm not used to talkin' 'bout the business of men in my wife's bedroom. Why don't we go to my office? It's properly set up for a serious discussion. I've got some papers that I want you to see that demonstrate how serious I am about meeting my responsibilities to you."

"Oh, I have no doubt you are serious. Isn't that what this whole affair is about? To wine and dine and impress me into letting you keep this plantation?" Richards moved towards the Lady's bed and ended this speech sprawled across it, as if it were his own.

Wallace stared in disbelief. "That bed's my wife's, sir."

"I would hope so. It seems a little too womanly to be yours, though I've seen stranger things in Paris," he responded. He put his hands behind his head and rested on a perfumed pillow.

Wallace stole several glances toward the door. He was willing Lady Wallace to remain downstairs. She would be apoplectic to see Richards sprawled across her bed and give him a tongue lashing that would destroy any progress he hoped to make. "I can assure you my office is a lot more comfortable to talk business. There ain't nowhere to sit in this room except the vanity and the sofa," he said, referring to a fainting seat in the corner.

"If I were you, I'd choose the sofa, even though pink is not quite your color and please don't bother trying to move me again, Jr. We are where we will stay. So why don't you sit and tell me your story."

Wallace deflates, wipes sweat from his brow with a handkerchief, and takes a seat.

***

The closet was stifling, as the still air mixed with her sweat. Joraye vibrated with fear. She expected the door to be thrown open any minute and her life to end, but it remained closed. She started hyperventilating, almost to the point of passing out. She pressed her hands against the sides of her head. She squeezed her eyes shut and mouthed silent prayers to keep the madness at bay. She could hear muffled sounds. They were talking about The Lady. If she could just stay quiet until they left, she might escape with her life. She would barely breathe if it meant her survival. Then she felt the tiny feet of a rat scamper across her ankles.

***

"Once I sell the nigger, I'll have a good chunk of what I owe you. You just gimme a couple months extra and I can get you the rest, no problem." Jr. Wallace was sweating profusely. He imagined a firing squad positioned on The Lady's bed waiting for that final command. He stammered through the next bit. "We are respectable and proud people, we Wallace's are. Unfortunately, we in a bit of a rough patch right now. But, as you can plainly see, we have every intention of upholdin' our obligations."

"I appreciate you and your lovely wife. Trust me. I thoroughly enjoyed the delicious meal and hospitality. You have a spirited wife who knows the art of conversation. The problem I see with your well-thought-out proposition, Jr., is that it seeks to modify the contract without additional consideration Does it not?"

"Yes sir." Wallace shot back. "But, like I said, I have every intention of honoring my debt. I merely hoped you might be Christian enough to extend the deadline under the existing contract, as a courtesy. You said yourself, you think my plan is reasonable."

"I did, indeed, and I did not lie. But, as you can understand, I have my own financial responsibilities that depend on on-time payments from my clients. You are putting me in a difficult position, Jr., though I am inclined to consider your offer.

"You are a true Christian, Mr. Richards. Just like I told the Lady. I never had any doubts."

"I am a businessman. Which means, by nature, I am an opportunist. That said, I look to make my transactions beneficial to all parties. I can see how important it is to you and your wife to keep this property and continue to enjoy the social status your family has earned and holds so dear. I can also appreciate the willingness of you both to make the necessary sacrifices to do so."

Wallace cocked his head, alert to something out of sync.

***

With the speed of a striking snake, and enough force to loosen teeth, Joraye's hand flew to her mouth. She did not scream. The rat scurried across her feet, pausing and wriggling its nose, excited by the scent of fear and desperation permeating the air, before disappearing into darkness. Joraye felt she was losing the battle. She rocked back and forth with increasing speed. Her mumbling was getting dangerously loud, as the tight space became more like a tomb than a closet. They would eventually have to leave, she knew. And Lady Wallace would eventually wonder about her hat, but when? By that time, with her heart pounding loud enough to be heard beyond the closet door, it might be too lat

"We belong here, sir. I be most grateful if we come to an arrangement," said Wallace.

"And the The Lady?" Richards queried.

"The Lady?"

"Would she be most grateful, like you?"

"My wife and I are of like minds. Why you ask?"

"In any transaction, parties must be willing to negotiate. Men whose wives are also willing can often turn any transaction positive. But enough about business," he concluded, pleased to have set Wallace on edge. "We have some fine cognac and cigars lonely for our company downstairs. Let us go and oblige." As they rose, their heads snapped toward the closet. Did they hear a box fall? Richards looked at Wallace who was already moving toward it. He opened the door, to find Joraye cowering in the corner.

"I sorry massa! I sorry! Please don't hurt me, please!" Her arms covered her head in anticipation of the strike.

"What the hell you doin' in my wife's closet, you thievin' nigger!" he yelled and yanked her up. She stumbled into the room.

"You take care of that nigger!" hissed Richards and quietly left the room, just as Simone came up the stairs.

"I'll teach you to steal from white folks," Wallace said. He advanced on her.

"I jus' get a hat for the missus. Please massa, Oh, please !" She covered her head and backed away, urine spreading over the floor.

"Sweet Jesus," he said. He backhanded her across the face with all the pent-up rage meant for Richards. When she fell, her head hit the bedpost with a muffled thud. She landed on the floor and remained motionless, the carpet turning dark beneath her in seconds. The door burst open and Simone charged in.

"Joraye!" she screamed and rushed to her, "Oh Joraye, no!" she wailed as she cradled her bloody head. "What she do massa Wallace! Please, tell me what she do?"

"The nigger was trying to steal from the Lady's closet and I caught her. See what happens when you do wrong in my house?" he shouted back.

"What's this?" Lady Wallace stood in the doorway, hands on her hips.

"I caught her stealing out your closet and I taught her a lesson."

"I sent her up here to get my hat, you imbecile! What did you do? Kill her?" Wallace stared blankly down at Joraye.

"Oh, missus, I think she dead, Joraye be dead!" Lady Wallace sniffed the air.

"Good God! Did that idiot soil my good carpet?! Get her out! Now!"

Simone tried to lift Joraye by the shoulders but was clumsy and couldn't get a grip.

"Wait!" demanded the Lady "Put something under her head, to save what's left of my carpet." Simone desperately looked around, afraid to grab anything. The Lady read her mind. "Oh, for crying out loud. Just rip your dress up!" Simone grabbed the hem of her dress and violently ripped off strips and formed a pillow to put under Joraye's head. "The dining room door is closed," The Lady continued, "Get her out of here without disturbing my guests. Get some niggers from the kitchen to help you. Go. Go! I said" Simone fled.

Brushing back a few stray strands of hair, breathing heavily, Lady Wallace turned to her husband, "You go downstairs and report that one of our niggers has had an accident, and we are sending for a doctor. Did you hear me?"

"I thought she was stealin'," he mumbled.

"Wake up!" The Lady spat out."You can't go back downstairs looking like a convict. One of the niggers tripped and hit her head. That's what happened. Isn't it?" Wallace is still dazed. "Isn't it?" He nodded. "This is a disaster," she said as she stepped over Joraye's body and hurried out.

***

"What you mean it Joraye?" Miss Edna demanded.

"Hurry!" Simone yelled to Miss Edna and the Rev., as she led them out the woods.

"Simone, you tell me!"

"It bad Miss Edna. It real bad," she said through sobs. "Massa think she be stealin' from the Lady closet, but The Lady ask her to fetch a hat. He hit her and she fall on the floor in the Lady bedroom. I think she dead, Miss Edna. We got to hurry!"

"Dead?! What you mean, dead?!'"

"There be so much blood, Miss Edna."

"Simone, you take the Rev. And y'all bring her to me. And be gentle with her!" she called out after them.

As they approached the big house, the door was open. A male servant was standing in the doorway, frantically waving them in.

"Come with us, Lawrence," Simone instructed. He followed, closing the door behind them. When Simone opened the bedroom door, Rev. R. fell to his knees before the body.

"Jesus, sweet Jesus," Rev. R said, as he stared down at Joraye, laying in a pool of blood. Simone rushed over and cradled her head.

"Come!" She demanded and they sprang into action. Simone continued to support her head as they navigated the safest way to lift her.

"Be easy!" Rev. R whispered. They made the excruciatingly long journey down the stairs and out of the house, while the guests remained ensconced in their separate rooms, none the wiser. Once outside, they quicken their pace.

Miss Edna had spread a clean blanket over one of the straw beds. They gently lowered Joraye.

"I think he mean to kill her, Miss Edna. I see a man leave the missus bedroom right before this happen, and he look worried. I think somethin' happen in there, and they think Joraye know."

Miss Edna put her head to Joraye's chest. No one breathed. "She has life in her," she announced. There was a collective exhalation. "But that could change in a minute." She went to the stove and dipped a clean towel into some hot water, let it cool then wrung out the excess water before she started gently cleaning the wound. She worked in assured silence. She put some ingredients in a cup and poured hot water over them and let them steep. She then strained the mixture over a small amount of flour to create a poultice that she applied to the wound with a clean wrap. Rev. R., Simone and Lawrence watched the procedure without uttering a sound.

"Simone, you go tell massa she dead." They stared at her in stunned silence. "If he think she alive, he come after her. Her heart still be beatin' and she got breath, so she may live. We know in the morning, but he got to think she dead, so she be safe."

"But what we do she live?" asked Simone.

"She stay inside til' it come to me what we do. What I do know, she die, T kill massa, and then he be killed too."

"This happen 'cause of me, Miss Edna, Joraye die 'cause of me," Simone sobbed.

"Hush, child. This the Devil's work if I ever see it. You tried to save her is what you tried to do, Simone. You never forget that." Having counseled Simone, she continued on with the business at hand, "Tomorrow morning, we make a grave for her so he think we put her in the ground. Gather some folks and bring 'em to a spot in the woods. We make a show of laying her to rest, so massa think he rid of her. She be safe then."

They marveled in silence at the thoroughness and complexity of her plan.

"Before you and Lawrence go, gather 'round Joraye. Let's all put a hand on her while Rev. R pray." Everyone placed a hand on her.

"Jesus, my sweet Jesus, giver of life and breath, please, my Jesus, hear our plea for the life of yo' servant, Joraye," began Rev. R. "She come to you by the hand of the Devil, who would take her life and we come before you to say nay! He shall not prevail! You! You are the life and the light! You! Are the healer! You! Are the redeemer!"

"Yes, Jesus." Chimed in Simone.

"Yes Jesus!" Echoed Lawrence.

"We beg you, dear Lord, to shine yo' holy light on Joraye tonight, that she may be living proof of yo' power over Satan, and over death. You are the worker of miracles, sweat Jesus, and we humbly, with a deep, abiding love for our sister, Joraye, beg You to show us a miracle tonight. That we may say look what our Lord Jesus has done! Our Jesus b alive! Our Jesus be love! Our Jesus be mag-ni-fi-cent!"

"Yes," whispered Miss Edna. "Yes! Yes, my Jesus!"

"In His everlasting name, we pray. May you shine the light of life on our dear, sweet sister Joraye. Amen."

After a round of amens, Miss Edna said to Simone and Lawrence, "You best be going now. You know yo' story, Simone?"

"Yes ma'am. I know it well"

"Be sure and tell him we put her in the ground tomorrow. Don't forget."

"I won't. But I believe God gon' hear Rev. R's prayers," she said.

With only Miss Edna and Rev. R in the cabin, an uncomfortable silence filled the space. There was unfinished business between them. It was Rev. R. who broke the silence.

"I be goin' now, Miss Edna. I will pray and meditate on a miracle for Joraye."

"Yo' prayer was strong tonight, Rev. She in the best hands now."

"Thank you, Miss Edna. You been a faithful servant. I know God work through you to save her. God bless you and give you strength."

After he left she moved a large pot close to Joraye and got out a clean nightshirt and placed it next to the pot. She dipped a cloth in the warm water and began to clean the rest of her body. When Joraye woke up, she did not want her to find this soiled evidence of fear and desperation.

***

Simone went straight to the kitchen. Dirty dishes lay in climbing stacks. She put on an apron and joined in, hoping for the right moment to approach Jr.

Wallace. She walked into the study and started clearing plates. When Wallace saw her he stood and motioned for her to follow him out.

"She gone?" he asked.

"Yes, Massa Wallace. Miss Edna say she be dead," Simone answered, not having to pretend tears.

"Is she sure?" he challenged.

"She be sure, and also want me to tell you, that we gon' lay her to rest, first light tomorrow."

"You do that," he said, now strangely awkward. He was about to head back into the study, when he saw Richards heading his way. Simone rushed off.

"Looks like I'll have to replace that nigger thief, Mr. Richards. Seems she hit her head and died trying to get away."

"That is a tragedy, Junior. But such is the life of a thief.

CHAPTER 42

Miss Edna was startled into consciousness by loud knocking on her door. She put a hand on the right forearm of her inert charge then bowed her head in a silent prayer, grateful that she was still warm to the touch. While keeping watch, she had fallen asleep in a chair next to the bed. She felt stiff and out of sorts. Lawrence spoke through the door.

"Come on, Miss Edna. We goin' out to the yard now."

"You go on, Lawrence. I'll be there in time," she answered and slowly lifted herself out of the chair. She walked around to the head dressing and found very little blood on it. She carefully placed it back and started to prepare for the services.

***

Jr. Wallace also woke up out of sorts. He had planned the evening so carefully, with everything worked out to the last detail, only to have it explode spectacularly. He wondered, briefly, if the witch had put some kind of curse on him. This seemed plausible given the disastrous events. *And what was that last bit about my wife being grateful?* he wondered. He wondered as well how that would play into Richards' decision. Wallace was the first to admit that he and his wife didn't get along, but Richards was right to want some respect from the woman and not the bad feeling she gave him whenever he was around her.

He remained hopeful, since his proposal was not rejected outright, that they might not have to add another shameful chapter to his tome of failures.

Richards needed to think about it like any good businessman and then would see that it made sense. When he had given his wife what he though was the good news, she laughed outright and called him a fool for believing anything the man said or promised. But she had also thanked him because, even though it was unintentional, the impromptu wake gave her a chance to say goodby to a few her guest that she might actually miss.

He heaved his feet over the side of the bed and rubbed his face, hoping to kick-start his brain. He peeked out the window and noticed a small gathering of slaves. There was a makeshift cross stuck in the ground and he figured it must be for the funeral of that nigger that died the night before. If there was any good that came out of the night, that was it. There was no telling what she had heard. Even though she lacked a part of her brain, she could still let slip that she heard him begging to keep the plantation. That would further damage his reputation that was already on life support. As a bonus, Richards seemed pleased that he was able to take care of the problem so quickly. *Why didn't she just say something when they came into the room?* he thought. She could have easily explained that The Lady sent her up. He would have told her to get out and be done with it. Instead she had the guilty fright of a cornered criminal and he had every right to suspect her. Niggers were always stealing. None of them could be trusted. He didn't mean to kill her. He just needed to show her what happens to thieves. That she stupidly hit her head would not be on his conscious. *Well, that should discourage any of the others from stealing*, he mused. He turned his attention to more pressing matters.

A hole was dug then covered with a mound of dirt. With the addition of a makeshift cross, Joraye's grave looked passable. That was the extent of the funereal atmosphere. Miss Edna had let on that Joraye was on the mend, though not out of the woods. The overwhelming sense of relief prompted celebratory "amens" along with shouts of "praise Jesus" and hands raised skyward. She had to remind them that somber faces and a few tears would look more believable to massa and anyone else unaware of the ruse. The mention of massa had the intended effect and the mood shifted immediately. They joined hands around the makeshift plot and took the opportunity to continue prayers of healing. When the service was over, Miss Edna sent them off with a stern warning that Joraye's life would truly be in danger if anyone felt the need to gossip.

She entered her cabin to find Joraye as she had left her, stone still, but breathing. She had dealt with head wounds before and knew that blood, even a lot of blood, did not always indicate a worse outcome. The only way to know was to watch and wait and pray. She started building a fire and her thoughts went to Joraye's future, which included possibly losing the baby. She had no doubt if that were to happen, Joraye would very likely choose to follow the baby into heaven. She said a silent prayer and continued warming the cabin and preparing breakfast.

Who will this girl ever trust again? she wondered. Joraye went to the big house only because of Miss Edna's prayers and assurances that nothing bad would happen to her. Now she was clinging to life. Those horrible events would be proof of what she feared most, that no one could save her. Not Miss Edna, not Rev. R., not even T. At least in madness there was no pretense of hope or salvation. Its dark constancy left her with the expectation of life's horrors and seldom disappointed. If she determined her survival meant reclaiming the safety of hopelessness, it would be like losing another child for Miss Edna.

She shook off these dark thoughts with limited success as she went about her day, all the while keeping a close watch on Joraye and on the door. Her cabin had become like a secret prison on some angry, rocky seashore where every visitor would be treated with suspicion, all while Joraye was tucked away and out of sight. Fortunately, day moved into night with no surprise callers.

There was no change in her patient's condition. She was still breathing regularly, *but maybe too deeply,* thought Miss Edna. She feared that she might be in a state where death had not yet paid a visit but life was nonetheless moving on.

She was cutting up turnips and had gathered them in her hand to put them in the boiling water, when she heard a barely audible moan come from the other side of the room. A few turnips fell on the floor, as she rushed to the bedside.

"Be still, baby," she cooed and gently rubbed her cheek, "You in Miss Edna's cabin now."

Joraye opened her eyes. "Miss Edna?" she said weakly.

"Yes baby, girl?"

"I thirsty Miss Edna, real thirsty."

"I know you are. Here, take jus' a little sip." She held a cup to her lips.

"My head hurt real bad. Why my head hurt, Miss Edna?"

"I know, I know it do, baby. I put some medicine in the water. You feel better in a bit." Joraye took a sip. "Can you drink jus' a little more?" Joraye nodded and Miss Edna helped her take another sip. "That better?" She tried to sit up. "Oh no, baby, you keep still." Joraye flinched. "Let that medicine take some of the pain away. It won't take long, jus' let it do its work. You feel much better."

"He hit me, Miss Edna. I remember. He hit me," Joraye said. Tears streamed down her face. "You promise I be alright, Miss Edna. You promise, but he beat me. He maybe kill my baby!" Her sobs grew powerful. Miss Edna moved to comfort her, but Joraye turned away.

"I know, Joraye. You right to turn away after I promise you be safe. But you know I die if I thought somethin' like this happen after we pray 'bout it. Guess the Devil be so powerful in that house he always find a way. But I swear you never go back there again. You ain't got to forgive me, but I hope you can see how I be tryin' to keep you from harm since you come to me, 'cause I feel for you like you my own. You also need to know yo' baby still inside you. God be workin' hard to keep it safe, and I be sayin' special prayers too." She paused to wipe away her own tears. "This so hard for me, Joraye, to think I let this happen to you. It cut me deep, and I tell you, it put me in my grave I lose you now."

Joraye calmed as she listened to Miss Edna. Then she tentatively reached out for her. "I want my baby. Please, Miss Edna, I can't lose my baby," she cried.

Miss Edna held and rocked her. "I know. God know too. That why the baby still inside you. We gon' keep prayin' and you jus' keep believin'." Joraye nodded. "Nothin' but love be here, and it be powerful."

Joraye was asleep almost as soon as she closed her eyes. Miss Edna patted her arm and knelt in prayer. This is why she would never forsake her God. He could deliver miracles. The rest of the night Joraye, fell into a deep and uneventful sleep. Her breathing was slow and steady, as she continued to move further from danger.

Miss Edna watched her sleep, she tried to imagine what had happened. She was able to pick up bits and pieces from Simone, who made it clear that her life was in danger, should Jr. Wallace discover she was alive. But why? What had she seen or heard that would make Jr. Wallace want to kill her? She would not ask Joraye to repeat it. Whatever devilment those white men were up to, they could take to their separate hells. She had far more important matters to tend to, like what to do with Joraye. How would she be able to keep her forever hidden from Jr. Wallace? She would be in grave danger if he found out she was alive. Miss Edna Knew this in her bones. She also knew she was not going to let that happen. She wasn't sure how, but not knowing something had never been a hindrance before. What she did for a living had made her nothing if not resourceful.

***

She woke with a start, in what seemed to her like a few minutes when, in fact, the sun was peeking through her door. What jolted her awake were the seeds of a plan. It would be dangerous, maybe impossible, but it would guarantee their safety.

The sun threw light on Joraye, who was still sleeping comfortably. As Miss Edna looked on that peaceful face, her plan seemed too cruel to contemplate, but she knew it was the only way if she and her baby were to survive. Joraye might even think of it as some sort of cruel joke, but it was no joke. It was the only way.

A gentle knock shook her out of her thoughts and put her immediately on edge. She walked up to the door and whispered, "Who there?"

"It Rev. R, Miss Edna." He announced softly. She opened the door and put her finger to her lips to indicate that he should be quiet.

"How she be?" he whispered.

"That be you Rev.?"

They turned to see Joraye struggling to sit up.

"Praise Jesus!" he practically shouted as he rushed to the bed. "Yes, it me, Joraye." He took her hand. "The Lord bring you back to us, jus' like I knew He would!"

Joraye smiled weakly. "Yo' prayer be strong, Rev.," she said.

Miss Edna moved to the bed. "Be careful, baby, yo' head might still be strange."

"It be much better," she said then added, "I need to tell you somethin' Miss Edna." She looked over at Rev. R and dropped her head. There was silence for a moment, and then Rev. R understood they wanted a private moment and stepped outside. Miss Edna called him back in.

As Miss Edna led her back to bed she said, "I want to sit, Miss Edna. Been too long on my back."

"Ok, but if yo' head don't feel right, you let me know and you go right back to bed." Joraye nodded and sat slowly.

"You be looking strong, Joraye. You be proof that God still work miracles," said Rev. R.

Joraye smiled and started contemplating her hands. She asked, "When T comin' back?"

"Soon, sweetheart, real soon," Miss Edna answered, not knowing what else to say.

"He be real mad he know what happen," Joraye added.

"You don't need to be thinking 'bout that right now."

"That man Richard's, he be talkin' somethin' 'bout business. Then he talk 'bout the missus and massa got real scared. Massa know I hear it. That why he hurt me. I think I die in that closet. I try not to even breathe, but he open the door and grab me."

This report ended in shuddering sobs. She wrapped her arms tightly around herself and started to rock.

Miss Edna knelt beside her. "I told you he not gon' hurt you now. Look who be here. It be me and the Rev. and T be back here real soon. You with folks who love you and gon' protect you. The Devilment in that house be over for you now."

"God brought you back to us 'cause He got work to do with you, Joraye. You be special in is His eyes and that what you got to believe," added Rev. R gently. She quieted.

"You want me to make you somethin' warm to drink?" asked Miss Edna. Joraye nodded.

Rev. R continued. "You know, I see folks have trials in they lives that you can't begin to know, Joraye, and you know what put they mind at ease?" She shook her head. "They give all that worryin' and all that fear up to God. He got a plan of salvation for His believers. Like I say, he got a plan for you too. He plucked you out of Satan's hands for a reason and don't you ever forget that. You in THIS house now. Let me tell you the spirit of God be strong and alive in here. Do you believe that?" She nodded. "So you ain't got nothin' to concern yo'self with when it come to the big house. Like Miss Edna say, all you got to do now is let God keep on makin' you better, like He been doin'."

He turned to Miss Edna, "I also hope God be tellin' Miss Edna to be makin' us more than jus' warm milk. I don't know 'bout you, Joraye, but I got more than a little appetite right now." Joraye smiled.

"See now Rev., God jus' be continuin' to answer prayers, 'cause He bring me yo' head to crack these eggs on," said Miss Edna. This quip got a hearty laugh out of them both. "Y'all laugh all you want, but bring yo' hard head over here, Rev. so I can get to work." She warned Joraye, "You don't want to laugh too loud, baby. Can make yo' head start hurtin' again. Best you be real quiet for a while. I'm gon' make us all a little breakfast, and we gon' have us a little celebration of God's presence in this house. How that sound?"

"That sound good, Miss Edna. Guess I do be hungry."

When breakfast was over, Miss Edna said that she and the Rev. needed to go for a short walk. This did not go over well. Joraye was terrified to be alone. Only after several minutes of reassurances were they able to leave. For good measure they waited until she was asleep.

***

The silence stretched on as they walked. The events of the last few days had overshadowed their argument. Now that they were alone together, it was the elephant in the room looking startled that no one noticed him.

Miss Edna was first to speak. "Looks like God hear yo' prayer."

"He hear all our prayers, Miss Edna. We all sinners." Time was short. She got to the point.

"I be thinkin' 'bout what to do, now she better."

"Simone say massa come after her, if he found out she be alive," Rev. R said.

"I believe he would too, so I be thinkin' 'bout a way to get her out. That what I want to talk to you 'bout.

What I be thinkin' be scary for her, but it be the only way to get her past massa. She can't be runnin' through no swamps with dogs chasin' after her and Lord knows what else. She lose that baby for sure."

"She be with child?"

Miss Edna nodded. "It early but she start to show real soon," she replied. "She afraid he leave her, she tell him. All her hurt don't make her think like she should. She 'bout to kill it, before we talk. Now she got a strong love for it."

"God bless you, Miss Edna. T gon' love you for what you done. Miss Edna gave a slight nod. But you say you be thinkin' 'bout something?"

"You hear of Mista' Kincaid?"

"I hear 'bout him from T."

"Well, he also buy medicine from me that get put on the wagon that go into town. I be makin' up some potions and such for him right now. Massa be makin' a trip into town in four days. That how we get Joraye out."

"How you figure to hide a full-grown woman Miss Edna? Ain't no place on that wagon you can do that?"

"This where I need your help Rev. Joraye ain't gon' like what I be thinkin'. You neither, but ain't no other way, and you got to make Joraye see it too. I be thinkin' that we put her in the box that I put the medicine in. It fit her right and nobody be thinkin' she in there. Then once we get to town, I convince Mista' Kincaid to take her. He a good man, and T told us how he be treated like family when he with Kincaid."

He stopped walking. "Miss Edna, she ain't gon' want to be put in no box like that. She feel like she in a coffin. You see the way she be right now. She ain't gon' want to do this. Also, she be Massa Wallace property. Mista Kincaid be stealin' her, if he keep her."

"I know it got problems but there ain't nothin' else that come to me, and time be runnin' out. I tell Mista Kincaid she die, he don't take her."

"You also gon' have to get her to leave T behind," he added. "That be a bigger mountain than that box. She not gon' want to go nowhere without him."

"I be thinkin' 'bout that too, and ain't nothin' to do 'bout it if Joraye want to live, and that's what we tell her. No way she able to raise T's baby here with massa ready to kill her. And you know, sure as I standin' here, once T find out she with Kincaid, he find a way to get to her. Don't know how yet, but we both know he find a way."

"The only way that happen is if he run, and he as good be killed, as make it to Joraye, and she gon' know that."

"He won't have to run. I think of a way to get Joraye away from here, I also think of a way for T. I got more time to think on that, but we got to get Joraye gone from here now, and that box be a problem. You got to help me with that, Rev. It gon' take all our powers."

"Between you, me, and God, we make this work, Miss Edna."

CHAPTER 43

"We was movin' along one minute then the wheel dropped into this hole and broke clean off, sir." Logan, one of Kincaid's white hires, explained the separated wagon wheel that lay on the ground.

"Looks like the whole hub separated from the axle. Must have been quite a hole," noted Kincaid.

"Yes, sir. Was covered up with some twigs and leaves and we run right over it."

"Can you fix it?"

"To do it right, we need to get it to a smith. I did see this happen once before. They just knocked out the hub and rigged somethin' until they could get it fixed proper."

"I'll find someone going into town that you can ride with. In the meantime, see what you can do."

"Yes, sir."

That was several days ago. No one came to the rescue. At his desk, Kincaid prepared for his trip to Owenton in the now unlikely event that it was still on. Miss Edna had teased him with some new remedy that could help folks breathe better when their lungs were bad. She said it was some necklace and claimed it worked wonders. He was looking forward to adding it to his medicine chest.

There was a polite tap on the door before it opened. Rabbit bounded past Tommie and placed his head on Kincaid's thigh. Kincaid answered with the requisite ear scratch. Rabbit snorted his satisfaction.

"Don't just stand there staring. Come in," Kincaid gestured for his daughter to enter.

"Did they fix it?" she asked, clearly anxious.

288

"Not yet. But they tell me it should be ready for the trip."

"Ok," she said before turning to make her escape.

"Anything else you want to tell me?"

"I'm almost done. I promise I won't miss nothin' else before we go."

"Anything."

"Huh?"

"You won't miss anything else before we go. This happens again and you won't be going on the next trip."

"Mrs. Gloadstone is just mean, Daddy. Everybody says so."

"Did you miss two assignments in a row or not?"

"Guess so," she said to the floor.

"Mean or not, she has every right to expect you to get your work in on time. Doesn't she?"

"Yeah."

"I want to see those assignments before we go."

"I'll get 'em done."

"Good, 'cause I like you riding with me."

She kissed him. "Come on Rabbit," she said with urgency. Rabbit opened one eye indicating he had heard. But he wasn't about to move as long as Kincaid continued scratching. "I said, come on, Rabbit." She grabbed his collar and he waddled out, triumphant.

Kincaid had put them on the delicate journey to normalcy which meant scaling back expectations and responsibilities. He wasn't sure how much pressure would be too much and kept a close watch, ready to pull back even more if necessary. So far, Tommie had risen to the challenge and benefitted from the tonic effect that routine provided. Still, she was right about Gloadstone. The milk of human kindness had curdled some time ago in that one. Any show of empathy was a check the box exercise that belied her true nature. But she still had the right to insist her students meet their responsibilities and it was time that Tommie met her's. He loved these outings with her and looked forward to them with as much anticipation as she did, *but I have to show her I mean business,* he resolved and committed, once again, to standing firm.

These trips also offered the possibility that Tommie might see T, which Kincaid had started to question. She would be thrilled with the wave or nod of acknowledgement they might share, only to become pensive and sulking on the ride home. He wasn't sure if these emotional highs and lows did more harm than good, but that would be over soon enough, if all worked according to plan.

His tentative attempt at parental discipline would be moot if the wagon wasn't fixed. A few neighbors had offered the use of theirs, but so far no one delivered on their proposed generosity. It would be difficult, but he could skip this trip if need be. There were no immediate health emergencies, even though this could change in a heartbeat. Tommie would be disappointed but not surprised given her knowledge of the wagon. All in all, he figured there would be little to lose if he didn't make this trip.

CHAPTER 44

Joraye slowly improved. The day after Rev. R's visit, she was more confident navigating the cabin unassisted. Her head hurt less, but there were still sudden dizzy spells. Miss Edna gently explained what she had done after she was brought to the cabin and Joraye was initially appalled.

"People be thinkin' I dead? What if T find out?"

"No way he find out. I put the fear o' God in folks. They don't say nothin'. They be lookin out for you too." Even as she comforted Joraye, she was glad to be getting her away from the place. She knew it was just a matter of time before the big house found out. Joraye could stay jailed up in the cabin for only so long. Miss Edna assured her that she would not have to live like this much longer. while revealing nothing about her plan. She assured her that all would be revealed at dinner that evening with Rev. R.

***

"Every day you look more like yo'self," Rev. R said as he walked over and gave Joraye a cheek peck. "I ain't never see nobody turn 'round so fast."

"Thank you Rev. I do be feelin' better."

"And I can tell Miss Edna be doin' some conjurin' in the kitchen that make grown men weep," he said, attempting to keep the mood light, mindful of what was coming.

"You hold back those tears and come get busy. Take that pot off the fire and put it on the table," Miss Edna instructed instructed. Once the pot was moved, they took their seats, Rev. R blessed the food and they started in.

"Jus' like I be sayin', forgive me if I starts to weep," he said, after a spoonful of the stew.

"It be real good, Miss Edna," Joraye concurred.

"Thank you both. I 'preciate it," she said, more subdued than usual. "So, baby, I want you to listen to what the Rev. and me been talkin' 'bout. We got a plan that gon' make you safe but you gon' need to be brave to make it work." Joraye became wary at the abrupt seriousness of Miss Edna. She could tell that something was making her nervous and this put Joraye on edge, but she signaled for Miss Edna to continue. "We talk 'bout what happen in the big house, and how massa come after you, he know you alive." Joraye looked down and was silent. "Well, the Rev. and me believe the only way to keep you and yo' baby safe, be to get you off this plantation and away from Massa Wallace."

"What? How you do that, Miss Edna? And what 'bout T?"

"I know it don't sound like nothin' you be thinkin' 'bout, Joraye, but listen to what Miss Edna be sayin'. She pray on it and be usin' her wisdom to think of a way to keep you and the baby safe," added Rev. R, hoping his support might comfort her. Instead, it tapped into a fear that had been haunting her all day.

"But it don't move, Miss Edna! My baby don't move!" she wept. Miss Edna turned toward her and took her hands.

"But it still with you, Joraye. That's what you need to know. As long as that baby still with you, God be havin' a plan for it."

"He workin' to keep yo' baby safe," said Rev. R, "but you got to be safe too. That all Miss Edna tryin' to do. To make sure you stay safe to raise yo' baby."

Miss Edna and Rev. R shared a glance that signaled they were on their way to potential disaster. Miss Edna took a deep breath and continued.

"Too much can happen that we can't even know right now, if you stay here. You never be free from worry."

"But what if T don't want to go?" she asked. "Why you look at each other like that?"

"This the part where we need you to be brave, Joraye," Miss Edna said quietly. "We ain't got time to wait for T to get back."

"But you said he comin' back soon. That what you said!"

"He is, Joraye, but we can't wait. We got to do somethin' now."

"Do what now?"

"You hear T talk of his old massa, Mista' Kincaid?"

"He say he good to him. He say he buy him back one day, but T don't believe it. Why you ask?"

"T tell Rev. and me he be good too. So we be thinkin', he be good to you too, he find out you T's woman."

"No! I not goin' no place without' T!"

"That what I know you say, Joraye. I tell Miss Edna the same thing," Rev. R said. "But listen. We got to use what the Lord give us, and He give us this chance now. Miss Edna be thinkin' what be good for everybody. Think 'bout this, Joraye, when T find out what happen, you know he want to go after massa. He be killed he do that, and you know it. It better you not here and be safe. Massa can't get to you, he don't know where you be.

Miss Edna took over, "T like Mista' Kincaid. He take good care of you. He also know he got to stay alive he ever want to see you again. I swear we get T to you as soon as it be safe." Joraye grew pensive. She pondered what was proposed but was not convinced.

"But T be real mad, he know I leave without him. He never leave without me."

"He a man, Joraye. It different for men. They be strong. He can fight and protect hisself. We tryin' to protect YOU now. Ain't you think that what he want us to do?"

Joraye looked from one to the other with resignation, nodded. "But how you get me to Mista' Kincaid without Massa Wallace know?"

Miss Edna rose from her seat and moved to the bed. "Come here, baby," she said, and patted the bed. Joraye didn't move. "Come, Joraye. Everything we talkin' 'bout give you and yo' baby a chance at life." Joraye rose slowly and joined Miss Edna. "You know massa going into town in a few days. And you know how you help me prepare medicine to give to Mista' Kincaid, which we put in that box." She indicated the box in the corner. Miss Edna looked down at Joraye's hands then met her eyes. "Well, sweetheart, that box be yo' way to freedom."

"What?!" She leapt up as if the soft bed had become a hot stovetop. "You can't be thinkin' to put me in no coffin, Miss Edna!"

"Ain't no coffin, Joraye! It jus' a box to get you outta here and I give you somethin' to sleep so you not even know you in there. You go to sleep and wake up safe with Mista' Kincaid. Oh, Joraye, you think I want to do this? I wish you could jus' walk down the road in full daylight. But you can't! And you not able to run through no woods while you be with child." She looked to Rev. R for support.

"What you think we be doin' here, Joraye?" he asked gently. "We all be tryin' to come up with the best way to get you outta' here before massa find you. If you got some way you think be good, let's talk 'bout it. Miss Edna say what she think be best. But it be you in that box. We do somethin' else you think it be better. We jus' ain't got time to waste."

A long silence followed.

"You say I be asleep while I be in there?" Joraye asked cautiously.

"Yes, baby, you not even remember the trip when you wake up, and I be watchin' over you the whole way. I swear you be safe.

"What if massa look inside before we leave?"

"In all the time I be takin' medicine to Mista' Kincaid, he ain't never look inside. All he care 'bout is he get paid."

"How you plan on T gettin' to me?"

"We got time to worry 'bout T, but massa leave in two days and you need to be on that wagon."

"What 'bout you, Rev.?"

"I told you I think it be a good plan."

"I mean, when you come?" Miss Edna and Rev. R register their confusion.

"What you mean by that, Joraye?" he asked.

"I mean, when you come to be with me and T? He say you be our family, and he be strong 'bout it. I know he not gon' want to leave you behind. He be real sad you not with us." Rev. R stole a glance at Miss Edna, who would not meet his eye.

"Well, Joraye, we all feel like we be family, you, me, T and Miss Edna," he began, not sure where to take this. "But this between you and T and yo' baby. Miss Edna and me work to make sure you be together. I got real strong feelings for T. He be a friend to me like no one else ever be. But my callin' be here."

"That what T say 'bout you too, Rev. He say you like a friend he been wantin' and ain't never found before. He say he got you right here," she put a hand on his heart. R looked down. When he looked back up, he made no attempt to hide the tears.

"Then I be the luckiest man on earth, and T and me, we have a real long talk when he get back, Joraye. It hurt me we can't all be together, but I make him know we always be family, even though he be with you and I be here. God call me to minister to these folks here, Joraye. This be my flock, and I jus' can't turn my back on 'em."

"Rev. be right," Miss Edna added gently. "We still got souls that need savin', right here. We be needin' him to keep our faith strong like his daddy did. Like the Rev. say, we always be prayin' and thinkin' 'bout you and T." Suddenly, Joraye's eyes got big and her hands shot to her stomach.

"What's wrong, baby?" Miss Edna raised her voice in alarm.

"It move! Miss Edna! My baby! It move!" Her eyes were wide with fear and shock.

"Oh, Miss Edna, it my baby, my baby!" she rocked and caressed her stomach.

"Praise JE-SUS!" Miss Edna exclaimed through her own tears. She grabbed Rev. R's hand, their differences taking a back seat to this miracle.

Rev. R. prayed, "We give thanks to You, Almighty Jesus, we give thanks, maker of miracles and savior of man!"

"Yes, Jesus!" Miss Edna responded.

"For saving this baby, Yo' baby! That will forever be a testament to Yo' majesty and power! We give our lives to You! We give thanks to You and in great and Almighty Jesus' name we pray, amen."

Quietly Joraye announced, "I think I be ready now, Miss Edna. I got to save T and me's baby. So I do what you say."

The first time in the box did not go well. All of Joraye's fears of being entombed came screaming forward and only the thought of keeping the baby safe gave her the strength to try.

"Come lay on the bed," Miss Edna instructed Joraye. When Joraye was on the bed, Miss Edna sat beside her.

"Okay, now close yo' eyes." Joraye did. Then silence. And more silence. After a few minutes, Joraye opened her eyes.

"What you want me to do, Miss Edna?"

"Nothin'. How you feel right before you open yo' eyes?"

"Like I was 'bout to go to sleep."

"That what I want you to do. Jus' what you did now. Soon as you lay down in the box, close yo' eyes and think you in the bed and jus' breath like you was doin'. I give you the medicine to help you sleep right before you get in the box, and I promise you be sleep before you know it."

By the end of the day Joraye felt ready. But this was only the first part of the plan that had to fall into place, it was also not the most critical. Even if they managed to get her to Owenton undetected, Kincaid had to agree to take her. Even though he was a man of indisputable character, everyone has his limits. He had to be willing to put himself in danger. Joraye was the legal property of Jr. Wallace. If he refused there was no contingency plan.

***

The day of Joraye's macabre journey to freedom had arrived, complete with all the trappings of rising from the dead. Everything was going to plan. Before Joraye was placed in the box, Rev. R drilled several discreet holes in the lid to ensure she would get enough air. Miss Edna made sure that Joraye was sleeping comfortably before four strong slaves who were in on the ruse carried the box to the wagon. She was now sitting on a bench beside it, waiting for the journey to start. If this were like all the other times, Samson or Jr. Wallace would hop up front and they would be on their way. If this was the one day that they decided to check the box, then lives would probably end.

Miss Edna straightened her skirts, played with her necklaces and did anything else with her hands to relieve her anxiety. Finally, it was Jr. Wallace who climbed up and took the reins. *Praise Jesus,* thought Miss Edna, they were on their way. She allowed herself only the tiniest bit of optimism knowing that a thousand things could still go wrong.

"Wallace!" Miss Edna sat bolt upright. They turned their heads to see The Lady standing on the porch. He pulled to a stop. "One of the kitchen niggers burned her hand. Tell the witch she needs to get her something for it." Miss Edna stood up trying hard not to look like the trapped animal she felt.

"Go on, then, and be quick about it. We ain't got time to waste." Paralyzed with fear, she didn't move. "Didn't you hear me! Go!"

"Yes massa." She stumbled out on legs that threatened to fail her at any minute. She forced herself to control her breathing, just as she instructed Joraye and hoped it would also control the trembling. Every cell in her body was telling her not to look back toward the wagon, even though she was desperate to ensure that Wallace remained up front. But it could be this small thing that aroused suspicion and send him to the box.

"Come on, then," coaxed The Lady, as Miss Edna took advantage of her age to slow her progress.

"Think this might it, missus." Lady Wallace turned as a female servant approached her holding a small bag.

298

"Go down and show her," Lady Wallace commanded.

She moved past The Lady. "This be it, Miss Edna?"

"That's it, Monique. Put some of that olive oil with lime water and be careful. Burns be extra painful."

"I be careful, Miss Edna," Monique said and returned to the house.

With a sudden spring in her step, Miss Edna returned to the wagon. It took will power summoned from her Jesus not to collapse on the top of the box. As it was, she had to lean on it for a minute to catch her breath before returning to the bench. When the house was firmly behind them Miss Edna shifted her position to block Jr. Wallace's view. She gingerly slid the lid open just enough to give Joraye even more air.

***

While Miss Edna rode nervously in the back of the wagon, Kincaid was informed that his wagon was still not repaired. Seemed that axles were in short supply with the ever-increasing influx of homesteaders and dreamers. All would not be lost, though. Knowing of this possibility, he had come up with what he hoped would be a satisfying alternative for his heartbroken little tomboy.

Yatesville Lake was about two hours away, and it was famous for its excellent fishing. It was one of her favorite things to do and it might still be warm enough for a swim. T had the wisdom to suggest that she get back into the water as soon as possible after the accident. He explained that if she didn't, she might be too scared to ever get back in. As a result, she was an even stronger swimmer. This trip to Yatesville would do just fine, Kincaid concluded, mostly because of the journey. For him, the most valuable part of their trips into Owenton was the opportunity for an unhurried conversation with his daughter. So they would pack a picnic basket, saddle up a couple of horses, and be on their way to a great day of swimming and fishing.

A great day of fishing did not sit well with Rabbit. He wanted to go to town. When he saw them working on the wagon the night before, he jumped in the back and spent the night, lest they get some evil idea to leave him. When there were no preparations to leave in the morning, he trotted purposefully up to house and barked a few times to get some movement. Time was wasting. When it became clear they were not going, he followed everyone around wondering how they were going to make it up to him, and then he heard "boat". He liked "boat" and was now trotting alongside the horses ready for his own day in the sun.

Before they set out, Kincaid decided to send a single rider to town with a couple of empty saddlebags and instructed him to bring back whatever he could carry. *No need to make Miss Edna's trip an entire waste*, he thought. He was confident she would be able to sell whatever remained and if not he would make her whole on the next trip. Satisfied, he did what he could to remedy the situation. They set off to the lake.

***

Miss Edna kept a watchful eye on Joraye. They had another half hour to go and her breathing remained steady and deep. But Miss Edna was fearful for the baby. She would not express her concerns to Joraye. *She may have a perfectly healthy baby. Lord knows she deserved the special joy she was feeling now,* thought

300

Miss Edna. Nevertheless, she knew some babies born to mothers that had been through what Joraye experienced were sometimes born "not right". Some were slow and others had various physical ailments. There was simply no way to tell. She was nervous that Joraye was unconscious for a time. That was unusual and concerning, but the baby was alive. God seemed to be listening to their prayers, so far. She held out hope that He would continue. She had no concern about what she gave her to help her sleep. This was the same dose she had given other mothers with child when they got beside themselves, and their babies had come out just fine.

She also did not have a moment's doubt that getting Joraye off the plantation was the only thing to do. There could only be discovery and death if she stayed. All the unanswered questions regarding her future with Mista Kincaid would have to be put in the hands of the Lord. As she stared down at Joraye, she was jolted with the realization that she might never see her again. In their desperation to get her to safety, it had been a passing thought and now landed heavily. Memories of her stolen children came rushing up and she wiped away tears that threatened to turn into a flood as she thought about also losing Joraye.

She was pulled back to the present because the wagon slowed. Following her own advice, she took a few deep breaths to calm herself and prepare for this next critical task. Since Kincaid had a shorter distance to travel, he usually arrived first.

"Looks like we beat the little bastard this time," Jr. Wallace shouted toward the back of the wagon. He pulled up to a hitching post with several other wagons.

"What'd you say, massa?" Miss Edna asked, poking her head out.

"I said Kincaid ain't showed yet. I ain't waitin' round for him. If he takes too long, you best look for someone else to buy your witch's brew."

"I know he be here, massa. He ain't never missed comin' out," she said, nervously scanning the street.

"I'll be in there," he said, indicating the saloon. "You call me when he gets here."

"I will massa." Wallace disappeared into the saloon. One of the two slaves that had been riding with her asked in a near panic, "What we gon' do now, Miss Edna?"

"Let me think!" She barked back.

"Miss Edna, somebody be comin." In the distance, a wagon was making its way slowly down the street. It was too far to make out any details. They all stared anxiously. After a minute Miss Edna said, "That ain't Mista' Kincaid wagon," and they went back inside.

The box started to take on the funereal presence they had been trying to avoid. They stared at it in silence. No one dared articulate what hung in the air. The atmosphere grew thick and claustrophobic. There had always been only one option and now that it might be gone, the world had just turned sideways. It was simply unbelievable that in all the time Miss Edna had been selling to Kincaid, this would be the one time he did not show up. Joraye would be lost if she had to return to Wallace and the baby might not survive if Joraye took more of the sleep tonic. They were all looking at Miss Edna for guidance.

She was about to speak when someone shouted, "You in there, Miss Edna?" From darkness to light in seconds, as they recognized the familiar voice of Kincaid.

"Oh, yes! Mista' Kincaid, we in here!" She shouted back, almost falling out of the wagon, in her haste to get out. "And I got everything you asked for," she said as she straightened up next to him. "Boys, go on and put that box in Mista' Kincaid new wagon."

"Hello, Miss Edna," said Tommie, "T come with you today?"

"I sorry, baby, but he don't make it today. He told me to tell you, that he see you next time." She shared a look with Kincaid.

"Can you let him know I asked after him?"

"I will Tommie, and he be glad to hear it."

"Can I go now, Daddy?"

"Go on. Be back here in an hour." She hopped off the wagon and Rabbit followed.

"Everything alright with T? You seem a little anxious, Miss Edna."

"We jus' a little worried, when we not see yo' wagon," she replied.

"Truth be told, we almost didn't make it. Broke a wheel on my wagon. We were going to spend the day fishing. If that Harris boy didn't catch us to let us know we could use his father's wagon, we would be fishing right now. T is alright?"

"He still not be back yet. We be sayin' our prayers for him."

"Something on your mind, Miss Edna? You don't seem like yourself today."

"Mista Kincaid, terrible things be happenin' over at Massa Wallace place," she began quietly.

"Go on."

"It hard for me to know where to begin other than to say it not only medicine you got in that box."

"What are you saying, Miss Edna?" His anxiety rose. She did not answer. She walked to the back of his wagon and was helped up by one of the slaves. Kincaid

303

followed. She went over to the box and slid open the lid.

"Good God!" Kincaid's hand flew to his mouth. "Why, in God's name, did you bring a dead girl all the way out here?"

"She not dead, Mista' Kincaid. She sleep. But she be dead she stay over at Massa Wallace place. That why I bring her to you."

"What do you mean, 'bring her to me'?"

"Mista' Kincaid, she T's woman and she be with child." The color drained from Kincaid's face. "That why I think to bring her to you, 'cause massa think she dead already, or else he kill her for sure. T always talk 'bout how Christian you be."

"For God's sake! Get her out of that coffin!" He demanded.

"I don't want to do that if you can't take her." Miss Edna said, with a slight challenge. Kincaid was tight with indecision.

"Why does he want to kill her?"

"You in there, Kincaid?" As one, their heads turned toward the drunken voice of Jr. Wallace. "Somebody told me you in the back of that wagon. We beat your proud ass this time, didn't we, Kincaid? Yes, we did!"

Kincaid jumped out, stopping him before he got to the wagon. "Yeah, guess you did this time, Mr. Wallace," he said in exaggerated good humor while he put his arm around Wallace's shoulders and lead him away from the wagon.

"Didn't know we was so close," Wallace chuckled.

"No reason we can't be neighborly and do business together. Least that's how I see it." They reached the door to the saloon.

"You got a point there, Kincaid," Wallace mumbled.

"Miss Edna was just explaining about some of the medicine she brought me. Why don't you go on back in and have another pint. This one's on me. I'll be there right after I'm done with her."

Wallace lurched forward, and conspiratorially whispered in his ear, spit spraying, "You need to watch that witch, Kincaid. She put a spell on you, if you not careful." He laughed and headed back into the saloon. Kincaid wiped his ear as best he could and rushed back to the wagon.

"So what happened to make him want to kill her?"

"The Lady asked her to fetch a hat from her closet. Massa caught her in the closet and think she be stealin'. He hit her and knocked her out. Before he know she in there, though, he be conducting some personal business he don't want nobody to know. When he find Joraye, he think she know what they be doin'. That's why I tell him she dead even though she ain't. He kill her if he know she alive. She can't stay there, Mista' Kincaid. Please."

"And you say she's T's woman?"

"Yes, sir. T be outta hisself when he find out she gone. But she can't stay there. He be better, he know she with you."

"You say her name is Joraye?"

"Yes sir."

"And you say T doesn't know anything about this?"

"That's right. He know nothin' 'bout it. He gone when this happened."

"He'll go after Wallace when he finds out and get himself killed," Kincaid voiced all their fears.

"That be on me what to tell him. Right now it Joraye that need help. T don't do nothin' that stop him from seeing her again, way I see it."

"What an impossible situation." He looked over at Joraye. "I guess you better wake her up now."

Miss Edna removed a handkerchief from a bag and unfolded it to reveal a horseradish root. She held it under Joraye's nose. Nothing happened for a few seconds. Then a few more. No one in the wagon breathed as Joraye remained corpse like. Miss Edna's heartbeat sped up. What had always worked in the past was not working now.

"Everything alright?" Asked a concerned Kincaid.

"Just give it a bit more time," Miss Edna said. Then Joraye's head jerked from side to side and there was a collective sigh that was audible.

"It okay, baby. It Miss Edna. You safe." Joraye opened her eyes.

"We be there, Miss Edna?" she asked groggily. "Already?"

"It jus' like I told you, Joraye. You get here with no worry. I want you to meet Mista' Kincaid."

Joraye tried to focus on Kincaid, who leaned over and said, gently, "Please to meet you, Joraye. Do you mind if I help you out that box? Think you might want a little more space." He offered his hand. She looked at it, then up into his eyes.

"It be fine Joraye. You remember how T told you Mista Kincaid be a good man?" Miss Edna said. Joraye moved cautiously while Kincaid helped her out and guided her to a place on one of the benches.

"Now isn't that a lot better?" He asked.

"Thank you, Massa Kincaid?" She said kept her eyes to the ground.

"Call me "Mister Kincaid" Joraye, and I want you to know that Miss Edna told me everything, and I am happy to take you back with me where you will be safe to raise you and T's baby. But right now I need to meet Wallace before he comes back to this wagon. You sit here quietly with Miss Edna for just a little while and I'll be right back." He turned to Miss Edna, "Can you have one of your men take the wagon to the end of street? We want it as far away from the front of this saloon as possible."

""You a witch doctor now?" Wallace blurted out. He chuckled. Kincaid took a seat.

"You don't waste anytime starting your day, I see."

"Just a quick refresher after a long trip. You ain't gon' look down your nose at me 'bout that, are you, Mr. Kincaid? After we become so neighborly, and all."

"Not at all, Mr. Wallace. Refresh to your heart's content. Why don't we get to the business at hand?"

"You a lucky som'bitch, 'cause I got my wife to agree on $600, and that's down from $650."

"Well, as much as I want this to work out, Mr. Wallace, that would put a strain on me that I just can't take on right now."

"You better find a way. You ain't the only one want a nigger like that one. And don't gimme no more talk 'bout a Christian duty. The way I see it, I ain't done nothin' wrong here." In one stroke, Wallace thought he gained the upper hand.

"Can you promise me that offer is firm?" Kincaid responded, his heart beating faster.

"Since we bein' all neighborly, I can do that. How much time you need?"

"Four weeks?"

"Be back here in three weeks with the money or we ain't got no deal."

"What condition is he in?"

"All that stuff I talked 'bout last time was just me havin' a little fun."

"So, you didn't beat him to within an inch of his life?"

"Come on Kincaid, you know that a little whippin' don't mean nothin' to a nigger. They come to expect it after a while."

"No. I don't know that."

"Like I said, he's fine. The Lady almost didn't want him to go, 'cause he works like a goddam horse.

"I have a right to a slave in excellent condition, for that kind of money," reminded Kincaid

"You just be sure to be back here with the money in three weeks."

"Then three weeks it is," repeated Kincaid.

"Let's go, Tommie. Time to head back," Kincaid said as he approached her.

"That wasn't no hour," she protested.

"I know, but something came up. We have to leave now. Let's get a move on."

"Please, Daddy, just a half hour more? That's what you said." She was not giving up easily, which made Rabbit proud.

"I know what I said, but we need to leave now. Go get into the wagon," he said, more angrily than he meant to sound.

"Somethin' wrong, Daddy?"

"No."

"Where did the wagon go?"

"It's at the end of the street. Let's go."

Tommie had to run to keep up with her father. Rabbit sprinted toward the wagon and hopped into the back. This incursion was followed by a stifled scream.

They dashed to the wagon and found Joraye, Miss Edna, and the other slaves huddled in a corner, with Rabbit looking curiously at them, tail wagging, ready to play.

"Rabbit! Sit! commanded Kincaid. Rabbit obeyed. "I'm sorry. He took off before I could stop him. You don't have anything to fear from him, unless you scratch behind his ears. Then he will never leave you alone." Rabbit understood "scratch" and "ears" and his tail thumped against the floor.

Tommie stood, mouth agape.

"Her name is Joraye, Tommie, and she is coming to live with us." Tommie turned her head sharply towards her father in wonder and confusion. "Go introduce yourself," he said. Tommie walked up to Joraye and held out her hand.

"My name is Tommie." Joraye tentatively took the proffered hand. "You don't need to be scared. Rabbit is real friendly," she added.

"He got your friendly eyes," said Joraye. To everyone's astonishment, she kneeled, "Come here boy." Rabbit walked up to her, tail wagging, and Joraye started scratching behind his ears. Rabbit chuffed his satisfaction. "Had me a dog like this a long time ago. He a good one like this one."

"Ain't God good," said Miss Edna.

"We should get going," said Kincaid.

"You right, Mista' Kincaid," agreed Miss Edna. She moved over to Joraye. "Look like you made a good friend," she said, indicating Rabbit. Joraye was looking down. When she looked up there were tears in her eyes. Miss Edna hugged her. "Oh, my baby," she managed through her own tears, "I loved you like you my own, from the first. You always be a part of my heart." Joraye's tears flowed freely. "You gon' be so happy with yo' new family. T gon' be with you real soon."

309

"Oh, Miss Edna, Miss Edna," was all Joraye could manage. She hugged her tight.

"Me and the Rev. come see you soon's we able. You hear?" She held Joraye's face in both her hands, "Remember, you got a life in you. You got to be strong for that baby. You come a long way. Don't you never forget how strong you be when life get hard, you understand me?" Joraye nodded. "I pray for you each and every day."

"I pray for you too, Miss Edna, each and every day," she whispered. Miss Edna kissed her on the cheek then walked over to Kincaid and took both his hands in hers.

"You truly are a man of God, Mista' Kincaid. I see why T speak 'bout you like he do. I mean what I say 'bout prayin' for you and Tommie every day." She looked down at Rabbit, "and maybe even that ol' mutt too."

"Tommie, you stay back here with Joraye," he said as he helped Miss Edna climb out of the wagon.

CHAPTER 45

The Wallace's were in flight mode. Their cover story of accepting the wedding invitation of a dear relative was only partly true: the wedding was of an acquaintance, and they hadn't been invited- - they had asked to attend. Their motive was self-preservation. T would be returning in their absence, and they wanted to be gone. His reaction to Joraye's death would be a volcano even Samson could not subdue.

The other enslaved shared their disappointment. Many imagined T exacting a bloody revenge. There were hushed discussions about past revolts and magical thinking that this might be the catalyst for a large-scale reckoning. They stood ready.

Samson had been instructed that, whatever happened, T had to remain alive with a minimum of visible scars. It would be a little over two weeks from the time he got back until he was due to be delivered to Kincaid, or to anyone else who could come up with payment. This was made clear in their last conversation when, unbeknownst to Jr. Wallace, Kincaid was leaving Owenton with Joraye.

"That nigger's gonna be a wild animal and you know it. You sayin' I can't take a whip to him?" questioned Samson.

"I'm sayin' anything you do has to be healed up in a couple of weeks. You do what you got to. But I want anybody lookin' at the nigger in a couple of weeks to see a fine healthy specimen. We clear?"

"We clear."

Miss Edna moved around her empty cabin feeling the loss of Joraye one minute and anxiety over T's return the next. She prayed for the safety of her own children every night. But it had been years since the pain of those losses felt so fresh. Joraye's absence was a reminder of all she had lost. She reflected on how she had grown from a skittish, frightened little mouse, into the woman that she was now, and what a gift it had been to experience that growth. She would forever be grateful to God for giving her another child to love before she died.

Now Joraye was starting a new life with strangers. Though she trusted Kincaid to do right by her, there were no guarantees. There were days and nights of hand wringing. She hoped T would see the wisdom in her decision. *Right or wrong, she in Kincaid's hands now and away from the certain death that be here,* she thought. She could only hope her powers of persuasion were in full force to stem T's certain bloodlust once he found out about Joraye. She made it clear to everyone involved that he could never know Jr. Wallace' involvement. There would be at least one real funeral if that happened.

Rev. R gave thanks to God, upon hearing Miss Edna's dramatic retelling of the trip. She recounted how Kincaid almost didn't make it, which drove home the sheer audacity of the undertaking and the miracle of its success. Joraye was truly blessed, if Kincaid was as good as Miss Edna described him. Now T's return loomed large and potentially tragic. He was twisting in knots but not entirely for the same reasons as the Wallaces or Miss Edna.

T's reaction to Joraye's "death" was certainly foremost in his thoughts but also on his mind was the question of his own future. These last several weeks were the first time they had all been apart since becoming a family. Would the time apart make T decide that he only had room in his life for Joraye? Would he be imagining a wholly natural life with her and decide there was no room in that life for him? These were the thoughts that had him staring into space, as he sat before an untouched meal or missed hearing someone calling his name.

With him gone, the doubts sprouted up like the weeds in the Lady's rose garden that he now tended. It was a task he had asked to perform and that normally brought him a great deal of pleasure. There was no pleasure now. This is where his faith became an ally. He believed what he told Miss Edna about God bringing T into his life. He had had faith that God would keep T there. When Joraye suggested he go with her to Kincaid's, he was moved by her innocence. Whereas for him, doubt and indecision constantly hovered around the edges, she embraced their new life fully without a trace of shame. T pulled her from her mental inferno, and she trusted him with the same unquestioning faith that Rev. R trusted his God. That T was open with her about his feelings for him, was yet another marvel of the man.

Nevertheless, T would have to make a choice, and the choice would have to be Joraye. Once he found out Joraye was with child, he would move heaven and earth to get to them. *Just as he should*, thought Rev. R. For this reason he was prepared to let him go. He would take T's hand and release it to Joraye; he would stay forever secure that what they had created was real. With this thinking, he could come to terms with the impending, inevitable separation.

CHAPTER 46

Clouds started to roll in as the buckboard wagon rolled into Jr. Wallace's plantation. Sitting atop was an overseer from the Sr. Wallace plantation and in the open back a shackled and chained T. The first faces to greet him were Miss Edna and Rev. R, along with Simone, Lawrence and several others. When Rev. R's eyes met T's, the tortured, smoldering face he looked into gave no indication of where his heart might be. Rev. R's anxiety moved up a notch.

T noticed that several slaves averted their glances. He picked up a current of discomfort that went beyond curiosity at his homecoming. When he did not see Joraye, his stomach lurched. He did another quick scan of the crowd and grew more agitated. He tried to stand to see further out, but his shackles stopped him, and he started to buckle against them.

"Hold up, T! You need to calm yourself if you expect me to unlock you," said the overseer. Breathing heavy, heart pounding, T grew still. When he was unshackled, he leapt off the wagon and sprinted toward Miss Edna's shack.

"T! Wait!" Miss Edna called out. By the time she and Rev. R caught up to him, he had entered the shack.

"Joraye! Joraye, it T!" When he heard nothing, he turned to Miss Edna. "Where Joraye? Miss Edna! Where Joraye?!"

"They didn't tell you?" came a voice from behind that made everyone stop dead. Samson was standing with a whip in one hand and a gun in the other. "The idiot be dead." Miss Edna, anticipating an attack, placed herself between the two men before the overseer stopped speaking. All T could do was take one bold step forward.

"Where-is-she," he hissed.

"Probably out back with the rest of the shit. You be there with her real soon, you come at me again." T rushed to the back of Miss Edna's shack and up to a fresh grave, just as the clouds broke and rain poured down, hard and heavy. "Welcome back!" he heard the overseer shout.

"This be where Joraye is?! He demanded. The crowd had thinned out to take shelter. He fell to his knees and started scooping out mounds of dirt. There were gasps as the few remaining people turned away. Through the wind and rain Rev. R called out.

"She alive, T! "Joraye alive!" He did not hear, as he grunted and strained, using both arms to move mud that slipped right through them. Rev. R attempted to approach him, but Miss Edna grabbed his arm and kept him with her. T attacked the grave in a mad rage, as much punching the mud as trying to throw it away. More rain came. T continued throwing mud out of the hole. After a few inches, his hands hit hard dirt. Other parts of the ground were hard.

"This ground ain't been dug," he shouted. "Where she be?!" Miss Edna signaled for Rev. R to go up to him.

"She alive, T. Joraye alive and safe."

T sat with his back to a crackling fire. He was wrapped in a thin blanket and sitting on a stump in Rev. R's cabin. After he recovered from the shock, Miss Edna refused to begin an explanation until he was warm and dry. She decided the simplest way would be best.

"Joraye with Mista' Kincaid."

"What you mean Mista Kincaid?" he blurted out in disbelief.

"I answer that, but first you tell me you think she be safe with him, that he take care of her?" His face was a cloud of confusion, anxiety and mistrust.

"He a good man. Joraye safe. But why you send her away?" Then without warning he sprang up and threw off the blanket. "If Wallace do somethin', Miss Edna, I swear, I kill him."

She grabbed his arms. "He ain't do nothin' to her." She shared a look with a startled Rev. R, who remained silent.

"Talk real to me Miss Edna," T said, not convinced. "Why you send her away before I get back? Why you make people think she die?"

"She with child, T. She save yo' baby from being snatched by Massa Wallace."

"Baby? What you mean baby?"

"She be scared to tell you, T. She think you be mad and not want her."

"How she think that? She think I don't want our baby?" His hurt is palpable.

"You got to understand T, she don't think like other women 'cause of what happen to her. She still got some fear, and it don't be yo' fault. She don't mean no harm to you. She not tell no one 'cause she think massa take the baby anyway. But I tell her she don't know what God got planned for that baby and we jus' got to pray and let Him guide us. I also say you be 'bout the happiest man on earth when you find out 'bout it."

"The hand of God be on Miss Edna, T, when she talk to Joraye. She look like a new woman, she be so happy to carry yo' child," assured Rev. R.

"Miss Edna, you know what I feel 'bout God, but what you did be the nearest thing to God I ever know. You be a truly good woman," T said with quiet conviction.

"Give Him the glory, my son. I say what God want me to, and I be glad Joraye listen."

"I got to get to her. I can't stay here," he said.

"And you will," Miss Edna answered quickly. "What you got to know now is that she safe and can't nobody else know." He nodded agreement. "The baby move before she left. Yo' child waitin' to see you," she answered, along with her own silent prayer that she spoke the truth.

"We know you got to be with Joraye and yo' baby, T, and Miss Edna and me gon' help you." Rev. R said.

Miss Edna continued. "You rest tonight, here with the Rev. You say yo'self Joraye be safe. We can take a little time to make sure you get to her with no harm comin' to you."

"So you make people think she die so nobody ask after her." Miss Edna nodded. "How you do that?"

"Jus' say she catch a bad fever."This time she does not look in Rev. R's direction.

"How you to get her out?"

"We hide her in my medicine box I take to town. God was with us that day."

"And you sure she all right?"

"She waitin' for you and she fine. Mista' Kincaid be a gift from God, the way he treat her when he know she yo' woman. Tommie also be real nice to her. Even that dog cozy up like he know her."

"Rabbit," said T quietly.

"He be mean looking, but be like a lamb when you scratch behind his ears."

"You do real good by Joraye, Miss Edna and I 'ppreciate it." She put a hand on his shoulder.

"You know I think of her like my own, T. I do anything for that child." She squeezed his shoulder.

"I'm gon' leave now so you can all rest. Come by tomorrow before you go to the fields."

Rev. R broke the awkward silence. "I be thinkin' all kinds of things while you be gone," and went to lift a pot of stew over the fire.

"He leave me alone to work, most time."

"The Sr. Wallace ain't like his son," said Rev. R

"Maybe not. But ain't nothin' 'bout it good. I be snatched off this place like a dog."

"All that over now, T, and you got a new baby. Joraye be real glad to see you. She almost not go without you, but everything happen jus' like it should." He had been working around the fire this whole time, avoiding eye contact. T got up and moved toward him and put his hand on one of Rev. R's arms. Rev. R stared at the hand. They were both still as statues.

"You come too," T said low and pointedly. "You got to come with me."

Rev. R dropped his head and didn't move for several seconds then turned back toward the fire. "You know, Joraye say the same thing," he said over his shoulder.

"She right. You know she be right. Don't you?"

"She right and you right, but I can't go." He said quietly, as he rose and sat on the bed.

"You don't want to be with us?"

"That be the only thing I want, if I could, T, but God gimme these people to look after, and I can't walk away from them. They be my calling."

"So God say walk away from me and Joraye?"

"No. He tell me to let you go to yo' woman and yo' child. You the man that need to keep them from danger, to watch over them. I got people to watch over too. But you know what I also be thinkin' 'bout? I be thinkin' that if you feel this way 'bout me it be easier

318

for me to send you to Joraye. When you was gone what I scared 'bout most is that you be sorry for us and want to forget. Now I know we real."

"But what you want for yo' life, Rev? You got a right to that too." Rev. R is silent "You so worried 'bout these people not having somebody to teach 'em God. What about that man with the bad leg? He do it before you come along."

"Jerome don't teach. He jus' say what's in the bible."

"So. You ain't leavin' 'em with nothin'. And you get what you want too. Look to me like this the answer yo' God be showin' you.

"We always be family, T, even if I be here. Won't nothin' ever change that. If there be a way to all be together, I'll praise Jesus. But you got to get to Joraye, even it be without me. Miss Edna make it safe jus' like she do for Joraye."

"She ain't gon' fit me in no box and I can't wait."

"You won't have to. But you got to be safe."

***

They were gathered at Miss Edna's table, pre-dawn, discussing T's next move. "Why you want to take the chance you be killed?" Miss Edna asked. "Them woods give you up once already. God might show us another way, like he did with Joraye. We got to give Him a chance to speak."

"But how long it be?" T paced in exasperation. "Joraye be havin' the baby before I get there.

"You jus' got back, T, let me pray on it like I did with Joraye. See, I pray on it and then I be sleepin' in my chair right next to her and God speak to me and

319

now she safe. He do the same with you. "I know it," answered Miss Edna. T stopped pacing. Nobody spoke. A sense of helpless foreboding permeated the space.

"No, in a few days, soon as the ground dry out some, I leavin'," he said with finality. "What you think 'bout Jerome, Miss Edna? He preach good?"

"He was called a long time ago to bring people to God," she answered and turned to Rev. R in confusion.

"That what I say too," T offered up.

"Why you ask 'bout Jerome?" She continued to be confused.

"I got to stay," Rev. R said, "jus' like we talk 'bout."

She understood. "He can't go, T. He be doin' the right thing by stayin'. I know you and he be close, but we need him here. Too many things go wrong you both run."

"I not leave my family behind, Miss Edna."

"I know," she said, no longer at odds with the truth. "But it matter more that you get to Joraye and that baby and it jus' be too dangerous with you both out there."

He stared at Miss Edna, as if about to protest, then turned to Rev. R "You got to come soon as possible."

"I know, T. I pray to God to find a way."

"And I be prayin' for a miracle like He gimme with Joraye," added Miss Edna.

"You go ahead and pray for yo' miracle, Miss Edna. You too Rev. but I be gone in three days."

Miss Edna looked down, took a deep breath, and then said, "You need to do some things first, if you set on this path," she said.

"What you mean."

"I need you trap about six squirrels and bring 'em to me, alive."

T and Rev. R exchanged confused looks. "I take food with me, and I can't be carryin' 'round no squirrels," answered T.

"They not food. They be for the dogs. When you in the field tomorrow make sure to wipe yo' sweat off with three or four rags. Do that every day until you go. Also, bring me some of the straw you sleep on. I got some cages I use to hold little animals for some of my medicine. I put the squirrels in those cages with yo' straw and the rags with yo' sweat. Then right before you leave, I set them off in all directions so that the dogs go after them 'stead of you."

"How you know to do all that?" Rev. R asked in amazement.

"You live long enough you learn some things." She said then added, "I'm gonna give you some garlic. Soon as you get past the plantation rub it all over. This ain't the way I want you to go but if it got to be this way, all this will help."

***

They were gathered in Miss Enda's cabin in final preparations. She had put together a sack of herbs, roots, and potions along with some dried meat, fruit and nuts. They mapped out a route that would keep him deep in the woods and give maximum cover. However, when massa released the dogs, speed and Miss Edna's ruse with the squirrels and the garlic would be T's only friend. A head start was the best friend of a slave on the run.

"This be real good, Miss Edna," T marveled at her travel supplies. "You the closest to a mama I ever have and I see you again, I promise you." He embraced her.

After a minute she broke away and looked him in the eye, "You a strong man T, who take what he want from life. When it be people you take, it be on you to make sure you do right by 'em. You understand?"

He nodded. "I got no life without Joraye and the Rev., Miss Edna. It be simple like that. They be my life."

"I know that and I still be talkin' to God to give me understanding 'bout it but you all always be my family, nothin' ever change that." She walked over to Rev. Rs chair and placed a hand on his shoulder. "You a good man, Rev., and God and everyone else know it and don't you never doubt that." He put his hand on top of hers because he could not speak. After he took his hand away she went to gather up two bags that held the squirrels.

"I gon' let these go now then you got to leave real soon. Don't wait for me to come back. And don't forget what I told you 'bout the garlic and she left them alone.

***

After a few hours she quietly entered the cabin. Rev. R sat alone at the table with both hands in his lap, looking utterly diminished. His eyes were glistening pools. She knelt beside him and gently rubbed his shoulder.

"I.." he tried to speak. "I.." he tried again and was overcome.

"I know, baby. I know," she whispered and continued her soothing touch until he calmed.

"Thank you," he finally murmured.

"We love that man and God bless us to put him in our lives," she said as she stood.

Rev. R slowly and stood up. "I go now."

"You stay Rev. Don't need to be by yo'self right now."

"I be fine. Got to think 'bout tomorrow." This momentarily silenced them both. It was going to be a dangerous day. "I pray 'bout it tonight when I pray for T."

"Me too," added Miss Edna. He nodded and left her cabin.

***

There was nothing. No feeling. No desire to pray, barely a desire to breathe. Rev. R lay on his bed and absorbed the thickness of the dark, his eyes wide open. He would pray, eventually. He had to pray, that would save him, but this moment, this exact moment, there was nothing. The numbness offered its own comfort, a surcease from darkness so encompassing as to threaten no return. So, he just breathed.

Slowly the images came. T in the darkness, the moon lighting his way. T looking at the map. T wiping his brow. "I see you," Rev. R whispered in the dark. "It's me, T, jus' look beside you, it will always be me." Then he began, "Dear, sweet Jesus. . ."

***

After two days with no hounds and no trackers, T was gaining confidence. He had been beaten and bloody on the floor of Jr. Wallace's barn by this time on his last attempt. The miracle that was Miss Edna had given him everything he needed, and he was following her instructions to the letter.

The Old Ones

It was cold, but not winter cold, and so far, there had been no rain. If he could last for three more days, he would see his Joraye, or maybe it was less, it was hard to tell. He was rushing to his true life and he could be there tomorrow.

He found a clearing that would keep him out of sight. He had been using every last reserve of energy to keep up a strong pace during his nighttime sojourns, and quickly fell into a deep sleep. A slight breeze had picked up as Joraye and Rev. R took turns weaving through his dreamscape. The images were not ones he knew. They were of a time and a place where they lived as the family he made without fear or shame. Then the breeze suddenly turned warm and caressed his face like a soft blanket. He came awake to see Rabbit's grinning face and angel eyes staring down at him.

*N*ow those old black folks, the ones that tasted breezes and talked of shadows, put their candles out, put their blankets on, and prayed their million prayers for impossible things. A final sleep for the lucky ones, the others would wake, once again, to a world where:

The whips still whipped...

The chains still chained...

And Jesus would watch the trees bare strange fruit...

Acknowledgements

Thank you, Ira, for being the first to say that there was more to discover and challenging me not to settle. If this effort succeeds at all it's because you kept asking the good, hard questions. Your imagination and passion were crucial in setting this piece off.

Thank you, Jay, for your critical eye and suggestions. You were the first!

Thank you, Noelle, for asking, "Are there chapters?"

Thank you, Andrea, for coming back into my life with grace, support and guidance. It means the world!

Thank you, Rafi, for seeing the spark of something and paying it forward!

Thank you, Hester, Stephanie, Rudy and Ron for your critical eyes and support.

Finally, thank you Donnie, for your tireless proofreading support. I am humbled by your willingness to spend hours parsing lines, pointing out mistakes and often scratching your head and insisting on clarity. You may be my sister but an angel says it better.

Made in the USA
Columbia, SC
24 January 2025

52530144R00183